Delilah's
DESSERTS

A **tangerine street** ROMANCE

A NOVEL IN THREE PARTS

Delilah's
DESSERTS

A **tangerine street** ROMANCE
A NOVEL IN THREE PARTS

Melanie Jacobson
Heather B. Moore
Julie Wright

Mirror Press

Cover Design by Rachael Anderson
Interior Design by Cora Johnson
Edited by Cassidy Wadsworth Skousen & Lisa Shepherd
Published by Mirror Press, LLC
ISBN-13: 978-1-947152-34-2

The Tangerine Street Romances
Can be read in any order

Welcome to Tangerine Street

Tangerine Street is a must-see tourist stop with a colorful mix of one-of-a-kind boutiques, unique restaurants, eclectic museums, quaint bookstores, and exclusive bed-and-breakfasts. Delilah's Desserts, situated in the middle of this charming collection of shops and cafés on Tangerine Street, is a bakery that offers a different variety of desserts each day. The emotions that Delilah bakes into these desserts have a strange effect on customers, sometimes altering the course of their lives . . .

PART ONE:

A Taste of Magic

PART TWO:

The Art of Love

PART THREE:

Much Ado About Cupcakes

PART ONE

A Taste of Magic

One

Delilah stepped back from the giant mixer and brushed a stray lock of her hair out of her face, careful not to smudge herself with her batter-covered hands. It had been a few weeks since she'd played with a new flavor, but Dylan's happy energy as he'd bounded out the door this morning had infected her. She'd rushed back to the bakery in the mood to try something new and bright. She had a good feeling about how this blueberry and lemon pavlova cupcake would turn out.

Well, assuming she could figure out how to approach the meringue. And did she want to inject the lemon curd like a ganache into a truffle? Or should she—

A loud crash sounded from the shop front, and she clapped her hands to her head and winced, the clatter still ringing in her ears. That was the aluminum sample platter Jessie was supposed to circulate among customers to entice them to try the newest item, a chocolate cannoli.

Sure enough, the door to the kitchen swung open, and a

pink-cheeked Jessie popped her head around it. "Sorry, Delilah. But we only lost two little pieces this time."

Delilah nodded. It was much better than the full plate of cake bites Jessie had spilled the week before. "It's okay. I'll bring out more in a few minutes. How's the line?"

"Long!" Jessie said and disappeared.

Delilah dug into the cabinet for another passing tray and gave it a quick swipe with a clean rag before fetching more fresh cannoli shells from the fridge and piping in the sheep's milk ricotta filling.

Sleepy Seashell Beach was waking up to new flavors, and it pleased her that she'd underestimated the demand for the pastry. She'd known Evan Rockham at the five-star Mariposa Hotel kitchen would appreciate them, but almost a third of their foot traffic customers had added cannoli to their order too.

Another hit. She smiled. She'd made them while dreaming of a sun-drenched Tuscan hillside, and people could taste it in the filling.

She plated the next batch of samples for Jessie. Her favorite employee wasn't the most graceful, but if it meant keeping Jessie's sunny attitude and ease with the customers, Delilah could handle a dropped tray every week.

She backed through the kitchen door and carefully turned with the cannoli, making sure Jessie was nowhere near her. But it wasn't Jessie who made her freeze when she saw the line; it was the sheer number of faces waiting to buy desserts. Her desserts.

"I'll do the samples. Just keep ringing them up," she murmured. Jessie nodded and continued her conversation with the little white-haired lady dithering between a Mocha Marvel and a Dream Fudge cupcake.

The sharp scent of acrylic paint cut through the usual warm butter and sugar smells in her little shop, but Delilah didn't mind. "Hey, Roxy," she said to her friend crouched at the north wall. One paintbrush held her newly platinum hair in an adorable messy topknot while she wielded another to paint a candle onto a fluffy-looking lavender cupcake. "Want a piece before I feed the line?" Delilah whispered.

Roxy smiled around the third paintbrush clenched in her teeth and shook her head. Delilah grinned back and stepped over to the next person waiting to order. "Would you like to try our new Tuscan cannoli while you wait, Mr. Nelson?"

The old man shook his head even as he plucked up one of the samples. "I thought you were crazy to branch out from the cupcakes that made you famous, but I was wrong."

"Thanks," she said, pleased to have won over her crustiest customer.

The flannel-swathed hipster behind him also grabbed a sample. "I think you're a genius," he said around a mouthful.

"No amount of sweet-talking can get you in the kitchen yet, Max." He was a newly graduated culinary student who begged her weekly for a job. "I promise, as soon as I have enough to meet the payroll, I'll hire you out of the Mariposa kitchen and make them hate me forever."

"Evan won't mind," Max promised. "I like being a sous chef, but pastry is my life."

"I need that on a T-shirt," the plump housewife behind him muttered.

Delilah laughed and offered her a sample too, which she happily accepted. The line stretched all the way to the door, but Delilah knew she could buy their patience with samples, then jump behind the counter to help Jessie fill orders.

She'd almost reached the end of the line when the bell tinkled to announce a new customer. She glanced up with a smile, but when she realized who had just walked in, her tray hit the ground with a clatter more spectacular than anything Jessie had ever managed.

A tall, lean man stood in the doorway. His olive skin and dark hair were as common as the blond surfer shags that filled Seashell Beach, a town that was proud of its Mexican heritage, but this man would have stood out in any crowd.

It had been ten years and a million lifetimes ago, but there was no forgetting Luke Romero.

"Delilah Dawes," Luke said. A slow smile spread above the distinct cleft chin that made him striking. "There's a face I never thought I'd see again."

Delilah struggled to find words, even a simple hello. The pulse in her neck pounded so hard words couldn't push past it. She didn't realize Roxy had come to help her pick up the scattered cannoli until she heard her friend's soft, "Whoa."

"Is that—" Roxy started to ask, staring at his chin, but Delilah stepped back, careful to land on Roxy's foot, and a pained squeak strangled the rest of her question.

"Yes," Delilah said to Roxy, and then she cleared her throat and ordered herself to pull it together. You can't screw this up. "Hi, Luke. Long time no see."

That corny statement could not have been more loaded with freight if the whole longshoremen union had stacked it for twenty-four hours straight.

"That's an understatement."

Yeah. He obviously also felt all the weight of things unsaid. He glanced around the shop. "So this is your place. Looks like business is great."

"Yes." She grabbed on to the statement as a desperate excuse to disengage from him until she could reorder her universe back to what it had been three minutes ago. "I would love to catch up, but ..." She waved to the samples still littering the floor, then bent to collect them, grateful finally to have broken the spell he'd cast on her.

She glanced at her watch. Twenty more minutes before Dylan got here, and she needed Luke out of Delilah's Desserts before that.

"No problem," Luke said. "Let me help."

He was already half crouched before she barked, "No." Startled, he froze, and she pasted on a smile. "I've got it, thanks. Let me handle this, then I'll pick out an order for you myself."

He stepped to the back of the line. "Don't worry about me. Do your thing. It'll give me time to look over the choices."

Time. No. She didn't have time, but she didn't argue. She swept the ruined samples onto the tray and hurried to the kitchen, flinging them in the trash before racing back out to help Jessie manage the line. Max was standing at the register and studying the display case like his future rode on picking the right cupcake. Well, his didn't, but hers did.

"Describe your mood in one word, Max," she ordered.

"I love it when she does this," the housewife behind him said to no one in particular.

Max thought about it. Delilah glanced at her watch.

Sixteen minutes. This would work. It had to work. "Max," she snapped.

"Mellow," he said. "I feel mellow."

She was already moving for the case. "Ring him up for a vanilla bean," she said as she boxed it.

"But that's so basic," he complained.

She gave him a squinty-eyed stare. "Have you had my vanilla bean?"

"No, but—"

She squinted harder.

He swallowed. "Okay, vanilla bean."

She wanted to scream as Jessie counted out his change.

Fourteen minutes.

The housewife stepped up to the counter. There were still three people behind her before it was Luke's turn. Unless they all knew exactly what they wanted, this was never going to work.

"I'll take a dozen cannoli, but only half of them are for me," the housewife said, and her unapologetic cackle made the line behind her laugh.

Even Delilah grinned as she practically dove through the kitchen door for the pastry fridge. She would pack the lady's order plus some for Luke, give them to him as a goodwill gift, and send him away with a fervent prayer that he never came back.

She snapped the cardboard box printed with her rolling pin logo into shape, nestled the first dozen cannoli in it as fast as she could, and closed the box with her Delilah sticker. When she did the same for Luke's half dozen, she wished she had something besides a box with her name on it to send him home with—she didn't want him to have even that much of her.

Twelve minutes.

She raced back through the kitchen but slowed to a walk when she hit the front, not wanting to draw any more attention to herself. She handed the housewife her box, and the woman had one half eaten before she even reached the door.

She handed Luke his box too. "That's my newest offering. Enjoy them. It was good to see you again. Wish I could chat, but I need to help Jessie." She might have had questions for him if she had a few more minutes to ask them, but time ticked as loudly as the pulse in her temple.

"Oh, you didn't have to do that. I can pay."

"Consider it a gift. So sorry, but I need to get back to work." She flashed him a tight smile and slipped behind the counter. The weight of his gaze pressed against her nerves, and she glanced at Roxy to find the artist studying her. Roxy would have questions. Delilah would not have answers.

Ten minutes.

Luke pulled a cannoli from the box and took a bite.

Please, please, please.

She kept her eyes on the case, pulling the cupcakes the next customer ordered while straining to hear the tinkling bell that would announce he'd left. It came a minute later, and she looked up in relief only to see a new customer walk in. Luke had taken a seat at one of the two small café tables.

Eight minutes.

She glanced as often as she dared. Normally it made her happy to watch a new customer enjoy her baking, but there was nothing normal about this. He chewed slowly, like he was really concentrating on the experience. That was how she best liked people to enjoy her food, but not today.

Six minutes.

This was impossible.

Her hands fumbled one of the cupcakes to the floor as her panic mounted.

"Hey, that's my thing," Jessie joked. "We can't have both of us dropping food, boss."

Delilah forced a smile. "I'll take it out of my own paycheck." She scooped up the smashed cupcake and reached for another.

Five minutes. If she was really, really lucky.

Luke finished his cannoli, and she held her breath, ready for him to leave. Instead he picked up another one. She cursed herself for making good food.

Three minutes. Her stomach hurt.

Just before he could bite into it, his forehead wrinkled, and he set the cannoli down to pull his phone from his pocket.

"Romero," he said, and he listened for a minute. "I'll send it over. Give me fifteen minutes."

He closed the box, and she could tell he was about to look for her to say goodbye, so she stooped to the lowest shelf of the display case to reach for a key lime tartlet. It gave her the perfect excuse to watch his feet walk out of the door barely ten seconds before Dylan's feet walked in. The aftermath of the adrenaline rush dropped her onto her backside for the space of two long breaths while she contemplated the narrow escape she had just made from disaster.

Two

*L*uke leaned back against his rental car and let his editor have her say. "Marie, I'll do the story. You know I will. But I can't fly out until next week."

He didn't know it was true until he said it. He had just become a useless pile of iron filings to the magnet of Seashell Beach, and it had everything to do with Delilah Dawes.

He listened to Marie until she ran out of steam again. "If you can find another freelancer ready to do a month in Nepal on three days' notice, book them. Otherwise, I'll take the assignment a week from today."

Marie's heavy sigh dampened the line. He'd won.

He slid the phone into his pocket and stared down Tangerine Street toward Delilah's storefront, a lemony splash against the blue-washed coziness of the other stores marching away from it in either direction.

He'd walked into her bakery on a whim, wondering if it could possibly be the same Delilah who had disappeared on him ten years ago, the cinnamon-scented local girl who'd tangled up his thoughts—and eventually his sheets—for the best summer of his life.

It was her, all right. Yet it wasn't her too. She'd grown into something contained, the wild edges mostly tucked beneath her soft apron, the beach curls he'd loved to wind around his fingers gathered into a subdued ponytail at her nape.

Except one of her shirt cuffs had come unrolled, and she had a streak of flour trying to paint a white streak through her dark hair and across her forehead. Those were glimpses of his untamed Delilah hiding beneath her neatly uniformed facade. Some things would never change.

Other things had. She'd grown more beautiful. She still had a trace of freckles across her nose, but at least twenty much-needed pounds had turned her angles into curves. Her hazel eyes were as sharp as ever, missing nothing behind the dark fringe of her lashes. He had no doubt she'd taken in his every detail in the second before the tray crashed to the floor.

Her reaction had satisfied him the same way he'd been satisfied when he slipped off the cliffs at Acapulco instead of doing a graceful dive; his guide had laughed right until he slipped too. At least Luke hadn't been the only one whose world tilted off axis for a minute today.

He took a couple of steps back toward the bakery before stopping. He had work to do, but more importantly, he'd have to let it sink in—for both of them—that he was back in town.

He slid into the convertible Mustang rental he'd convinced the magazine to pay for. "How else can I evaluate the quintessential California experience of cruising the coastline with the top down without a convertible?" Marie had growled but approved it. Now as he drove toward the Mariposa Hotel and let the wind blow away the fog of his run-in with Delilah, he was glad he'd risked his editor's wrath to get the car.

The Mariposa was a major upgrade from the scruffy hospitality Seashell Beach had offered before the luxury hotel had opened. He thought he'd miss that—the ramshackle spirit of the beach town in his memories—but the Mariposa had integrated beautifully.

The effect seemed to inspire healthy change in the town. He'd recognized several of the old surf shops and taco stands from his college days, but they all sported new paint, and new businesses like Delilah's Desserts had made their home in between some Seashell Beach institutions, bright beads strung on a boardwalk of resurgent stores.

Delilah.

His breath caught for a minute. Even beneath the bakery smells of warm yeast and butter, he'd picked up the barest touch of citrus and cinnamon. That scent had weakened his knees the first time he'd caught it across the sand where they'd first met. He'd never had a chance back then.

Guilt pricked his conscience as he replayed the crash of her tray and her shocked face. Then he gripped the steering wheel tighter, the Mustang's speed climbing as he sped past the hotel toward the undeveloped reaches of the coast highway.

He had nothing to feel guilty about. He wasn't the one who had disappeared with no warning all those years ago.

He was too restless to sit and work in a hotel room right now. Instead, he kept pushing north. In twenty minutes, he'd be at the college he'd attended against his parents' wishes, the one he'd trekked down from every day his sophomore year. At first it was to surf, and then it was for Delilah, either to spend a day on the waves with her or to drop her off after she had spent the night with him.

The sign for the university exit flashed into view, and the Mustang practically flung itself from the freeway. Five minutes later, Luke was out of his borrowed car and deep down memory lane as he walked the campus path from the library to his old apartment.

The first year after Delilah took off for New York was a blur soaked in cheap tequila and barely passable schoolwork. But he'd pulled himself together finally and did what he should have done all along: pushed his parents out of his education completely, taken out loans, and blasted through his final semesters so he could graduate and leave his memories behind the way Delilah had left him.

He sighed and took a bench on the lawn littered with napping and studying students. It must be near the end of the semester, he realized. Maybe he should drop in on one of the psychology classes to see if they could tell him what his brain was thinking, help him work through all the feelings that seeing Delilah had pushed to the surface.

He should have braced himself for her, the only girl—woman now—who had broken his heart. But he'd managed to convince himself that it was some other cooking-obsessed Delilah who had opened a bakery in her hometown. And now he felt . . .

Like a bug that had flown full force into a windshield.

Like a sand castle that had just been walloped by a rogue wave.

Like the cannoli samples scattered over the bakery floor.

But also like the warmth and sweetness in the shop's air had clung to him and followed him here. Even the wind roaring past the open convertible failed to strip it off of him.

He didn't understand the feeling. But he wanted to. And that meant finding Delilah again tomorrow.

Three

Delilah dropped into a kitchen chair and let her head thunk to the table. Then for good measure, she thunked it again. Then one more time after that.

"What are you doing, Mom?"

She squeezed her eyes tighter and held her breath, but when she exhaled and opened her eyes, her brand-spanking-new problem hadn't disappeared. Not unless an Oz-bound tornado had funneled down and snatched Luke away to somewhere far and exotic.

It wasn't such a wild hope. She'd Googled him over the years. Of course she had. He worked as a travel writer for the biggest magazine in the business, and his byline popped up from locations all over the world. Just . . .

Why couldn't he be in Borneo and not sleepy Seashell Beach? If only he'd never come here at all. Not ten years ago. Not now.

Except that would mean no Dylan. And Delilah wouldn't trade Dylan away for anything.

She brushed her hair from her eyes and smiled at her son. His eyes crinkled in worry as he watched her.

"I'm trying to pound some sense into my head. You ever feel like doing that?"

"Only all the time. Mostly you're all right though."

She burst out laughing. "I meant pounding sense into your own head, but I see how it is."

He grinned at her and took a bite out of the grilled cheese sandwich she'd made him.

"How was school?" she asked. "Any . . . problems?"

His smile slipped, and she almost regretted bringing it up. But she had to stay on top of the situation, and pretending like it wasn't a problem wasn't an option.

"It's fine, Mom."

"Yeah? Everyone treated you right?"

He shrugged. "No one treated me bad today. It was fine."

"You'll let me know if Marcus or Gabe bothers you again?"

"I promise." But he didn't meet her eyes. He wasn't old enough to be a good liar yet.

"Dylan . . ."

He looked down at the table.

"Tell me, kid. I promise not to stress."

"It was nothing. They're just stupid."

"So there was some teasing today?"

"Yeah, a little."

He wasn't going to volunteer the information. It had to be bad, then. He usually folded with the slightest pressure from her. "Dylan, the longer you take to tell me, the more stressed I get."

He groaned. "It's just the thing this weekend."

Her stomach double clenched, once because she'd

forgotten about it and again as she realized what the teasing must have been about. "The father-son camp out?"

He nodded. "They're making fun of me for . . ."

For not having a father.

Except he did. And that father had walked through her bakery door not two hours before and cracked open her neatly ordered existence like a pecan shell.

What was she supposed to do about that? Because Luke Romero had no clue about Dylan's existence, and she'd sworn he never would.

Four

uke pushed open the door to Delilah's Desserts and once again caught her scent beneath the smell of fresh paint and the warm baking smells wafting from the kitchen. He grabbed one of the tiny tables and slung his laptop bag over the chair before he approached the cashier. The line was four deep this morning, but he didn't mind. It gave him more time to study the store.

The platinum-haired muralist was back at work. Or at least she was back at the mural, but rather than painting she was staring at him with a look he couldn't interpret. He felt like a figure model as she assessed him from head to toe. It wasn't like being checked out so much as it was being . . . evaluated.

Her lips pursed, then she nodded and went back to her work as if he'd disappeared.

Okay . . .

Delilah's shop wasn't exactly what he would have expected from her. It was clean and contemporary, with butter-yellow walls, white trim, and the occasional touch of blue lending it a beachy feel. He'd have expected the Delilah he knew to paint the walls dark purple and hang fortune teller beads over the door.

Then again, he'd also have expected the Delilah he knew to have aged fast and gone brittle, but that was definitely not what he'd seen yesterday.

Well. He'd changed in the last ten years. Why shouldn't she?

He eyed the display case. Yesterday it had been full of comforting flavors like cannoli and cupcakes with notes of cinnamon or citrus. Or maybe that was Delilah? Today's complicated chocolate flavors marched in rows behind the glass: dark chocolate ganache, blackberry tarts, deconstructed red velvet trifles, and was that . . . He squinted. What was a sesame and yuzu cupcake? After eating all over the world, he had no food fear, but that certainly wasn't a cupcake flavor he'd run into. He was definitely ordering it.

A cell phone chirped ahead of him in line, and he jumped. A buzzing sensation had been playing along his nerves since he walked through the bakery door, and he paused to interpret it. It was more like the way he'd felt before rappelling down the Qumran cliffs in the Judean Desert than when he'd hidden from angry Bedouins in Tunisia. An impending adrenaline rush percolated beneath his skin, the slow simmer before the boil.

The bell announced a new customer, and a cloud of old-lady gardenia swallowed him a second later.

"Tsk," said the voice behind him, and he turned to find a tiny woman swathed in a brilliant pink, plumeria-printed muumuu. "I hate it when it's a moody day. Ganache," she added with a grumble.

"Pardon?" Luke asked. She seemed to be speaking to the room at large, but he didn't want to be rude if she meant him.

She pointed to the case. "All those sophisticated flavors. She always gets unnecessarily complicated when she's in a mood."

"I'm sorry," Luke repeated, feeling as if his wits had been chloroformed by her perfume. "Are you saying Delilah bakes according to her mood?"

She squinted up—way up—at him. "Tourist, huh?"

"No. Well, yes, but . . ."

She waved away the rest of what he was going to say. "Whatever mood she's in, that's what you get."

Interesting. Very interesting. "So what happens if she's happy?"

"Apricot macarons," the tiny woman and the guy in front of her sighed in unison. "Not macaroons." She glared at him as if he'd confused the two aloud. "Macaroons are coconut drop cookies. Macarons are different. They're delicate little French sandwich cookies that . . ." She sighed instead of finishing her sentence.

"Wow," he said. He didn't bother explaining how many freshly made macarons he'd eaten in Parisian patisseries. "That good, huh?"

The tiny woman didn't answer, but just gave him a dreamy smile like she was so far inside the memory of the apricot macarons that she'd forgotten his existence.

"Moods don't sound like an efficient business plan," he said under his breath. Shouldn't Delilah keep some classics on hand?

"That's exactly why her business is blowing up. I wish she'd hire me," the guy ahead of him said. It was an apricot macaron tone of voice.

It made the skin at the nape of Luke's neck prickle, but

he couldn't figure out why. Man, with all the colors the painter was adding to the wall and the rich smells wafting from the kitchen, he was definitely overstimulated. Maybe he should grab his sesame and yuzu cupcake to go and eat it out by the beach so the breeze could clear his head.

The kitchen door swung open, and Delilah backed through it. One look at her poured into her white jeans beneath the bow of her bakery apron, and he changed his mind. He'd finish his cupcake right here.

She bore a tray of samples again, but this time when she spotted him, the cake bits didn't hit the floor. She didn't look surprised to see him. She also didn't look happy to see him either.

She made her way down the line, offering the tray to the waiting customers, exchanging greetings with the regulars. The woman behind him asked, "Got pumpernickel today?"

Delilah stopped in front of Luke and held the tray out, her smile turning plastic. "Not today, Miss Betty. I have a feeling I'll make some tomorrow."

"Ooh," said Miss Betty. Her gaze followed the direction of Delilah's strained smile to Luke's face, and he had to fight a fidget as Miss Betty's eyebrows rose like she'd received critical intelligence about him.

"Cake bite?" Delilah said, clearly wanting him to take his piece so she could move on.

"Sure, if it's anywhere as good as the cannoli." He plucked up a piece, but before she could breeze past him he added, "I'd like to talk to you when you get a minute."

The bell announced another customer, and Delilah's expression relaxed the tiniest fraction as she nodded toward it. "I'm almost always out of minutes. Sorry. Joys of small business ownership."

"Almost always isn't always. I'll take my chances and wait for a lull."

Her face frosted over again. Not the sugar kind. The ice-cold kind. "I need the table space for customers, but there's a great café about two doors down, and you can work in there. People do it all the time."

He popped the cake bite into his mouth and took his time savoring it as first one layer of flavor and then another rolled over his taste buds. It was complicated and interesting, and he had a sudden itch to read Proust or do some speed work at the boxing gym. Or maybe even do speed work while reading Proust.

"This is delicious," he said. "You're two for two, and I don't even like cake. I'll just settle myself at the table and buy different desserts until I've had a chance to try them all."

"Wonderful," she said, in a tone that said the opposite.

She finished serving the line and disappeared back into the kitchen, and after ordering his sesame and yuzu cupcake, Luke sat down at his table and prepared to wait her out. He had all day. In fact, he had all the way until next Tuesday, and he was suddenly fine with waiting as long as it took—and as many cupcakes as it took—to dig deeper into the mystery Delilah had become.

Five

*D*elilah fumbled her phone from her purse and dialed her neighbor's number.

"Hey, Delilah. What's up?"

"Hey, Cindy. I'm so sorry to ask this, but could you pick Dylan up today when you grab Scotty? I'm slammed, and I don't want him to have to wait around for me forever if it doesn't slow down."

"That's great! Means business is good, right? We'd love to have him. I'll get him."

"Thank you," Delilah said, and she wondered if the intensity of her gratitude startled Cindy. But Delilah would be thankful every single day for her mellow neighbor who didn't seem to have any judgments or criticisms of her single parenting or any problem jumping in to help without making Delilah feel guilty for asking.

She did anyway, of course. She tried not to take advantage of Cindy's kindness unless it was urgent, but this . . . Keeping Dylan out of Luke's sight was about as urgent as it could get, short of a severed limb or other catastrophe.

For the next two hours, she popped out of the kitchen between bouts of whipping up dishes to serve as samples when the line got long. Luke stayed put, glancing up from his laptop to smile at her even as he accumulated a growing pile of cupcake wrappers and serving doilies. At one point, Jessie stuck her head back to report that he'd eaten a half dozen desserts so far.

Finally, around the time of their normal lull—post-midmorning snack but pre-lunch—Delilah poked her head out to find that the store was indeed empty.

Except for Luke.

Who only smiled at her again.

She turtled back into the kitchen.

Gah.

He wasn't going away, and she needed him to go away without making him suspicious. She eyed him through the small glass window in the door. He'd turned his attention back to the laptop, and as he smiled at whatever he was reading, the memory of the first time she'd seen him swept over her.

He'd been smiling then too as he waited for her reaction, the girl he'd catcalled on the beach to impress his friends. She knew their type—every last one of them. Frat boys from the university who blew off classes to surf and pick up the local girls. But the local girls weren't easily impressed with the out-of-town flavors, and she was harder to impress than most. Nineteen years old and she'd been jaded for a long time already.

Normally, she'd ignored the stupid frat boys, but he'd been specific and creative in his "compliment," so she whirled and stopped, her hand on her hip, resting above the sweet a—

Well, above the part of her figure he'd just crassly admired.

"What now?" she asked.

He was still smiling. "What do you mean?"

"I mean, you shared your feelings about my butt, you have my attention. Congratulations. Now what?"

A couple of his dumb frat boy friends did that low, *oooooh* sound, like she'd one-upped him, but she was barely getting started.

His smile had slipped a little. "I was paying you a compliment."

"And? I heard it. What am I supposed to do? Say thanks for making me the center of the attention I don't want?"

"Maybe you shouldn't be walking around in that little bikini then," one of his buddies piped in, but at that, Luke's smile had disappeared completely.

"Dude, she's wearing a swimsuit at a beach. Shut up."

But Delilah wasn't interested in letting him off the hook. She'd escaped her house in the aftermath of another fight with her stepfather, and the last thing she felt like dealing with was more males trying to clutter up her mental quiet.

She took a step toward the ringleader, and he actually flinched.

"No, I really want you to tell me. What did you think would happen when you yelled your thoughts about my body to the whole beach? That I would come over and throw myself at your feet? You don't even know me. You want to impress a girl, have a conversation with her so she can at least figure out you like her for her mind and not because she's—" She broke off and scowled at him. "What was it? Bootylicious?" She spat another booty-related name at him, flipped off his friends, and headed down the beach toward the sandy bike rental shack she worked at in the mornings.

Luke had appeared in the shop fifteen minutes later to sheepishly introduce himself, apologize, ask her name, hand her a fresh bunch of daisies, and ask about her favorite book.

That was all it had taken. That bashful grin, that sincere apology, and the realization that he was super hot when she wasn't mad at him, and the wildest summer of her life had begun. When the first of his friends had gone off to put on ties and work the summer internships their parents lined up for them, he'd blown off his parents and stayed behind, plundering his trust fund to pay the rent on the apartment they had all to themselves.

She should have been smarter. She'd always been a smart girl, regardless of her stepfather's accusations. But something about the summer and his smile and the way they talked like equals and not like she was a dumb townie, the way he composed silly, delicious poems to her freckles off the top of his head right before he kissed them. Something about all of that, and well . . .

She didn't regret Dylan or her choice to have him and keep him. And she didn't regret vanishing into thin air when the Romeros, Luke's parents, became a threat to the growing fetus she loved madly and irrationally from the start. And she had never regretted keeping herself and Dylan safe from Luke's spinelessness in the face of his parents' wishes. But she would always regret that the only time she'd ever fallen for someone had been for a boy who hadn't deserved her.

Irritated with herself for hiding, she marched out to the front and plopped herself in the seat opposite him. Avoiding him hadn't done anything. Time to change tactics.

"Why are you here?" she asked.

His eyebrow shot up.

"It's not that weird of a question," she said to his unspoken one.

"I expected something more like, 'So what brings you into town,' not an interrogation."

She fought not to grit her teeth. This was the same kind of garbage his parents had done to make her feel small, his tone policing, implying she didn't know how to handle herself right. And she hadn't with them, right up until the moment she'd fooled them utterly. But she couldn't back down until she confirmed that he didn't know a thing about Dylan.

When she didn't take the bait, his forehead wrinkled, and he pushed again. "Why are you so suspicious?"

He'd gone from smiling to alert, studying her like she had something to hide. Great. Now *he* was becoming suspicious of *her*, the exact opposite of what she was going for. She drew the deepest breath she could without cluing him in that she was struggling for calm and tried a different approach: a smile.

"You're right. I'm stressed trying to get this place into shape for summer tourists. Sorry. Let me try that again. What brings you into town, Luke? It's been a long time."

"Ten years, right?" His easy smile returned, but she still felt the unspoken weight of her abrupt disappearance in his words. "I had no idea you were still around. When I saw your sign, I wondered if Delilah's Desserts could possibly belong to the Delilah who anger-baked in my apartment kitchen at 3:00 a.m. And it is."

Relief flooded her. He hadn't come looking for her. Finding her had been a coincidence. An unlucky one for her, but this was definitely not a man on a mission.

She hoped her own smiled stayed passable. "You still haven't explained what brought you back to Seashell Beach. Are you here on business?" She flicked a glance at his laptop.

He closed it, not as if he were hiding anything from her, but in the same way she would put her cell phone down when she wanted to give Dylan her undivided attention.

27

"I'm working on an article. I'm a travel writer."

She acted like this hadn't turned up in her extensive Googling of him. If he didn't know she owned a bakery in town, he must not have done the same kind of research over the years.

But then, why should he? She was the girl who had ghosted on him without a word at the end of a memorable summer. He had no idea she had his kid.

No. *Not* his kid. Absolutely not his kid.

Her kid. Always.

"Travel writing sounds interesting. I wouldn't have guessed that for you."

He'd been studying civil engineering, which was a hair too close to blue collar work for his parents, who were already distraught that he wasn't attending an Ivy League school. They'd tried to push him toward architecture, something they could find a way to spin as prestigious to their associates, like he was so much more evolved than his law school-bound friends.

"I wouldn't have guessed it for me either, but I love it," he said.

She knew that. It came through in his articles. She'd just been banking on those articles keeping him off in places like Fiji or Madagascar.

"That's great." It sounded lame, but all she really wanted to do was shout, "Get out! Of the whole town! Leave!" so she figured her subdued reply was a victory.

"I shouldn't be too surprised that you're doing something with food, but . . ." He trailed off, studying the shop. "This is perfect, but so different from where I thought you'd end up."

"Let me guess. You figured I'd end up in some cutting-edge San Francisco restaurant doing elaborate pastries and sporting a hundred percent more tattoos."

She got the first peek of the lopsided grin that had won her over in the bike rental shop. Thankfully, she was way past falling for a charming act now. Children had a way of setting your priorities straight.

"Something like that," he admitted. "But it's great to see you thriving here."

"So glad you approve." She felt a twinge of guilt over her sarcasm. He'd been sincere.

Instead of bristling, his smile grew. "You've still got bite."

She wouldn't be drawn into banter with him. She only shrugged.

"So tell me more about the shop," he said. "How long has it been open?"

But she didn't want to catch up on their missing years. She wanted to start the countdown to the next ten years of not seeing him. "Sorry, it was great to see you, but I've got to check on some cupcakes. I hope your article turns out well. At least it won't take long with such a small town." She gave him a wave, but his next words stopped her cold.

"This'll take a while. Seashell Beach is even better than I remembered it. I'm going to pitch this as a story on undiscovered Pacific jewels. I'll have to do some digging to do it justice."

Her heart slammed once against her ribs at the word *digging*, and she turned toward him as casually as she could. "That sounds interesting. How long does something like that take?"

"It takes as long as it takes. Every place is different. How come you can't hire that pierced kid?"

She blinked at him, confused by the sudden change in subject. "Umm, what?"

"I've heard him say two days in a row that he'd die to work here. I'm guessing it's not the first two times he's mentioned it. Why can't you hire him?"

"I'm a small business. I have more work than I can do, but not enough to pay for more help." She clamped her mouth shut. Why was she telling him about her finances? "Speaking of which, I need to get back to—"

"I want to make your bakery the centerpiece of my story."

He'd flummoxed her again. She'd never used that word, but she couldn't think of another one to describe the exact feeling that his non sequiturs provoked. She tried to pick through her confusion. "Are you switching to food writing?"

"Food writing tends to be intertwined with travel writing. It's very much a part of a place. Same as architecture and geography. That's why I like travel writing. I get to explore all of that."

"Okay. But I've been open two years. I'm not exactly an institution. Write about Woody's. If you want to talk about the DNA of Seashell Beach, that place is it."

"I'll cover Woody's too. The thing is, there's been a lot of change here, but it's working better in Seashell Beach than it is in a lot of other coastal towns. Most places, the new competes with the old, and there's a weird tension, visually and otherwise, but not here. It all works, and I think Delilah's Desserts is a metaphor for that. If you give me full access, I promise you that the second this hits the internet, you'll see your business double from people looking for the next undiscovered hot spot. You'll be overrun by hipsters, but they'll bring their money, and you can hire that kid to help you count it all."

She didn't want to be persuaded, but she'd reached the limits of what she could do without a major jump in traffic or a major capital infusion. She refused to go any further into debt to expand, but it also killed her that she could see her trajectory stretching in a flat line indefinitely.

"What kind of access do you need?"

She almost thought she glimpsed relief in his eyes, but he looked and sounded exactly the same when he answered. "I'd need to sit in here for a full day tomorrow to observe you and the store, but mostly the vibe of the people who come in and out, how everything integrates."

No. No way. She couldn't have him here, in her face, all day long.

As if he could sense the rejection coming, he shored up his argument. "I wouldn't press anyone for interviews, just the ones who are totally open to it, and I'd only talk to you during the slow times. I don't think it'll take more than a day. I'd do it today, but I've got an architectural walkthrough scheduled at the Mariposa and some crazy local legends to chase down."

"The wishing well?" she guessed.

"The wishing well. Oh, and something about a fortune cookie café. Anyway, I need to go check into that, but I promise you, if you'll let me work out of here tomorrow, I'll stay out of your hair, but you'll get a massive bump in business when the story runs."

She wanted to say no. Every self-protective instinct she had wanted him gone, but then she had two warring mother instincts: one to protect her cub by getting Luke out of Seashell Beach as fast as possible and one to seize an opportunity that would allow her to provide for Dylan better so that they didn't have to skip some of the activities his friends enjoyed without a thought. Luke was offering her possible long-term financial stability if she could work out how to keep Dylan out of his way in the short-term.

It wouldn't be that hard. Well. Logistically it wouldn't. But it would take her swallowing her pride, and that never went down easily. But if she asked for Cindy's help, she'd get it, no questions asked.

She had to do this.

31

"Sure, a story about the bakery would be great. And yes, you can set up in here if that helps you write it faster." She hoped she sounded casual about it. That's how she should have been playing things all along instead of sharp edges and spiky suspicion. It was more proof she lost her common sense whenever Luke was concerned.

"Great. I'll see you tomorrow."

She gave him a friendly wave and scowled as soon as she turned her back to him, fleeing for the safety of the kitchen. She rummaged for her rye flour. Oh, if ever there was a pumpernickel day, tomorrow was it. She'd set those loaves to rising and bake all her anger out and right into the bread. There was a reason she almost never made it: she almost never got this mad.

Six

*L*uke stared at the arches of the Mariposa as Deanne, the manager, gave him a tour. He still loved architecture, which was why it figured prominently in his articles. Funny, but in a way, Delilah was the reason he'd never pursued it as a career.

He'd almost switched his major from civil engineering even though it meant doing what his parents wanted— something he avoided. But then that disastrous weekend happened when they'd met her and done such a thorough job of humiliating her that she'd disappeared. After that, his only driving interest had been doing the exact opposite of anything they wanted.

Deanne led him down a path toward a distant hedge of hibiscus flowers. "I assume you've heard about our wishing well?" she asked.

"I have. Tell me more about it."

"The developer of the Mariposa spotted it when he was visiting his ancestral village in Mexico. The town was deserted, but the state officials gave him permission to bring the well here on the condition that he'll return it if they ever request it. It's over three hundred years old."

He ran his hand along the time-worn stones. "Are the rumors true?"

"That it grants wishes? Yes and no," she said, a small smile playing around her mouth. "You can wish for whatever you want, but it grants your heart's desire even if you don't know what it is."

"Do you believe that?" He was curious about the secret smile he'd glimpsed.

"Against my own common sense, yes."

"Sounds like a good story."

"It is. Maybe you should try it and see if you get a good story out of it too."

He crouched to examine the tiles painted with butterflies. "No coins on me, but maybe later."

"As you wish," she joked, and he grinned up at her.

"Thanks for the tour," he said, rising. "This is an excellent specimen of Spanish neocolonialism. The developer did a beautiful job of integrating it with the rest of the city."

"He'll be pleased to hear you think so, especially since you have a trained eye."

She excused herself to see to other hotel matters, and Luke stepped out of the hedge to stare at the Pacific. It was doing its best to impress with a bluer-than-usual color and high, crashing waves. He hadn't planned to surf because he hadn't planned to be here long enough to fit it into his schedule, but now he almost itched with the need to get out on the water.

Seashell Beach was stirring up all kinds of interesting longings, he realized as he watched more waves roll in. He'd thought about Delilah a lot over the years, wondered why she'd left him so suddenly. They'd been young, too young to talk about forever, but old enough to fall in love. It had hurt when she'd taken off, but he'd talked himself into blaming it on their age. He'd been barely twenty-one and only two years older than her. No one knew what they wanted at that age.

At least . . . not what they wanted from life. He'd been very sure he wanted Delilah in every way possible.

She'd seemed as into him as he was to her, but obviously he'd missed some clues along the way. And he'd thought he was okay with that, eventually letting the unreturned voicemails and text messages trail off, letting the sting of her vanished social media accounts fade, lapsing into occasionally wondering what she was up to now and then.

But talking to her today, seeing her try to rush him out of her store and remembering the feel of her lips beneath his, watching her unconsciously wrap her arms around her middle in an act of self-preservation as she talked about the bakery and remembering the way her waist had felt beneath his hands . . . it stirred everything up. The past. The hopes he'd had for their future.

She wasn't indifferent to him, whatever her words said.

And to his shock, he wasn't indifferent to her. She wasn't a pleasant memory, a faded summer fling. She was vital, full of new layers on top of the complicated ones she'd had even at nineteen, and he wanted to explore them the way he used to be able to, when he'd seen her core, parts of her heart and mind he knew she'd never let anyone else see.

When he'd pitched the story on coastal towns, it was with the intention of coming to Seashell Beach. He'd thought it was nostalgia for the last time he remembered his life being purely uncomplicated and happy, the place where the rest of the world had disappeared. But it wasn't Seashell Beach that had done that.

It was Delilah.

And even though she obviously didn't want to be doing it again, she was. He was very, very okay with that.

In fact, it sent a prickle of anticipation up his spine, an electricity he couldn't remember feeling in . . .

Ten years. Of course.

He had to figure out a way to get past her defenses, to see if this could become reciprocal.

He wanted that. He couldn't believe how much.

A twinge of guilt over smooth-talking his way into her bakery tomorrow came and went quickly. If anything, he'd underplayed the effect his article would have on her business.

Besides, he wasn't the one who had hurt her, so why was she giving him the straight arm? She'd hurt him, and although he wanted to know the reasons why, he'd already forgiven her the second she dropped her cannoli everywhere. She wasn't over him. Not by a long shot.

He worked for the rest of the night, reading through old digital archives of Seashell Beach to steep himself in the history, but it was hard to focus when all he wanted to do was plot how to chip away at Delilah's armor.

By the time he woke up and returned from a sunrise beach run, he had a plan. Or at least a philosophy. He couldn't come on as strong personally as he had professionally. He'd stay relaxed, tease her gently, work in reminders of the Summer of Delilah and Luke, coax her out of hiding. But he'd have to do it without getting in her way.

It would be tricky, but the same itchy feeling he'd had while watching the waves yesterday came back; he just wanted to dive in.

He was at the bakery early, an hour before it opened to customers. Luckily, Delilah was sliding something into the display case when he knocked on the glass door. He read her surprise across the store.

"I didn't expect you so early," she said when she unlocked the door. Puffs of flour clouded her shirt, and a streak of dark chocolate ran along her jaw. It killed him.

"I was hoping to see behind-the-scenes stuff before you had too many distractions."

"That makes sense, I guess." But her shoulders had stiff set to them.

"Can I watch you work in the kitchen? I might have questions, but if I ask at a bad time, shake your head, and I'll drop it."

"Uh, okay. Use that table in the corner and meet me in the back."

She turned, not waiting to see if he followed. He heaped his things on a chair and sped after her. She was punching a brown blob like it had done her wrong. He stayed out of reach.

"Is that kneading?"

"It's punching."

Ask a stupid question . . .

He tried again. "Why?"

"Because it's done rising, so I have to punch it down and shape it."

"It smells different in here today. What are you baking?"

She nodded down at the dough she was still giving hell. "Pumpernickel bread. You're smelling the yeast and rye flour instead of the usual sugar and white flour."

He said nothing more, not wanting to annoy her enough to kick him out.

After a couple of minutes she stopped punching and sighed. "Could you . . . It makes me nervous for you to sit there like that. Maybe it's better if you ask questions."

"I'm good at that. Why don't explain what you're doing?"

So she did, walking him through the process of mixing the dough, letting it rise then shaping it into loaves.

It wasn't even six o'clock, and he was already tired just listening to the process. "What time do you come in to get this all started?"

"Five o'clock, usually. I time everything so I have a full case and at least one piping-hot breakfast pastry ready to go when I unlock the door for customers."

"How can you get all this done by yourself?"

She shrugged. "I only make about a half dozen things a day. That helps." She nodded at the huge commercial mixer. "I do things in large batches, because it takes the same amount of time as a small batch, so it's more efficient that way. There's a lot of prep work I can do ahead."

"Like what? Freezing dough?"

"That's good for some cookies, bad for cakes. It depends. But yes, make-ahead dough I can pop in the oven. Big batches of frosting. Thursday is frosting day. I make as much as I think I'll need for a whole week."

"Is it hard to keep up with everything?"

She paused to wipe her chin against her shirt, transferring a chocolate smear before she went back to shaping more loaves. "Yes. Sometimes. I've hired employees to handle the nonbaking stuff like customer service and keeping the pantry organized. It all helps."

"But you'd like an assistant baker?"

"Someday. Maybe if you write a good enough article." She gave him the first sincere smile he'd seen from her. It was small, but it was there.

"I will," he said. "You're doing the hard part. I only have to explain it. I bow to your awesomeness in keeping this whole place going."

She shrugged again, like she didn't care that he was

impressed. She probably didn't. Nineteen-year-old Delilah hadn't cared about other people's opinions of her. He dug that this was another thing about her that hadn't changed.

"It's hard, but I don't mind because I love it and no one is my boss."

"That fits," he said.

"What do you mean?"

"It's hard to imagine you ever working for someone else. You always liked doing things your own way." He realized he'd misstepped when her expression darkened. "I mean that as a compliment. It's why I picked my job too. I can mostly do what I want without interference."

Her expression cleared, and she ignored him for a few minutes while she popped the loaves into one oven and moved on to another one to pull out a sheet of individual crusts.

"What are those going to be, and how do you decide what to make?"

"Black currant tartlets."

"Black currant, pumpernickel ... which isn't even a dessert." He fell quiet for a minute, realizing she hadn't answered the second part of his question. "I hate to admit, but even though this is my third day in a row in here, I don't see a pattern to your menu."

"I bake what I feel like baking. No mystery."

"But bread? At a place called Delilah's Desserts?"

She slammed the oven door shut. "Pumpernickel is slightly sweet. They'll get a hot slice with melting butter, and they'll like it."

"Or else what?"

"Or else they don't come back."

"Isn't that a bigger problem for you than them?"

She smiled again. "They always come back."

He propped himself on the empty counter behind him

and fought a smile so she wouldn't think he was laughing at her. "I'm getting more local color than I even hoped for."

She didn't answer, just readjusted the sunny ball cap she wore instead of a hairnet and set to spooning something creamy into the cooling shells.

A few minutes passed when she seemed so absorbed in her task that he wondered if she remembered he was still there. He cleared his throat, and she jumped. Yeah, she'd forgotten. He needed to work on that. "So why Seashell Beach?"

"You said it yourself. It's a hidden gem." She didn't look at him as she answered.

"You seemed pretty happy to leave it behind before."

He hadn't said it with any heat, but her hands froze and then resumed scooping. "It was time to come back."

"You like it that much, huh?"

She gestured vaguely toward the Pacific. "What's not to like?"

He changed the subject to something safer, asking questions about different equipment. She didn't ask him any questions about himself, but he didn't let it deter him, interjecting little bits about himself if he could do it without wedging it in by force. He hadn't seen her shoulders tense in at least twenty minutes. That was progress.

When her morning worker showed up, he melted into the background completely, watching the dynamic as she gave the girl firm but kind instructions. A few minutes before opening, he went out to set up his laptop and smiled when he saw the short line already waiting for Delilah to unlock the door. Front of the line was the Miss Betty from the day before. As soon as the lock clicked, she pushed past Delilah, who anticipated this and jumped out of the way.

Miss Betty's long nose quivered, and a look he would bet was as close as she got to bliss crossed her face. It was a slight lifting of her wrinkles before they drooped downward again. She marched to the cash register and barked, "Well?" as if she'd asked the poor girl a question.

Delilah brushed past her and murmured something low, and Miss Betty's wrinkles deepened in irritation. "I'm not being mean," she said loudly.

Delilah shook her head. "I mean it. Be nice to Jessie, or no pumpernickel bread for you."

Miss Betty scowled. "You don't have any in the case. Did you make it out of air this time?"

Delilah disappeared into the back and returned with a dark brown loaf clasped between her oven-mitted hands, steam rising from the crust. She set it on the counter and sliced off a piece before slathering it with butter.

Wow. He would definitely need a piece of that.

Jessie handed the slice on a plastic plate to Miss Betty, who demanded, "What are you giving me a slice for?"

"Because you asked for pumpernickel?"

Luke admired the way she held on to her patience.

"I want a whole loaf."

"We don't sell it by the loaf," Jessie said, obviously bracing for how this information would be received.

"Of course you do," Miss Betty said.

"We really don't," Delilah said, unruffled. "I make a lot more selling it by the slice."

"And how many slices do you get from a loaf?"

"Twelve."

"For two dollars a slice?"

"Plus butter, yes."

"So I'll take my twenty-four dollar loaf, and I'll pay twenty-five if we can stop this asinine debate."

Luke's jaw dropped, but Delilah only smiled and disappeared into the kitchen to return with a loaf-sized paper bag. Jessie rang her up and greeted the next customer. Luke couldn't help it—he edged past Jessie into the kitchen, leaving her to answer the next customer as to whether he was the health inspector and was he shutting down Delilah's Desserts? Oops.

Delilah didn't tense when he walked in again. That was a good sign.

"Hey, sorry, but someone just paid twenty-four dollars for a loaf of bread?"

"Yeah."

"That happens a lot?"

"Only on pumpernickel days."

"Other breads don't sell as well?"

"I don't make other breads."

"Why only pumpernickel?"

"Why anything? Why macarons or cannoli? I like them. I like pumpernickel."

"Got it." He went out and got in line. He needed some of this bread. So did everyone ahead of him. When Jessie handed him his slice, he tucked a dollar in the tip jar and eyed the dark brown piece, butter running down the sides. "What's so special about the pumpernickel?"

"Try it," she said with a grin. He took it to his table and followed orders.

After his first bite, he had to set the plate down and take a moment to breathe through his sudden quasi-religious experience. Holy smokes, had she laced it with crack?

It was rich and nutty and sweet, and the butter must have come from sugar-fed angel cows. But the flavor was also . . . He couldn't quite explain it. There was something . . .

He took another bite. There was a tang beneath all of it,

a taste he couldn't quite place, almost like pepper but not, and it only made the sweetness sing. He didn't eat much pumpernickel, but this wasn't like any he'd had before. What was it?

He opened up a Google search. Rye flour and whole rye berries, milk, cornmeal, yeast, cocoa, brown sugar, molasses. He could see how the ingredients qualified it for a dessert bakery. Could it be molasses he tasted?

He took another bite. No. That wasn't it. He looked for another recipe when one of the search results caught his eye and startled a laugh out of him. The laugh turned into a choke just as Delilah emerged with another loaf.

"You okay?" she called.

Checking on him was a good sign, but he hadn't quite recovered enough to answer, so he gave her a thumbs up. She set the loaf down and came over anyway. "Did you choke on the bread?"

"I choked on a laugh."

"Because you were eating my bread?" Her eyebrows drew together.

"No, because I was trying to figure out one of the flavors I'm tasting, and I ran across some interesting pumpernickel trivia."

"You're kidding."

"I'm not. I'm a good writer, but I can't make this stuff up. The word pumpernickel means devil farts."

Her eyes went wide, and he wondered for a split second what she would say. The old Delilah would have found this hilarious.

The new Delilah did too. A smile split her face, and then a snort escaped her, followed by a . . .

"Did you just giggle?" he asked.

43

"No. But I laughed. Devil fart," she muttered, walking off and laughing again.

Huh. He would never have guessed it would take devil farts to gain some ground with her, but he had no doubt he'd chiseled one more bit of her armor away.

The bell tinkled at least every two minutes as more customers streamed in. Around nine, the platinum-haired painter showed up and smiled at the line, then smiled wider when she saw him. "Word got out it was pumpernickel day." The bell rang immediately.

He nodded at his third slice. "I understand."

She winked at him and settled herself in front of the mural.

A half hour later, Delilah carried out another loaf from the kitchen and announced, "Last loaf!" which met with immediate protests. "One slice per customer." It was still gone by ten.

After that the line finally dwindled, and Jessie set about wiping down tables and sweeping up crumbs. When the bell stayed silent long enough for it to officially be considered a lull, he went back to the kitchen again. Delilah was rolling out more dough, her arms coated to her elbows with flour and a tendril of hair hanging in her eye, which earned her another streak of flour across her forehead when she brushed it away.

"It's finally quiet out there," he said.

"Morning lull. Always happens."

"So does your early start mean this is about lunch time for you?"

She paused and looked at him. "Usually."

"Can I join you? I wondered if you'd mind introducing me to the Chinese café I keep hearing about."

"How can you be hungry after four slices of pumpernickel?"

"You were keeping count?" It pleased him that she'd paid attention.

Instead of answering, she went back to rolling dough. "I can't leave the store. Sometimes we get an unexpected rush."

He wanted to laugh. He was no amateur in Delilah. More memories had been flooding back, and he was already anticipating her next moves and objections. "How about if I bring back takeout?"

"Fine."

It wasn't a wildly enthusiastic response, but he knew a victory when he saw one, and he hustled out of the bakery before she could change her mind.

Seven

Had Luke always been so . . . persistent?

Delilah refastened her ponytail and went back to rolling out the sugar cookie dough for the big-as-your-hand cookies she'd make tomorrow. Miss Betty's loaf purchase had put her in a good mood, and sugar cookies with bright pink frosting and sprinkles sounded appealing.

The morning with Luke so far hadn't been the nightmare she expected, especially after she'd found him standing at the door far earlier than she'd planned. He'd been good as his word not to bug her. He hadn't asked her anything that would force her to skirt around the subject of Dylan, but he had asked questions about her work that most people didn't. Not many people had asked her about why she made what she made.

She was glad he hadn't pushed too much on the flavor he couldn't quite place in the bread. There was no way to explain it without sounding crazy.

Pumpernickel. Devil farts. She snorted again in spite of herself.

When Luke appeared twenty minutes later, a bag of the best takeout in town dangling from his fingers, she realized she didn't feel even one stressed-laced pang at his reappearance. It was nice to breathe comfortably again.

"Are we eating back here or out front?"

As much as she didn't love the idea of Jessie eavesdropping while she cashiered, she still preferred a public setting to being alone with him.

"If you're cool with me reclaiming my own table, let's eat out there."

As he cleared his laptop, she took the bags but stopped short and glared at him. "Wait a minute. You didn't even ask me what I wanted."

"I think I made a pretty good guess. I'll run back and get something else if I was wrong."

He handed her a carton and a pair of chopsticks. She opened it and couldn't keep a smile from twitching her lips. "Dragon meat."

"Yeah."

Every Chinese restaurant had some version of it, a lightly fried and heavily sauced beef without interference from vegetables. He'd told her once that when he was little, his nanny had convinced him to eat the dish by telling him it was dragon meat, and his curiosity had won out over his pickiness.

She and Luke had eaten it often when they . . . dated? Was that the right word? It sounded so casual for something so intense and consuming, but nothing else felt right for something that had also flamed and died so quickly.

She busied herself with fishing some of the beef out and enjoying the genius of Chef Cái's cooking again. She hadn't eaten there in at least a month. She should take Dylan soon and make sure they got seated in Emma's section. Emma had been pretty preoccupied with wedding plans lately, but Delilah knew she could have made more of an effort to connect on her end too.

"This is as good as anything I've had in China," Luke said after a few bites. "Seashell Beach is killing it with their food game."

A soft warmth washed her cheeks because she knew he meant her food too. "The Fortune Café has been around longer than me, though. It's on its way to becoming an institution."

"I definitely think that's the path you're on. Your places have the same idiosyncratic I'm-going-to-do-it-my-way vibe. It's cool."

Her cheeks warmed again. It almost panicked her. What was happening? Why wasn't Luke anything like the man she'd always figured he'd become, the model son to his parents with a distinguished architecture firm and a high-profile career?

How had he become . . . this? She needed to do her own investigating. She cleared her throat. "So do you write a lot of travel articles about foreign destinations?"

"Mostly foreign, actually. I don't do many domestic assignments."

"How many countries have you been to?"

"Ninety-ish."

She shook her head. She'd never even driven the six hours down to Mexico. "Do you have a favorite?"

"No. There are a few I didn't like, but I find something to fall in love with everywhere I go."

Something about the way he watched her made her want to squirm, but she didn't. Instead, she picked out another piece of dragon meat and considered her next question. "What do you love about your work?"

"All of it. It's a constant adventure."

As a whisper of disappointment feathered through her chest. She realized she'd been hoping for something more. Something deeper. But it didn't matter. Not really.

"What?" he asked.

She glanced up at him, startled.

"You shrugged," he said. "When I said I loved the adventure. You shrugged like you were blowing that answer off. Why? Is that less noble than being everyone's sugar dealer?" A note of teasing underlined the words, but she took the question seriously.

"I wasn't trying to be dismissive. I don't know. It just made me wish I also had a trust fund and no obligations."

For the first time since he'd shown up in the store, his face closed off to her, turning into sharp planes and angles.

"I haven't touched my trust fund in ten years."

She was too startled to be ashamed of misjudging him. "Ten years?"

He didn't repeat it, only kept his steady gaze on her as the weight of that decade fell between them, pulling them closer to a conversation she didn't want to have.

She hadn't even half finished her lunch, but she began to gather up her chopstick wrapper and napkin.

"Why'd you leave?"

She pretended she hadn't heard him, tucking the fortune cookies and extra duck sauce back into the carryout bag.

"Delilah." He waited until she was looking at him. "Why'd you leave?"

She should have prepared an answer to this, but she'd figured the question couldn't come up without some serious conversation leading up to it, and she'd had no intention of having any of those kinds of conversations. But she couldn't fault him for wondering. She would have too.

"I was overwhelmed," she said. "I was immature and everything was happening too fast, and I needed to escape before I forgot all the things I'd planned to do."

"Escape." A hint of anger flashed in his eyes.

"I'm sorry. That's the wrong word. I ran away, not escaped. I wasn't ready. That was all." It was a massive understatement. Or maybe a half-truth. The full truth was that she hadn't been ready for the insulting offer his mother had made her when she'd figured out Delilah was pregnant before she'd even told Luke.

She hadn't been ready for the venom and the threats. She hadn't been ready for the conversation she'd overheard between Luke and his father while she'd agonized over whether to tell Luke about the way his mother had treated her. But that overhead conversation had sent her running for the first bus out of town and down to LA with her growing stowaway safely out of the Romeros' reach.

He didn't look satisfied with the answer, but she was done answering questions. As if he sensed she was about to ghost on him again, if only to the kitchen, he smiled and leaned back into the chair. "I guess I get that. You were young and we were . . . intense."

That was an understatement. Lava was intense. Thunderstorms were intense. They were . . . fusion. Lightning. Magic.

All the way until she realized it was an illusion, and she was his pastime.

But she repeated the word to calm the waters. "Intense. Yes. Nineteen does that to you."

He nodded. "Just to go back a point or two, I never touched my trust fund after you left. I got a job, paid for my last three semesters of school, and my only income is what I earn with my writing. I think it's the reason I'm happy."

"I'm impressed," she admitted.

51

"What about you? Are you happy?" he asked.

"Yes." She was. In most ways that counted, anyway.

He reached for a fortune cookie that had escaped the bag, tapping it against the table. "So I hear the fortunes here come true. Does that make you nervous?"

"No. I'm not sure I believe it. It's only for your first cookie from there, and I've already had mine. It didn't come true, so you can probably eat that pretty safely."

"What was your fortune?"

"Something about a soul mate. The usual. I don't even remember." She remembered every word, but she didn't feel like admitting to her disappointment that her sentimental wish for it to come true hadn't panned out.

"What is it about this place," he mused, turned the cookie over and over. "Wishing wells where things come true, fortunes people believe. Is it part of a particularly clever tourism campaign? Was it like this before, and I don't remember?"

"No, there's always been some of that in the air here. We just spent more time up at your apartment than we did in Seashell Beach. You probably didn't notice, that's all."

"I was pretty distracted in those days." He caught her eye again, and this time it was harder for her to look away, but she made herself.

"I should—" she said, starting to stand up, but he stopped her with a question.

"So what's your gimmick?"

"Excuse me?"

"Can people see something about their future if they eat your pumpernickel bread? Or maybe your baking casts a spell on people." He laughed. "I would totally believe that, actually."

He was closer than he knew, but she'd never explained

the truth to anyone, and she didn't plan to start with Luke. Still, the compliment kept her sitting a little longer.

"No gimmick, unless you count good food."

"That's the best gimmick."

"Then guilty as charged." They smiled at each other, and she wondered why this time it didn't make her want to dive for the safety of her kitchen.

He cleared his throat. "Would you be willing to play tour guide for me for one afternoon? I always learn more from the natives, whether it's Oman or Paris. Or Seashell Beach."

"Sorry, I can't," she said almost before he finished.

"Wow," he said with a laugh. "You're not even going to try to let me down easy, huh?"

"I didn't mean that to be rude. I'm always jammed up with work. And stuff."

"Jessie?" he called. "When does business die down for the day?"

"Three-ish. It's pretty quiet after that."

His eyebrow went up, and Delilah rolled her eyes. "That doesn't mean I don't still have work to do." She pointed at her chest. "Sole proprietor, remember?"

"If you'll give me three hours today or tomorrow, we'll call it even."

"For what? Buying lunch? I'll pay you back."

"No. For bailing on me ten years ago."

"No dice," she said.

He flashed her a grin. "Damn. I thought that would work."

"No, you didn't."

"No, I didn't. But this might. What if I promise to give you three hours of free labor if you'll be my tour guide?"

That was definitely more tempting—except for the part

where the last thing she wanted to do was spend more time with him. "Fair, but I really don't have the time."

"But having a local show me around will get my work done faster, which means I'm out of your hair and this town faster."

"Done," she said without blinking.

"Ha. I think my feelings are hurt that you jumped on that so fast."

"Three hours of your labor, you get a three hour tour, and we all return to normal."

"Deal. Now get back to work. You're distracting me."

"Shut up," she said without any heat. "We'll do your tour tonight, and I expect you back here at 5:00 a.m. as manual labor."

"Cruel."

"Work for your tour, buddy. I'm making your life easier," she said as she rose.

"Hang on. Don't you have to open your fortune cookie whether you believe it or not?"

She fished one from the bag and cracked it open. "Beware giant purple bunnies."

"It doesn't say that."

She handed him the paper strip that proved it did.

"What kind of fortune is that?"

"A typical one for the Fortune Café. Your turn."

"This is suddenly way less scary," he said. "I was half believing the stories."

"I don't know," she said, thinking about it. "Mine didn't come true, but enough have come true for people I know for it to be slightly more than coincidence."

"So I should be scared?"

"You should be a man and eat your cookie."

He smirked at her and cracked his open, scanned the strip, then, frowning, scanned it again.

"What does it say?"

He folded it in half. "Just another one of those vague fortunes that could be for anyone."

But she noticed as she scooped up her carton that he slid it into his wallet instead of sweeping it up with the rest of his trash.

Eight

uke pulled a shirt from his bag, a striped one that was slightly dressier than the one he'd worn in the shop all day. Would Delilah think he was trying to impress her?

So what if she did? It was exactly what he was trying to do. He shrugged out of his polo shirt and into the button-down, switching to crisp black shorts for good measure.

He couldn't explain why it mattered to him that Delilah notice him, really see him, and like what she saw. Not his wardrobe change: him, the way she'd seen the real him ten years ago when no one else could.

When he reached the bakery, she was waiting for him outside. She'd changed too. She still wore the white jeans that killed him, but sandals replaced her sneakers, and a filmy flowered top had replaced her work shirt.

She ran her eyes over him, quick as a blink, but he smothered a grin. She had totally checked him out.

"You ready?" she asked.

"Lead on."

They set off down the boardwalk, and he listened as she described each shop. She knew the story of every store, every owner.

"How do you know all this?" he asked. "Is it from growing up here?"

"Some of it, yes. But a lot of these places opened while I was gone. The owners come in and get pastries. I poke around in their shops. We talk. They listen."

They passed a candle shop as the owner came out to reposition the sandwich board advertising her seashell candles. "Hey, Delilah," she called. "How's Dylan?"

"Great," Delilah said and waved to the woman before pointing out to the horizon. "Do you see that?"

"See what?"

She squinted. "Oh, I thought I saw a white sail. Sometimes this old restored schooner sails close enough that you can see it if you look hard, but I must have been looking at a cloud."

"Who's Dylan?" he asked. Was it a boyfriend? He hadn't even thought about that. He'd seen her naked ring finger and figured it meant the field was clear.

"A mutual friend," she said. "Hey, remember this place?" She'd stopped in front of a bookstore they used to explore together. A display of children's books by a local author filled the front window, and she pushed open the door.

"Wow. Memory lane." The smell of new books hit him, but underneath it was a different smell than he remembered. It was the more mellow vanilla of old books tempering the scent of all the new ones. "Something's different. It smells different." He glanced around the store but couldn't see what had changed. The shelves were where he remembered them. It had been painted and spruced up, but there wasn't a huge change.

"The owner expanded to take over the space next door. If you go around those shelves, it opens into a used book section."

He followed her pointing finger and found himself in a space even larger than the original part of the bookstore, only used books stuffed this one, and the homey smell wrapped around him in a blanket of nostalgia. "Wow. Here I thought bookstores were struggling, but this place seems to be doing even better than I remember."

"It was struggling until he opened the used section. The old with the new has been magic for him."

"Magic," Luke repeated. It was as if that word threaded through every bit of this beach town. How had he not noticed that before when he used to cut class and escape down here to surf?

Delilah brushed past him into the used section, and he had his answer. Delilah had crowded out everything else back then.

No, not crowded. That sounded like an unwelcome distraction. Delilah had simply seared everything else from his consciousness except her.

The hairs on his arm rose even though only the hem of her shirt touched him as she passed. It wasn't even a surprise. This was the effect she'd had on him ever since she'd chewed him out the first time they met, her sunglasses pushed up so he could see the fury in her eyes.

This new Delilah didn't have that same barely contained fire. Shadows had crept in, walls had gone up . . . yet the heat she sent prickling along his skin was exactly the same.

"This is like a mini Powell's," he said, shaking off her spell.

"A what?"

"It's an iconic bookstore in Oregon. Same kind of thing,

where they sell both old and new books, and they're busy from morning until night. I did a story on them once for a Portland piece. The place is fifty thousand square feet, I think."

"I thought you said you didn't do many domestic stories."

"I did when I was first starting out to prove I could handle bigger assignments." He didn't mention that he'd included the iconic bookstore because wandering its stacks had reminded him of all the nights he'd spent curled up with Delilah reading to each other from their favorite books. That summer they'd fallen in love with a Lebanese mystic and poet, his verses seeming to paint the story of their own wild love.

It had been that, he realized. Love. He'd thought so then but talked himself out of it when Delilah disappeared. He'd blamed his fevered mind on the sultry summer and her wicked smile. True things didn't end that way, he knew, so it must not have been true.

That was the story he'd told himself, but standing here with Delilah now, he knew his rationalization had been the lie. Maybe those days had been impulsive and untamed, but they'd been real. Those feelings had been real.

Delilah must know it too, or she wouldn't be so guarded. She wouldn't have dropped a tray of food and hidden the first chance she got. She'd have greeted him as breezily as she did Miss Betty. But her instinct had been to run. You ran from things that might hurt you, and while he never had and never would, she obviously thought he could.

Whoa.

This was heavy, but the kind of heavy that gave him hope at the same time.

He scanned the neatly lettered category signs until he found Poetry. He wondered if there was a copy of that old poet's book and what Delilah would say if he found it. They'd spent hours reading those poems, marking them up, sometimes writing notes to each other when they saw each other in the lines. It had been a better literature class than anything in college.

He ran his finger down the spines until he got down to G and slowed, looking for the poet's name. There. Gibran. A worn spine of the exact same edition they'd read to each other faced out. The mystic's work was constantly reprinted in new editions—a few of the later ones sat with this copy—but he grabbed the worn one that looked exactly like the one they'd read from.

He pulled it and went to find Delilah. She had settled on the floor in the cookbook section, an old bread-making book open in her lap.

"Look," he said, crouching and extending it to her.

Her eyes widened, and a deep flush washed her cheeks as she took it from him. He smiled, guessing which memories had come flooding back to her. He bet they included tangled sheets too.

She opened it to the title page, running her fingers over the sketch of the poet, then leafed through a few pages before she stared up at him in total shock. "You kept this?"

"It was on the shelf. The same edition as ours and everything."

"Luke." Her voice was nearly a whisper. "This is our book." She turned to a page in the middle and handed it back to him, her finger pointing to a line in the poem. *I love you when you bow in your mosque, kneel in your temple, pray in your church.* Next to that she'd scrawled, *You are my church.*

Pain washed over him, but it carried something else in its current: need. The need he'd felt for her then. The need he had for her now. The need to see the Delilah he had known in this pulled-together woman who was showing the first cracks that let her old self through. And even something besides need. It was . . .

Wonder.

He had stood in the shadow of the Taj Mahal, a monument built by an Indian prince to his love, and hadn't felt the same sense of awe that finding their copy of this book at this moment detonated inside him.

"How is this possible?" he asked, turning the pages, watching as their handwriting intertwined in the margins of their favorite poems.

She shook her head, mute.

He rose and started out of the used section.

"Where are you going?" she called.

He paused for a moment. "I'm never letting this book out of my sight again." *Or you either,* he thought, his hand closing tightly around the spine as he strode to the register.

This sleepy little beach town was getting beneath his skin more than anywhere else he'd been in the world, but it was showing him a truth he'd known in his bones, the answer to why he didn't stay in relationships, why he moved restlessly from one country to the next, never anchored to a person or place: Delilah had also gotten under his skin all those years ago, and she'd stayed there and been a part of him ever since.

Delilah was quiet when they hit the sidewalk again. They passed a Salvadoran pupuseria and a souvenir shop without saying a word. She didn't even seem to notice them. They reached the next cross street, the one where her shop was located. They'd traveled only two blocks but a full decade back in time. Instead of continuing down the boardwalk, she crossed to the ocean side of the street, slipped her sandals off, and set off across the sand toward the rock jetty.

He wondered what she was thinking, but he suspected he'd get more out of her if he let her work through whatever it was than if he pushed her to talk. The tide was low but rising as she climbed the rocks. He stood at the base and looked up at her, not sure if he should give her space or join her.

After a minute she glanced down at him and patted the rock beside her, so he climbed up and took the spot. She didn't say anything as he settled down beside her, just kept her eyes on the ocean, her legs folded lotus style as if she were meditating.

Finally, she spoke. "Tell me who you are now."

"What do you mean?"

"I mean are you the same Luke you've always been? Are you different?"

He hedged, not sure what she was looking for. "Which one's better?"

"The one that's truer," she said.

"Fair enough. I'm mostly the same, I think. But some important things have changed."

"Tell me all of them."

He gave a low laugh. "Strip my psyche naked and lay it out for you? Is that what you're asking me to do?"

She stared at him without blinking. "Yes."

He scrubbed his fingers through his hair. "Women usually buy me dinner first before they ask me all my secrets."

She returned her gaze to the waves, and he immediately missed the warmth of it.

"I'll tell you," he said, surprising himself. He had the reputation of being laid back, but it was armor as true as hers, a shield that kept people from trying to see below his surface. They took him at face value.

But Delilah knew from the old days, from the pages in the book sitting in its plastic bag between them, that he was more than he let on.

He cleared his throat. "I live only on my salary. I'm done

with my parents' money. I picked travel writing because it took me far away from them and paid my way to see the world. I thought I'd figure out what I really wanted to be when I grew up while I explored it."

"Did you figure it out?"

"Yes and no. I see what I want to do. I haven't figured out how to do it."

"You're being vague."

"Yeah," he admitted. "But would you like to sit here and spill all your insides out all over the place for me right now?"

She granted him a small smile. "I guess not. So you've traveled the world, you know what you want to do, and that's not being a travel writer?"

"I don't want to give that up. It's become too much of who I am. Finding new places and the lens to understand them with, trying to translate it through words that will inspire people to pick up and explore places that make them grow too. I don't know. It would be hard to stop."

"So you definitely plan to be out there"—she waved, the graceful sweep of her arm encompassing the whole horizon—"more than you'll be here?"

"Here as in Seashell Beach?"

"No, here as in wherever home is."

"New York," he said. "And yes. I'm on the road more than I'm not. But I have the best office views in the world." And this time it was his turn to sweep the horizon.

"Are you happy?"

"I'm content."

She didn't say anything for a long time, and they listened as the waves crashed below. Silently she turned to him and touched a scar near his temple. It was so faint he never noticed it anymore. "I remember this. You got it here. That was scary."

They'd been down at the base of the jetty after a hot

afternoon of surfing, about to scramble up as the tide rolled out to check the tide pools for starfish. He'd slipped on a boulder and cut his forehead. It hadn't even needed stitches, but head wounds—even small ones—bled copiously, and from Delilah's reaction, she'd thought his end was near.

"I think it scared you way more than it scared me," he said, cupping his hand over hers. She didn't pull away. "You took good care of me though. You always did."

"You're different now," she said. Her thumb feathered along his cheekbone, and despite the fine ocean mist, her touch burned.

"You might be the only person who thinks so." But it was somehow right that she was the only person who could see that. She was the only one who'd seen beneath the surface back then too. "I'm sorry," he almost whispered. "It's this place. It's this book. It's you." He drew her palm down to press a kiss in it. Her skin smelled like vanilla, and he kissed it again, unable to resist a small taste to see if she was vanilla too.

She sucked in a sharp breath, and he lifted his head to apologize, but instead of pulling her hand away, she turned it to trail her fingers across his lips. Lightning shot straight through him, and he fought a groan. No one had ever been able to affect him like this. No one but her.

She drew back and stood. "The tide's coming in. Better climb down, or we're stuck until it ebbs."

He didn't want to climb down. He didn't want to leave their perch above the water until she answered the question he suddenly ached to know: how she could have walked out on this connection when he'd traveled the whole world and never found anything like it since?

But he stayed quiet and followed her back to the sand. The beach crowd had thinned to almost nothing, a few people dotting blankets, maybe waiting for the sunset.

Delilah led him back to the business side of the street and resumed her tour of the stores and their owners until the shops began to dwindle.

"Now what?" he asked. "I still have ninety minutes left in this contract."

"You mean the imaginary one made of air that we never signed?"

"That one."

She hesitated. "I could take you through some of the neighborhoods, show you some of our Seashell Beach quirks."

He didn't mention that he'd already investigated a few on his own. "That works. I've got a rental parked halfway between here and the bakery."

She nodded, and they walked back in silence. The silence was loaded but somehow not uncomfortable. He let his hands brush hers every now and then purely for the electricity it sent up his arm. Did she feel that? She must, because sometimes she let her hand brush his too.

She smiled when she saw the Mustang. "This is a long way from your wannabe hippie surf van."

"I loved that dumb, old VW bus as much as any hippie could. Not a wannabe."

"It is if your parents buy it for you."

He smiled to concede the point. "What does it make me if I'm driving a convertible on the company's dime?"

"A wannabe California boy."

"Tonight? Guilty as charged," he said, holding her door open for her.

She directed him up the nearest hillside, but instead of pressing on to the luxury homes, she sent him north through a far more modest neighborhood he definitely hadn't investigated and then into an older tract subdivision like a hundred others he'd seen.

"Not much local flavor here," he finally said as they reached the end of the main neighborhood street.

She smiled. "Just follow directions, frat boy. Turn left here."

The homes probably dated back to the seventies, California ramblers and bungalows with cracked driveways and towering olive trees. Finally, at the mouth of the last road in the neighborhood, she directed him to park along a curb and climb out.

He shot her a questioning look, but she only shot him a mischievous smile as they turned onto the little suburban street. He immediately stopped in surprise.

A laugh bubbled out of Delilah, and he wished he could feel it rumbling from her chest, trilling in her throat, spilling from her lips. He swallowed and forced his attention to the absurdist Wonderland confronting him. Every other house on the street sported a large, whimsical sculpture on its lawn. "What is going on here?"

"A couple of years ago, an old guy named Jasper Greene moved in with his daughter in their casita," she said, pointing to a house halfway down the road. "He was a famous sculptor in his younger days, but from what he tells me when he comes in for the blintzes he's not supposed to eat, he was sick of doing pretentious bronze castings for big corporate gigs. He thought the street lacked character, and he decided to give it some."

She walked him over to the first one, a shiny fish. "He put together a sculpture made of found objects he scoured for on these long walks he would take and built something to make his little granddaughter happy, a dwarf from a fairy tale she loved. He installed it right in the front lawn, and his daughter was mortified until the neighbors came over and told him he could use their yards if he made any more. And thus a new

Seashell Beach oddity was born. I like to check it every month or so for new ones. This is the most recent."

"Do you know how hard it is to find things that are genuinely quirky and not the trying-too-hard quirky?" he asked, crouching to admire the blue-and-gold fish made from old bicycle parts and discarded paint cans.

They examined every sculpture on the street, and he snapped pictures of each of them with his phone. "This is a gold mine. Thank you."

"Sure."

As they turned back to the car, he realized the sun had nearly set. He glanced down at his watch. Eight o'clock. The tour was over, and he couldn't ever remember being so disappointed about an evening ending.

He needed more time with her.

When they reached the car, he cast around desperately for a way to avoid getting in and driving her back to the store. Another sculpture garden, a lawn full of pink flamingos, something, anything.

He glimpsed white fencing further up the road. "Is that a park? With an ocean view?"

"You can see a slice of it from the swings," she said.

"Do you mind if we check it out? I hate missing a Pacific sunset."

"Sure."

They settled into the swings, and she sighed. "Sorry. Looks like we missed it after all."

He stared out at the flash of the water, more silver than blue now. "It's okay. It was just an excuse to prolong the evening."

She smiled. "I know."

He stood and pulled her to her feet. "Everything about you is better than I remembered. It's killing me not knowing if this is too." He pulled her against him and found her lips, brushing a kiss against them, a soft growl of satisfaction escaping him when they opened beneath his.

He'd meant to be soft and sweet, but it had never been that way with them. The moment her hands slid around his neck, her fingers threading through his hair, every good intention he had melted against the searing heat that swept through him, that rolled off of her.

He deepened the kiss, exploring her mouth, the ivory slide of her teeth, her sugar-scented breaths. She moaned soft and low and leaned into him. He walked them back until his back met the trunk of a broad eucalyptus tree and rested against it, hungry to take her weight as she strained against him.

He couldn't get enough of her, and when he finally broke the kiss, it was only to explore the soft line of her jaw in a trail of kisses to the hollow beneath her ear.

"I will never understand how you walked away from this," he said, resting his forehead on her shoulder. "But I'm so glad you're back."

She stiffened, and he went still, sensing a shift in her, waiting to see what she would do.

"Am I wrong?" he asked, pulling back to frame her face in his hands.

"No," she said, but a tear appeared, trembling on her lower lashes.

"What did I do? What's wrong?" He brushed it away with his thumb, desperate to fix what he'd broken.

She pushed away from him and pressed the palms of her hands into her eyes while she drew a few deep breaths.

"Luke, I—" She stopped as more tears fell.

"Hey, hey, it's okay. Whatever it is, it's okay. Just tell me."

She turned her back to him and wrapped her arms

around her waist, and he'd never seen a starker portrait of loneliness before she finally drew another deep breath and turned to face him.

"Luke."

"Delilah."

"I left because I was pregnant."

Nine

"What?"

"I was pregnant."

"I heard that. I just . . . what?"

He looked so lost, and she wanted to reach for him again, tell him it would be okay even as she told him the truth that was about to change her world, and possibly Dylan's, forever. How had things turned around so completely?

"That's why I left. I was pregnant. I was scared. I didn't know what to do. So I took off."

"Did you . . . What about . . ." He swallowed, and a sick wash of fear and nausea rolled through her stomach at what she was about to say.

"I had him. I kept him. He's amazing."

Luke looked as if the ground had tilted beneath him and the world had changed shape. He reached out a hand like he wanted something to hold on to, then lowered it to his side. He tried and failed to say something again, and then, he sat. Sat on the ground and dropped his head into his hands.

She didn't try to rush in or explain. She remembered how huge it had felt when Dylan became real to her even though he was nothing but a grainy, peanut-shaped blob on an ultrasound printout. Her world had changed shape that day too. She had no way of imagining how it would feel to have someone tell her that she had a nine-year-old she'd never known about.

But she didn't regret telling him. The moment that old volume of poetry had fallen open and she had recognized the spiky slash of his handwriting, she knew the thread that had connected them then had stretched all the way forward to now, and that he deserved to know, no matter what happened between them.

Luke drew a shuddering breath and found his words. "Is he happy?"

"Yes." It wasn't the question she had expected. Maybe she thought he would ask if Dylan was healthy, that he'd demand to see him. But not this most important question.

"Does he know that I don't know about him?"

"Yes."

Luke rose to his feet, slid his hands into his pockets, and walked until the fence stopped him, then vaulted over it and headed down the sidewalk. She stayed behind him, not sure what to do. At the car, she half expected him to jump in and drive off, but he braced his hands on the side and leaned over, his head bowed like he'd run a long race and used up his energy.

She stopped several feet away and waited, not sure for what.

"Why?" This time it was a snarl, and she stepped back.

"I told you, I was scared."

He whirled on her. "I don't believe that. Not for a second.

Did you think I was going to be angry? Blame you? I was there, Delilah. I remember how that baby happened."

She took a step back, startled by the force of his anger. Tendrils of it reached out to her like the fog gathering around them as the last light faded.

"I wouldn't have blamed you, and I think you know that. So tell me what it really is, because I never gave you a single reason to be scared of me."

"You're scaring me right now," she said quietly, but he flinched.

"I'm not going to hurt you," he said after a minute. "It never crossed my mind. But I do feel like I'm going to explode. I don't know what to do right now. I better take you back."

"No, Jasper's daughter can drop me off. It's okay."

She could see that it didn't sit well with him to drive off and leave her, so she pointed up the sculpture street. "Why don't you watch me walk up and knock? I'll wave if she's fine with giving me a ride."

He heaved a frustrated sigh. "Maybe that's best right now. But Delilah," he said, and a note of warning laced his voice, "I have a lot of questions, and I deserve real answers. And I'm going to want to meet him."

The thought made her sick. She had to find a way to explain all of this to her son, and she had no idea how she would do it, but she nodded. "I need to give him some time to get used to it. I don't know what I'm going to tell him, and I don't know how soon he'll be ready."

"It's been almost ten years for me already. I don't want to wait."

She lifted her chin. "You deserve to meet him. But it won't happen until he wants it to, and nothing is going to change that. If you try to go around me, there will be hell to pay."

"I wouldn't do that," he spat. "I never realized you had such a low opinion of me all these years."

She snorted. "I guess we're even then, because your low opinion of me back then was a shock too."

Confusion clouded his face. "What are you talking about?"

"Never mind," she said, rubbing her hands down her face. "I'm exhausted. We both have a lot to think about. Don't come to the bakery in the morning, but if you don't mind stopping by tomorrow afternoon and leaving your contact info, that would be good."

She skirted around him to the corner and walked up to Jasper's house. His daughter, Anita, answered, happy but confused to see her. When she explained what she needed, Anita snatched her keys from a hook near the door, and Delilah glanced down to the corner. Luke stood there waiting, and when she waved, he nodded and disappeared. She settled in for the short drive to her house, her mind half on Anita and half on how she was supposed to break this to Dylan.

The sitter had already gotten him down to sleep when she got home, so she paid the girl and crawled into her own bed, where her thoughts chased themselves so quickly and with so little logic that the mental tornado carried her down into a fitful sleep.

Luke wasn't waiting for her at the store in the gray dawn light, but she found his business card tucked into the door frame with his familiar scrawl on the back. *I'll be waiting.*

She knew it wasn't a threat, but she shivered anyway.

In the kitchen she pulled the first batch of cookie dough from the fridge and set to work slicing off perfect circles and spacing them on the baking sheet while the oven heated. She'd made the dough yesterday when the morning had passed uneventfully and she'd felt her first moments of ease since Luke had appeared.

This dough would be good, infused with that feeling of calm she'd carried in her as she made it. But she'd meant to make more today, and she couldn't. She'd had no idea she would betray herself so thoroughly before the moon rose last night, and if she tried to make more dough in her current mood, it would taste bitter.

She knew that people thought her menu choices were capricious and found them sometimes charming, but sometimes annoying if they wanted something she hadn't been in the mood to make that day. But it was those moods that gave the food she baked their flavor, and she had learned never to work against them. The food always suffered.

But even her worst mood, if she baked the right food, gave her creations a texture and complexity that people couldn't quite put their fingers on.

That was the flavor Luke had been trying to identify in the pumpernickel yesterday, but how could she say to him, "It's my anger. I only make pumpernickel when I'm angry because I ruin everything else I touch."

She couldn't. She'd tried once or twice to explain it to people she thought might understand—one of the sous chefs at the first LA restaurant she'd worked in, and later to another preschool mom she'd grown close to when Dylan was little. But both of them had treated her just a touch differently after that, and she'd never bothered explaining it to anyone again. She knew what she knew. Her happiest moments meant apricot macarons, her saddest were for savory pies, and right now she felt . . .

Like she couldn't make new sugar cookie dough.

Her mood was more . . . she wasn't even sure. Scared.

Defensive in a mama bear way. Guilty for how she had leveled Luke with the news. Confused.

She didn't know a word for all of that, but she knew what to bake, and she gathered up the ingredients she would need for rocky road bars, because nothing seemed like a better metaphor for a million things happening inside of her at once.

When those went into the oven, her mood had settled slightly, and as she frosted the sugar cookies and waited for the bars to bake, she was astonished to find a new mood growing and another change in her menu plans for the day. Her attention kept wandering from the frosting back to the kiss with Luke last night, the kiss that had been one long breath, one long gasp, one long shiver of heat and desire.

And that was how she found herself mixing up the batter for the most decadent cake in her arsenal, Death by Chocolate. But even as she topped it with cherries on perfectly piped icing curls, she knew that it hadn't been enough to exorcise the kiss from her system.

She was beginning to despair anything ever would, and despair could only lead to oatmeal raisin cookies, the saddest cookie of all.

It was quite a mixed display case when the store opened to her first customers, but by the afternoon, the display case was looking sparse when she waved goodbye to Jilly and headed out to fetch Dylan from school.

He flew out of the classroom, his shoelaces streaming behind him, and launched himself at her in a bear hug.

"I missed you so much last night, Mom."

"I saw you this morning, silly muffin." She had to wake him at 4:45 every day and drop him off next door at Mrs. Castro's house. Mrs. Castro gave her a key and kept a warm blanket for Dylan to settle back under to sleep until their kindly neighbor got him off to school while Delilah opened her doors to the first customers of each day.

"I know, but I tried so hard to stay up and wait for you last night, but I just fell asleep."

She gathered him into another hug. "I'm yours for the rest of the day. What should we do?"

"*Minecraft!*" he shouted, and she groaned while he laughed.

"All right, an hour of *Minecraft*, but then we're curling up with some Narnia."

"Deal," he said, and her breath caught because it was exactly the same way that Luke had said it the day before. And the more time she'd spent with Luke yesterday, the more she had caught mannerisms—a tilt of the head, a certain little smile that she'd seen on Dylan his whole life.

Maybe that more than anything else had finally convinced her it was time to tell Luke the truth. That and a sense that it would matter to him to know.

At home, instead of Narnia, Dylan convinced her to pack for their overnight camping trip, winning her over with his excitement. She'd worried that he was going to be embarrassed as the only kid there with a mom instead of a dad or an uncle, but he was all chatter as he carefully followed the diagram in his Wildlife Scouting book to make his bedroll.

She wasn't sure she wanted to dim the enthusiasm by dropping a bombshell on him: that he had a father who wanted to meet him.

Friday she baked up more cannoli, vanilla bean cupcakes, hazelnut tortes, and lemon pound cake. Good, solid, comfort foods as she soaked in the last few days of being Delilah and Dylan, a perfect set. It was possible that very soon they would become Delilah and Dylan and Luke and Dylan as they figured out how to be in one another's lives.

Several times she caught herself murmuring a prayer or a hope or a wish. *Let him love Dylan.* And sometimes, even though she had the grace to be ashamed, she found herself wish-hope-praying, *Let Dylan always love me just a little more.*

Luke respected her wish to stay away until she gave him permission to come back around, and she gave him grudging credit for it. It had to be eating him up, not knowing her time frame, not knowing how Dylan would take it. But Friday after work, for the third afternoon in a row, she'd driven past the hotel parking lot and seen his rented Mustang still in the lot. He was sticking this out.

At school Dylan almost vibrated with excitement. "It's time to go to the campout, Mom!" he said, grabbing her hand and pulling her back toward their little car. "I want to get there right on time."

"We don't even need to leave for an hour," she said, laughing, but she let him pull her along. At home he nearly drove her crazy repacking everything she loaded into the car. Geez, he hadn't even had a man in his life to teach him that; it must be coded into the male DNA.

She got them on the road early out of self-defense and listened to more of his happy chatter during the thirty-minute ride up to the campground in the foothills.

A handful of boys and their fathers were already there, and her heart sank when she spotted Dylan's most persistent bully, a bratty boy named Tyler. She led Dylan to the farthest edge of the clearing, and he didn't seem to give Tyler any notice as they set their tent up.

The troop leader, a gruff man named Dan, wandered over. "Hey, Delilah. Need help?" It was sweet of him to offer considering he hadn't been thrilled about having a woman come along in the first place, but she smiled up at him.

"No, thanks. We practiced setting up the tent a dozen

times in our backyard." They'd done it specifically so she wouldn't have to ask one of the dads for help.

However, as she attempted to pound in the first tent stake while Dylan held the other end of the tent pole in place, she realized she may have been too hasty in rejecting Dan's assistance. At home, the stakes had slid easily into the soft grass of their yard. Here, the ground was sun-baked to the hardness of brick, and her best efforts only led to two bent stakes.

"Mom, you almost done? I need to stretch a little," Dylan called from the other side of the tent. "Can I let go?"

"Just set it down for a minute, sweetheart," she said, and the tent fell flat while she stared down at the baked earth and wished she knew a really good old-school evil curse for it. She stole some glances at the other dads as they worked. They all carried heavy rubber mallets that they swung hard to drive the stakes down in three or four whacks.

She looked down at the regular hammer in her hand. Oops. Mistake one.

"Come here, kiddo," she said, pulling Dylan over to point at the chipped dirt. "The ground is harder here, so this hammer isn't tough enough to do the job." His expression fell, and she tickled him. "Don't worry about it, because I'm tough enough. We'll get it done. I'll just go borrow one of their mallets."

"No, Mom. Don't. We can figure this out."

"They won't mind. I'll wait until they're done hammering."

"So we're just going to sit here until they finish?"

"No, let's set up the cornhole game so there's something for everyone to do when the tents are ready." He looked relieved and hurried to the car to fetch the cornhole set they'd borrowed from Cindy. It was a simple beanbag game, but it never failed to keep the men and boys entertained during their Fourth of July block parties.

When Dan's tent—which she decided was more like the Tent Mahal than an actual tent—stood looming over the campsite, she went over to borrow the mallet, which he gave her only after she spent five minutes convincing him she really could do it herself with a heavier mallet and another five minutes enduring a lecture on best strategies for driving stakes.

Ugh. He was a nice man, but good heavens, it wasn't the rocket science he tried to make it out to be.

By the time she escaped back to the cornhole game, Dylan had disappeared, probably bored to death waiting for her while Dan had tried to put her to sleep with his mallet lecture. A minute later she spotted him just beyond the boundary of their own campsite, head bent as he scuffed the dirt road and listened to Tyler.

"Dylan," she called hurrying over to him. If she had fur, it would have risen.

"Hey, Miss Dawes," Tyler said as he sauntered past her back to the campsite.

"Hi," she muttered, not trusting the saunter. "You good, Dyl?"

"Yeah, fine," he said, but he didn't turn around, and his hands crept up to his eyes in a move she recognized as one of her own when she was trying to keep her tears from falling.

"What's going on, sweetheart? What did Tyler say to you?" She rounded him to study his face, but he turned to keep his back to her. "No, Dylan. We don't do that. We share the truth with each other, remember?"

He stiffened but let her turn him. Sure enough, tears had made tracks in the dirt he'd managed to accumulate in the twenty minutes they'd been there.

"Was Tyler teasing you again?"

Knowing his tears had already given him away, he nodded. "Yeah."

"What was he teasing you about?"

"It doesn't matter, Mom."

She lifted his chin and wiped the tears from his cheeks with her other hand, holding up her glistening fingertips. "These say something different. And I'm going to kill him, so I'd like to know why."

That got a small smile. "It's no big deal."

"Dylan . . ."

He sighed. "He said it was too bad my dad's a girl who doesn't even know how to put up a tent."

He'd gotten curious questions about his missing father when he was younger and more teasing in the last year or two as the kids grew older and learned how to find each other's soft spots. But this was the first time her reaction had been fear and not pure anger over someone hurting her child, because now she had to tell him that he did have a father.

He would be thrilled, and that was exactly what terrified her: allowing Luke and Dylan to connect would mean giving Luke the most power after her to hurt this child. But as she caught another rogue tear, she realized that having an absent father was already hurting him.

She'd have to do this soon. Tomorrow, probably, when they were back in their snug bungalow and there were no witnesses to the news that would change his whole life no matter how it went.

He let her hug him, one of the things that she adored about him. He never tried to slip out of her embraces the way his friends did to their moms no matter how much they teased him. And so she hugged him a little harder and said, "We're going to take this huge mallet, beat the snot out of those stakes, kill our old backyard setup record, and blow everyone's minds. You ready?"

He sniffed and grinned, scrubbing the back of his hand across his face. "Ready!"

"Race you!"

They barreled back into the campsite, laughing and teasing each other as they attacked the tent setup again. The mallet made more progress than the hammer had, but she still could only get the stakes halfway in. However, she didn't want Dylan to be the only one with a "dad" who couldn't handle the task, and a good tug convinced her that it would be enough to hold them for the night, especially when a grin split her son's face at how fast their tent flew up this time.

She spent the rest of the night sitting in front of her tent and watching Dylan with the boys around the campfire. They set the ends of thick sticks aglow and traced shapes in the air, ran around and played night games while the dads shot the breeze about who knew what. Baseball and jock itch cream, probably.

At one point, Dan approached her and invited her to join them, but she held up the book she wasn't reading as an excuse and promised she was fine with a little solitude and fresh air. She wouldn't have minded dropping in on the conversation, but she didn't want to give any of the absent wives a reason to mutter about her presence there. They were mostly fine with her doing the scout stuff with Dylan, and it was due largely to her keeping a huge distance from their men.

Finally, around ten, Dylan stumbled back to the tent half asleep. She crawled in after him and let him nestle inside the sleeping bag wearing his filthy play clothes. She'd have to boil everything to death when they got home anyway. Happy to see him end the night on a good note, she curled around her boy and fell asleep.

She didn't move until something brushed against her cheek and startled her awake. Blinking but unable to make out anything in the darkness, she waited. It came again, something soft against her cheek, something soft that felt all wrong.

She stifled a scream. What was in the tent with them? A bat? A large moth?

She waved her hand in the direction of the invader and felt—

Oh no.

The nylon of her sagging tent drooped against her cheek. At least one of the stakes had come loose.

With a bitten-back curse, she lay there and stared at the steadily sinking ceiling. She couldn't wake anyone to borrow a mallet, but maybe she could figure out a way to rig the tent from the outside, or kind of . . . screw the stake back in? With no confidence that she would find a solution, she crawled toward the tent door. The second she slid the zipper, Dylan started.

"Mom?" he whispered.

"It's okay, baby. One of the stakes came loose." No sooner were the words out of her mouth than they heard a soft pop and the tent fell down. She braced for a wail from Dylan, but he made no sound, and she groped her way back toward him.

"You okay?" she whispered as she freed him from the tent.

He nodded, but she heard the telltale sniff that told her he wasn't.

"Hey, it's okay. We'll go lay the front seats back and sleep in the car. It's better than these lumpy bedrolls."

But he only sniffed again.

"I'm so sorry." She pressed her forehead against his and felt the weight of her failure. Her failure to drive a stake, to put up a tent that would stay up, to be the parent he needed. "What can I do to make this better?"

"Can we go?" he whispered. "I don't even want to see Tyler in the morning."

She hesitated, but she had to admit that she wasn't interested in listening to Dan's tent collapse theories.

"Yeah, we can go," she said. "But we've got to be really, really quiet, because when they wake up and find us gone, I want them to think we're ninja-level escape artists."

He threw his arms around her neck and squeezed her. "Thanks, Mom."

It was surprisingly easy to sneak out of a campsite in the middle of the night. The sound of at least two dads snoring covered any noise they made, but they made very little to begin with, shoving their sleeping bags into the backseat without bothering to roll them, carefully picking up the tent poles so they didn't click together, folding the nylon tent with barely a whisper.

And then, with Dylan giggling in the backseat, they coasted out of the campground black ops style, headlights off and the car in neutral until they were well down the road.

In the morning, Dylan wandered in for breakfast an hour later than usual but looking no worse for the wear. She greeted him with smiley face pancakes and a hug, and then they curled up with Narnia, where he listened to the adventures of Prince Caspian for nearly a half hour before he began to squirm.

She could let him wiggle away and avoid the most difficult conversation of her life while he disappeared into *Minecraft* videos . . .

She closed the book and faced him on the couch, legs crossed, her expression as serious as she knew how to make it without scaring him.

"I have the most unexpected news you could possibly

imagine," she said.

"Good news or bad news?"

"Good news," she said, hoping it was true, and his face relaxed. "I had a visitor a few days ago that I never would have expected."

"Who?"

She took a deep breath and gathered his hands up in hers. "Dylan . . ." She swallowed, not sure how she was going to get it out, but when the worry creeped into his expression again, she forced herself to say it. "The man who . . . well, your father is back in town."

He blinked at her. "My . . . father?"

"Your dad, yeah."

"But . . ." He couldn't find any more words.

"His name is Luke," she said. "I knew him in college, and I haven't seen him since before you were born."

"I thought you said he didn't know about me."

"He didn't." He'd asked about his dad when he was five. She'd told him that she had never told his dad about him because Luke wasn't the kind of person who would make a good father, and she left it at that.

"But I thought you said he wouldn't be a good dad."

"Back then he wouldn't have," she said slowly, knowing every word she spoke would carry a ton of freight. "But I've been talking to him quite a bit for the last few days, and I think maybe he's a different guy than he used to be. He'd like to meet you." His fingers tightened around hers, and she squeezed back. "You don't have to. Ever."

His fingers tightened even more. "I think I want to. Maybe?"

"Whatever you want, and whenever you're ready. You get to choose."

He processed that for a bit. She loved that about him, that

he was so thoughtful, but he internalized so much. He did it to protect her from worrying too much, but she kept her mouth shut and let them him work through it to see where it led him.

"Did it make you sad when he came?"

She almost sobbed at the question. What a gift this boy was, that his first worry was for her.

"No, not sad. I worried at first because I thought he might be like he was before. But he seems to have turned into a pretty nice adult. I'm a tiny bit worried still because this is a major surprise, and I don't know what to expect, but no, I was never sad."

It was as if this reassurance gave him permission to be excited. "What's he like? What does he look like?"

She tapped the cleft in his chin. "You got this from him. And your eye color. Your lips are just like mine, and you have my ears. I think you're a pretty good mix of us both. And I think you're going to be tall like him."

"Is he nice?"

"He is. Kind, even. And funny. Very smart."

"I must get that from him too," he said with a sly grin, and he squealed when she swooped over to tickle him. "I give! I give! You're the smartest mom I know."

He leaned against the sofa and stared off into the middle distance for a minute. "I think I'd like to meet him. That's okay?"

"It's more than okay. It's perfect. How about tomorrow afternoon?" It was much faster than she'd expected to do this, but Sunday would be a good day for it. If there ever was a good day for introducing your son to your old boyfriend who also happened to be his dad. She always left the shop by noon to spend the rest of the day with Dylan, and now it looked like they'd figured out what they'd be doing tomorrow.

She sat with him for another minute until his gaze drifted toward the TV and his Xbox, and she smiled and waved him toward it. Within a minute he was exploring a new virtual world, and she didn't know whether to laugh or cry at how easily he'd accepted that he would be meeting his father.

Now she needed to call Luke and tell him and pray that he fell in love with his son enough for Dylan to feel it, but not so much that he rocked the boat she'd been keeping steady for her sweet boy for nine long, lonely years.

Ten

*L*uke set the phone down only because his hand was shaking too much for him to hold it.

Dylan wanted to meet him.

From the minute he'd driven away from Delilah, his whole purpose in life had become waiting for her to call and tell him that he would get that chance.

He didn't know anything about kids. The plan was for them to meet him on the grounds of the Mariposa for a picnic. He had no idea what the protocol was for meeting a kid you'd just found out you had.

Gifts? Should he bring him a gift? What did you bring a nine-year-old boy? Suddenly he couldn't be in his hotel room a second longer, and he grabbed his keys and nearly raced to the concierge. "Where's the nearest toy store?"

"On Tangerine Street. Mennick's Curiosities. It's a slightly fantastic store, but kids love it."

Good enough. He was parking in front of it less than ten minutes later. The store didn't open for ten more minutes, and he paced nervously as he waited, peeking through the windows to see if he could figure out what Dylan might like.

After the third time he peered through, the door swung open, and a kind-looking, older gentleman stood there, studying him with a small smile. "You look like you need a toy."

"I do."

"Come on in. What are you looking for?"

"Well . . . I don't know. It's for a nine-year-old boy."

"Yours?"

"No. I mean, yes."

If the man found this answer odd, he didn't show it. "Are you local? I might know him."

"No. Uh, yes. I'm not. He is. His name is Dylan."

The man eyes sparkled with renewed interest. "Do you mean Dylan Dawes?"

"Yes." Ah, damn. He hoped this didn't get him in hot water with Delilah, but he didn't realize Seashell Beach was so small that this man would know Dylan.

"Dylan is a great little guy," he said. "He comes in here every time he gets a good report card. I can probably help you figure out what he likes."

"I'd appreciate that," Luke said. The man, it turned out, was Thomas Mennick himself, and he took Luke past plastic robots and sports equipment, puzzles and art supplies, and led him down an aisle that reached back to his own inner child and delighted him with the sheer assortment of building kits. Tinkertoys, Lincoln Logs, LEGOs, magnetic blocks.

"He likes to build," Mr. Mennick said. "I know which sets he has already and which ones he might like."

Ten minutes later, Luke was at the register with six different kits.

"He'd be pleased with one, I'm sure," Mr. Mennick said. "I didn't mean to suggest you needed to buy all of them."

Luke shook his head and tapped the top of the pile. "You may have figured out that I have some time to make up for."

Thomas Mennick gave him another kind smile, and Luke appreciated the complete absence of judgment as the owner rang up the rest of the sale.

He lugged the presents up to his hotel room and sat on the edge of the bed wondering how he could possibly survive until the next day and their picnic.

Research. He would research nine-year-old boys and find out what they were like, what they liked to do.

Except three hours later, the research told him that they were all different and he was fundamentally unfit to be a father.

When it came down to it, he didn't know if a father was what Dylan would want. He might be interested in Luke as a novelty but nothing more. Maybe Dylan had no interest in a relationship even as Luke's mind had already jumped ahead to working on these projects together.

But he had no control over that, so he busied himself Googling lists of questions for talking to kids. When he had a list longer than he could ask in a year, he remembered that Mr. Mennick had mentioned something about how Dylan liked to read.

He did a search on which books nine-year-old boys were into, bought e-books in three different series, and spent the rest of the evening reading them in case they were books Dylan liked. He drifted off to sleep on the last one to a night full of dreams about a boy wizard.

Sunday morning he took his run and pounded through some of his frustrations. How could Delilah have kept this from him? He'd been good to her, never given her a reason to think he would hurt her emotionally or otherwise.

He understood that it was hard for her to depend on people. She'd had a rough time growing up. Her relationship with her mother barely deserved the word. Her stepfather at the time—her third—wanted Delilah to embrace his evangelical Christianity even as he measured her worth by how much leg was showing. The more skin, the further she had fallen from God.

Delilah had been a little wild, yes, drinking to match his frat brothers and contemplating daily what she would get for her first tattoo.

But she'd had a good head on her shoulders in other ways. The only reason she hadn't blown out of Seashell Beach the year before was because she was saving money to go to culinary school while she lived at home and worked two jobs.

Luke had respected that. He'd never judged her the way her stepfather had or let her down the way her mother had her whole life. If anything, he'd been crazy about her quirks.

It made her ten-year lie of omission that much worse for him. All he'd done was love her.

He'd get his answers, and soon. But not today. Today was about meeting this new little man in his life.

By a quarter to one, he was down on the Mariposa lawn with a picnic blanket the concierge had procured for him, an embarrassingly tall stack of presents, and a stomachache, as if he were the nine-year-old in this scenario. He stood at the edge of the blanket with his hands in his shorts pockets, and he caught himself bouncing nervously on the balls of his feet a half dozen times before he forced himself to sit. But then he couldn't stay still, and he was up and bouncing again, his eyes never leaving the back entrance of the hotel, constantly scanning for Delilah's dark hair.

He wished he would have asked her for a picture of Dylan. Why didn't he do that? He would know what to look for, what to expect. Dylan would have dark hair like both of them, but would he have Delilah's hazel eyes or his own brown ones? He hoped Dylan had Delilah's freckles. Every kid needed freckles.

Finally, just a couple of minutes past the hour, he saw Delilah's head weaving toward him, and as soon as they cleared the patio crowd, he saw the little boy next to her. He had no idea how to gauge a nine-year-old's height, but he was thin, and a shock of dark hair flopped over one eye. Delilah spotted Luke and paused. She leaned down to Dylan and pointed to Luke.

Dylan's hand rose in a small, tentative wave. Luke returned it with a big smile, even though his heart didn't feel right, like it was expanding and breaking all at once.

And then they were there.

Luke stuck his hand out to Dylan. "Hi. I'm Luke."

Dylan shook it and nodded. "You're my dad."

Luke couldn't even answer. Something was stuck in his throat, so he nodded.

Delilah stood there uncertainly and then looked past him. "Is this the picnic?"

"Yeah. Um, do you guys want to sit down?"

"That would be great," she said, and they did, each awkwardly folding themselves down to fit on the blanket. All Luke wanted to do was stare at Dylan, memorize his features, figure out which parts looked like him. "You have my chin," he said.

Dylan touched his cleft. "Yeah. I like it."

Expanding. That's what was happening. Luke's heart was trying to push outside of his chest.

Dylan's gaze kept traveling to the pile of toys. Luke

smiled. "I met your friend Mr. Mennick at the toy store, and he told me some of the things you might like." He almost asked Delilah if it was okay to have gotten them, but he stopped himself. He didn't owe her that, not after this, not after keeping Dylan from him. There was no excuse for this.

"Could I look at the magnets?" Dylan asked.

"Of course. You like building?" Dylan nodded. "Me too. Maybe you get that from me."

A look of surprise crossed Dylan's face. "I guess I do. Mom always helps me with this stuff, but it's not her favorite. She's just being nice."

"Hey," she said, pretending to look offended. "I'm a good helper."

"I know, but you don't like it the way you like baking or yoga."

"True," she conceded.

"I love it," Luke said. "Can I help?"

"Sure," Dylan said a little shyly.

They worked together at it for a while, opening and unwrapping the little packets of magnets and rods, deciding they wanted to build a scaffold just to see how high they could go. He asked Dylan questions while they worked, about school and his favorite subjects, soaking up each answer like it was California sunshine.

"You can ask me anything too. If there's anything you want to know about me, I mean," he said after Dylan answered several of his questions. He couldn't believe how much he hoped Dylan would want to ask him questions, but his crash course in child development the previous night had suggested that nine-year-old boys might not be really interested in adults.

Dylan surprised him though. "Do you have a mom and dad?"

"Yes, I do."

"So I have grandparents?"

"You do. I don't see them very often, though."

"Do they know about me yet?"

"No," he said. Delilah flinched and fisted the blanket in both hands, as if she was holding on with everything she had. "I don't know what I want to say to them yet. It's an interesting development to explain."

Dylan's expression only changed by a tiny fraction. Luke wasn't even sure he could say what it was. Maybe a tightening around his eyes or shoulders, but he realized he'd said something wrong, something that had closed the boy down a little, and he panicked, trying to figure out how to fix it.

"I want them to know about you," he said, "but they get kind of funny about surprises, so I have to think of the best way to tell them."

"Okay." Dylan bent to fiddle with something that didn't need fixing at the base of their scaffold.

Luke shot a panicked glance at Delilah, but her face had closed off completely. He was drowning and couldn't even shout for help.

"Do you see your other grandparents much?" he asked.

Dylan shrugged. "I have a grandma, but she has problems with her mood so we don't go there much."

Sounded like Delilah's mother had not improved in time. As far as he knew, his parents hadn't either.

"Can I tell you something that might sound a little weird?" he asked Dylan.

Dylan looked up, his eyes bright with interest.

"I don't have a super great mom like your mom. I wish I could tell you that you have really fun grandparents, but they're not really like that. That's why I do the job I do."

"You write about places you travel to?"

"Yes. To be honest, traveling for work is a great excuse for not having to see them much."

"Are they mean?" Dylan asked.

"Yes, but they don't mean to be. They just feel better when everything goes a certain way, and it's hard for them when there's wrinkles."

"I'm a pretty big wrinkle," Dylan said with so much composure that it startled a laugh from Luke.

"You are," said Luke. "But all of my favorite things are like that. Cool surprises that show up in my life."

"So you like surprises?"

"I love surprises."

"Surprise," Dylan said, and he smacked the tower down. Luke laughed again.

"Want to see who can build the tallest tower next?"

And they were off, building and knocking down a few more towers before Delilah cleared her throat and suggested they should eat. Luke busted into the hamper room service had packed with peanut butter and jelly sandwiches.

At two, she stood, and Luke scrambled up too, dreading what she would say next.

"We should probably get going," she said, and the tightness in his chest eased the tiniest bit when he saw a flash of disappointment on Dylan's face.

"It's okay," Luke said. "Did you guys drive here? I'll walk you out, and I can load all the stuff in your car."

"Maybe you should hold on to some of it for next time," Delilah said.

Luke's hands curled into fists as if he could hold on to the words next time.

There would be a next time. It was good to know he wouldn't have to fight her for it. Because he would if that's what it took.

He helped Dylan put away the magnet set and walked them to the guest parking.

Delilah said, "Muffin, could you take the keys and put this in the car? I'll be right there."

"Mom," Dylan said, looking mortified, "don't call me muffin."

A spasm of sadness crossed Delilah's face as he snatched the keys from her and unlocked a Toyota a few cars down.

"He's never been embarrassed for me to call him that," she said, watching him go. "I guess he wants to look tougher in front of his dad."

If she thought Luke was going to bond with her sympathetically over that, she was dead wrong. "I should have known about him his whole life. How could you do this?"

"Luke, I . . ."

"I can't," he said. "I can't listen to this right now. I just fell in love with a kid I didn't know about three days ago, and I can't listen to why I'm only just now getting that chance. But there will be a reckoning, Delilah. Don't think you can ever keep me from him again."

And he walked away before the rest of the angry words he wanted to hurl at her could escape.

Eleven

What had Luke said? There would be a reckoning? Was he hinting at a custody fight?

Delilah collapsed on the sofa, too tired after listening to Dylan chatter all night about his new dad, answering a million questions as she tucked him in, to make it as far as her own bed.

She was sure it had been the right thing to let them meet. She'd never seen her son so lit up. It had nearly broken her heart watching him with Luke that afternoon, working so hard to impress him, to be a tough little man and good builder.

And Luke had been perfect with him, attentive, complimentary . . . real.

She'd carried guilt like a second skin for the rest of the day, a feeling she couldn't shake no matter how hard she tried.

But to be fair, the Luke she had walked out on had not been the Luke she'd seen for the last week. He had been a much different, much weaker man.

When her cell phone alarm woke her, she was stiff from

sleeping on the sofa, and she bundled Dylan over to Mrs. Castro's and left him with a hug and a kiss.

She worried about Luke's vague reckoning threat all the way to the bakery. She wouldn't try to keep him from Dylan, but she probably needed to find a lawyer who could help her make sure that she didn't fall victim to the Romero family empire if he decided to use his trust fund for a custody battle.

As she walked up to her store at dawn, she recognized Luke's lean frame immediately. He bounced on the balls of his feet like he had yesterday before he'd spotted them.

She took a deep breath and stopped a few feet away, uncomfortable with the tightly coiled anger that rolled off of him. "I wasn't expecting you."

"It's been a big week for things people don't expect." His voice was hard and biting.

"Dylan likes you," she said quietly. Instead of pleasing him, his expression only grew darker.

"You owe me answers."

She did. Of course she did. "Come in. I have to get some things started, but I'll answer your questions."

He trailed her into the kitchen and staked out a spot in the middle of her workspace instead of keeping himself out of her way like he had the last time. She understood the message. You will deal with me.

"Should I start with why I didn't tell you?"

"Sure, why not. Sounds like an interesting story."

She didn't react to the sarcasm. She would be furious if she discovered that a magnificent human like Dylan was moving through the world and was actually hers and no one had told her. She reached back to the old pain, the raw place that still festered beneath the scar tissue.

"I found out right before your parents came to visit." She and Luke had been together for three months by then. No. Not just together—inseparable. His parents were in town before the university resumed classes in the fall, ostensibly to visit their son, but really to try again at convincing him to change his major.

"I thought I had the stomach flu. I went to the free clinic." It was open once a week for the undocumented field workers and trailer trash like herself. "The doctor told me I was probably pregnant. He was mad that I hadn't done any prenatal care and rolled out an ultrasound machine. And there he was, a little peanut on the screen. I didn't even care that the doctor was lecturing me."

She slammed the fridge door. "I hadn't meant to get pregnant. I want you to know that."

He made a small note in his throat. Not a grunt, exactly. Almost a sound of agreement. "I know. You were pretty focused on your five-year plan. So how did it happen?"

She couldn't help the snort that escaped. "Well, when a man and a woman like each other . . ."

"It was more than like, Delilah. It was for me. I told you that then. That's why I can't figure out why you didn't tell me about the baby."

She sprinkled flour onto the counter to prep for rolling out a pie crust. "Because I realized you were lying."

"The hell I was," he said. "First you decided whether I got to be a father, and now you're going to tell me how I felt?"

"No," she said, not rising to the anger in his tone. "You told me you were lying. Or you told your father, and I heard it."

He froze. "What are you talking about?"

"I got a printout of the ultrasound. I put it in my notebook when we met your parents for lunch for that day." She'd carried her notebook with her any time they went out to eat so she could take notes on the food, guessing what had gone into each dish. "I was going to tell you after your parents left. I figured you might need some good news after their visit."

"So what changed? Because that would have been hard news, and scary news, but I would have supported you no matter what."

"Your mom found the ultrasound picture." She almost hated to tell him, because it was a second betrayal by someone else who was supposed to love him.

"My mom?" The color disappeared from his lips as he leaned back hard against the counter.

"It fell out of my notebook. I didn't even know. She put it back without telling me. Until the next day at brunch."

She watched understanding creep into his eyes. "When she asked you to go for a walk with her. She said she wanted to get to know you."

"No. She wanted me to know she'd seen the ultrasound, and she didn't want some trampy girl from a second-rate beach town trapping their precious son with a baby."

He cursed, and she knew he could easily believe it of his mother. "What did she do? Did she threaten you?"

"She offered to buy me off. She said if I'd 'take care of it,' and break up with you, she'd give me ten thousand dollars."

"You took it?" he asked, the first note of contempt creeping into his voice.

For the first time, her own temper flared. "Of course I didn't. What I felt for you was real, even if you didn't feel the same."

He prowled toward her, an attempt to intimidate her with his size and proximity, but he must have forgotten that Delilah Dawes of Seaside Court Trailer Estates never backed down from a fight. She met his eyes and returned his anger-bright gaze with a cool one of her own.

"You keep accusing me of being a fake and a liar, Delilah. Stop. Every word I ever said about my feelings was truth. The way I felt about you burned me from the inside out, and you don't get to erase that."

The charge in the air changed, shifting from anger to a different kind of heat. His eyes darkened, and he bent toward her the tiniest bit. She felt her first frisson of fear. She'd lost herself in the crazy rush of fire that had swept through them in the park, and she wouldn't lose herself again.

She took a step back.

He took a deep breath and retreated to his perch on the counter.

She reclaimed her space, itchy to move and do and bake as she worked through some of her hardest memories. Because the next part . . . the next part of the story had hurt the most.

"I didn't care about your mom's money. I told her where to shove it. I assumed they would leave, and then I would tell you, and we'd figure out what to do. But the next morning, I ran out to grab us bagels, and when I came back I could hear you and your dad talking. The window was open."

He sucked in a sharp breath, like he knew what was coming next.

"He was saying something about how you should break up with me." As if she didn't remember the exact words. *You're better than this, Luke. She doesn't fit in with the life we raised you* for. "Do you remember what you said to him?"

Regret flashed in his eyes. "I do, but it's not what you think."

The bitter taste of the words crept up the back of her throat. "'She's a pastime, Dad. Don't worry about it.'"

"I wish you would have asked me about it," he said after a silence deeper than the Pacific.

"Are you really going to try to make this about me? You said the words."

"But I didn't say them for the reason you think." The anger had drained from his voice, and now he only sounded tired. "I understand how it must have sounded."

"Like I was a distraction? The hard-bitten girl who was so desperate for love she let down her defenses to the first boy who treated her nicely? That's how it sounded."

"But you didn't leave after my parents did. I had wondered if that's what did it, but it was a couple of weeks before you took off."

"Because it takes to time to close down your entire life and disappear. I put in my notice at work. I looked for apartments and sold my car for the deposit. And it took me some time to figure out how to track down your mom."

"Wait, *what*?"

Delilah nodded. "Yeah. I made her pay. I told her that I would disappear from your life completely if she doubled her offer."

"You took my mom for another ten grand?"

"Yeah."

"Good," he said, and a bitter smile twisted his lips.

"It was the only way I could afford to get out of here and go to culinary school."

He grew quiet again. By the time he spoke, she'd already rolled out four crusts. "My mom has known about Dylan this whole time?"

"No." She hesitated to tell him the next part, but it wasn't as if it could get much worse. "I led her to believe that I would handle the situation a different way. She doesn't know Dylan ever happened."

He scrubbed his hand over his face. "Okay." That was it. It was almost relief in his voice. "But where did you go?"

"Laguna Beach. They have a culinary school down there, and I had to stay in state to be eligible for the poor people insurance, and it was more affordable than the school in San Francisco. I lived in a tiny apartment and traded childcare with this girl who cleaned office buildings at night. We worked opposite schedules and watched each other's kids. I got a couple of grants for single mothers, and that got me through school without too much debt. Then I worked in LA restaurants and lived in crappy apartments until I saved enough to open this place. I wanted Dylan out of the city, and with the development here, Seashell Beach was the right spot."

"I need to think," he said. "If I leave and go for a walk, will you let me back in when I come back?"

"Yes."

He shoved his hands in his pockets, his head hanging low as he walked out, but she called his name when he reached the kitchen door.

"If I'd known you had become the man you are now, I would have told you sooner."

"Thank you for that, at least."

And he disappeared.

She worked quietly for the rest of the day, needing the comfort of simple dishes. Mini apple pies, brownies, pumpkin cupcakes. Every time she went out front, she looked for him. Every time the kitchen door swung open, she tensed and then sighed, wondering if she was disappointed or relieved that it wasn't Luke.

When she left the bakery at three to pick up Dylan, she found Luke waiting for her on the sidewalk.

"Are you going to get him from school? I'd like to come with you."

Instead of giving him an answer, she let him fall into step with her. "I don't have time to get into a long conversation or

I'll be late, but can you at least tell me your intentions? Are you going to see if you like this dad thing before you take off and disappear for months on assignments? Because that's going to be hard for him. Or are you wanting to step in and make up for nine years and be around all the time? Because that's going to be hard for me. But I'm a lot more worried about what's going to be hard for him."

He slid a key from his pocket and flicked his finger along its teeth a few times before he answered. "I rented an apartment on the north end. I'll be here when I'm not on assignment."

She needed to get Dylan comfortable with the idea of Luke being around more. "I don't think you should come to school with me." He stiffened and she hurried to explain. "Not yet. His friends will notice and ask questions he might not be ready to explain. But I'll give you our address, and you can wait there. It'll give me a chance to prep him for seeing you."

"That's fair."

She pulled out her phone and texted him the address as they walked in silence until they reached her car.

"Just one thing," he said, before she closed her door. "I only told my dad you were a pastime because I was afraid my parents would see you as a threat to their plans and try to screw it up. I would take back the words now if I could, Delilah. In my dumb-kid mind, I thought I was protecting you. But I never meant it, and nothing has ever hurt more than you disappearing like that."

She was about to protest him making it about him again, but he cut her off. "I'm not telling you what I went through was worse. I'm only telling you how much you mattered then."

He turned and walked away, and against her will, she wondered how much she mattered now.

Twelve

uke canceled his Nepal trip and picked up two shorter European assignments instead. In between, he came back home to Seashell Beach. And it did feel like home, more so with every return. He'd settled into a schedule with Delilah and Dylan because for now she felt more comfortable being around when they spent time together. They had an appointment scheduled with the family court mediator to work out custody, but Luke wasn't stressed. Delilah had been cautious but fair so far, willing to let him see Dylan as often as Dylan wanted to.

And Dylan . . .

Luke had fallen madly, wildly in love with his boy. He couldn't imagine a funnier, sweeter, more curious kid. It seemed like almost daily he saw some mannerism in Dylan that he recognized as one of his own: the way his mouth pulled up on one side when he was failing to keep a straight face, the way he rubbed one eyebrow when he was thinking hard.

Delilah . . .

That was more complicated. The more time he spent with Dylan, the harder it was to forgive her. He understood how the whole miserable misunderstanding had happened, how a nineteen-year-old girl who'd been dismissed her whole life by the people who should have loved her could believe the lie he'd told his father to keep her safe.

But it was hard not to hold all the missed time with Dylan against her. How could he forgive that? And yet . . .

Sometimes he almost wanted to. When he ate shepherd's pie at her table while they listened to Dylan talk about his day at school and she made him laugh with a comment about Dylan's devoted but slightly scattered teacher. Or when they went to the beach one day in the summer and he nearly lost his breath when she slipped out of her swimsuit cover-up and raced Dylan to the water, diving through the waves with him like an otter.

Then he would bring over another book to share, and Dylan would smile and say, "Mom and I already read that one. You'll like it," and his resentment festered again over all the firsts that had been stolen from him.

The hardest part was how much he missed them—Dylan—when he was gone. Now, at the tail end of the third trip he'd taken since finding Dylan, he couldn't believe how much he missed being home. It was a new feeling, and as he slung his travel bag into the trunk of the Mustang he'd bought, he couldn't wait for their court date in two days, when he could make it official—that he was a legal part of his son's life and *nothing* would be able to change that.

He swung by Delilah's place, knowing Dylan would already be home from school. Delilah was working in the yard when he pulled up, and she met him at the car.

"Hi."

"Hey," he said, climbing out. She'd become part of the

routine too. He almost didn't feel like a trip home was complete without connecting with her. It was funny how easy it was to fall into some habits. "Where's Dylan?"

"He's playing over at Scotty's."

"I'll go say hi."

"Wait." Something about her tone made his shoulders tighten. "I wanted to talk to you about the custody hearing."

"Okay," he said, trying not to panic. He wouldn't let her change her mind.

"We can't keep going on like this." The words seemed hard for her to get out, but they couldn't possibly feel harder to say than they did to hear.

"You can't back out now." He kept his voice flat, afraid he would lose control over it.

"No, I don't mean . . ." She swallowed and tried again. "I'm fine with shared custody. I just think it's time for you and Dylan to have your own thing now. I trust you. You should spend your own time together without me. He's ready."

Luke let out a slow breath, relief and a feeling he couldn't identify filling him up until she added, "This isn't healthy."

"What do you mean this isn't healthy? Is something wrong? Did he say he's unhappy?"

"No. I think it's confusing for us to spend time with him together. He needs to understand that he belongs to each of us, but that we don't belong to each other. You and me, I mean."

"Oh." He let that sit for a minute. "He thinks we're together?"

"Yes. I don't know if he thinks we're in a relationship or if he even pays attention to all of that. But he's starting to see us as a whole family, a mom and dad and kid, like Scotty's or any of his other friends. He needs to see us as separate. So no more family dinners. You can have your own time, whatever the mediator recommends for a situation like this."

He should have been happy about this. It's what he'd been working toward for almost two months now, but the idea of him and Dylan without Delilah didn't look right in his head. "I think it works pretty well as it is. Can't we just explain we're there as his parents but not a couple or whatever?"

She shook her head. "No."

That was it. Nothing more. Screw that. She didn't get to make unilateral decisions like this without him anymore. "I don't think we should change things so suddenly. We've already sprung a lot of change on him as it is."

"And he's turning out to be incredibly resilient. I don't want to go backward from that when he figures out that we aren't the family his friends have. I want him to get used to reality before he's invested in a fantasy."

It made sense. He knew it made sense, what she was saying. But it bothered him.

She slid her hands into her dress pockets. "I won't say anything to him about it until we talk to the mediator and see if he's got suggestions for how to present the change."

"So I can still stay for dinner tonight?"

"If you want to. But I don't think we should do too many more." She wouldn't meet his eyes, pulling out her phone instead. "I'll text Cindy and let her know you're coming for Dylan." She hurried into the house without waiting for his answer.

He wanted to say something, anything. Like "this is your fault," or "please change your mind," or "I might not be ready for this." But he didn't know if he meant solo parenting or Delilah stepping back. Away.

It was hard not to be angry at her sometimes. But it was also hard not to laugh at her jokes, melt over her cooking, or admire the hell out of her mothering. It was hard not to find excuses for brushing her fingers when he asked her to pass a dish or bumping his shoulder against hers with a shared sense of pride when Dylan scored a run in baseball. It was really hard not to lightly tuck the one lock of hair that always escaped her ponytail back behind her ear. So sometimes he did.

Maybe she was right. It had to be confusing for Dylan. And it would be a good thing for him to figure out his own thing with Dylan, how they fit when it was just the two of them.

Still, a sense of loss washed over him when the door shut behind her.

Thirteen

elilah waved as Dylan drove off with Luke, his hair flapping in the breeze and curling around the Mustang's headrest. Maybe she'd regain favorite parent status if she bought a convertible.

She settled onto the sofa with a smile and turned on her favorite cooking show. It was good that Dylan was so happy to be with his dad. Luke had totally stepped up. He traveled constantly, but when he was in town, he was present; Dylan got his undivided attention.

She always thought she'd had a happy kid before, but now Dylan thrived, walking with a new strut. The transition to solo visits for the past two weeks had gone well. Dylan and Luke took off without a backward glance, and she was happy that Dylan was so comfortable with him.

She felt bad for her jealousy, but it wasn't Luke who she was jealous of. It was Dylan.

Dylan, who got to hear Luke laugh and tell stories about

his latest travel adventure, who got to sit around doing nothing and just being, if he wanted to.

It was unworthy of her as a mother, and she knew it. But she'd recognized a growing need with each Luke visit, an impulse to turn into his touch when he tucked her hair back, or to twine her fingers with his when he asked her to pass the salt. She'd grown hungry for his scent, the tiniest whiff of cinnamon, as if she didn't have an entire bakery full of it she could inhale. She'd been cooking so many cinnamon-laced treats lately that for the first time since she opened, customers were beginning to complain.

She couldn't help herself. And that was the problem.

Luke had made it clear that she'd committed a wrong she couldn't right, and even though she wouldn't have changed her choices at the time, she understood his anger. Anyone worth his salt would be angry about missing time with Dylan. But when Dylan had casually mentioned how glad he was to have a "normal family" now, she realized she was trespassing. She didn't belong between them. She and Luke belonged to Dylan separately but not to each other.

She needed her distance anyway. She didn't know how long it would be before Luke saw how much his smiles had come to mean to her, how she recognized the potential of the boy he'd been fulfilled in the man he'd become. How she loved that.

Loved him.

Loved him with something deeper and wider than she had thought she could contain.

Dylan had multiplied her capacity for loving until she brimmed with it, so overflowing that some days it could only pour out into hugs for her beautiful boy and pour into beautiful pastries that made customers weep.

And then came Luke, and she learned that there may not

be a limit to her capacity to love. But she had sealed herself off from that possibility with her choice years ago, so rather than spill it messily all over Luke and catch Dylan in the sticky middle, she let Luke drift out of range before everything inside of her burst out and flooded him. It was the best thing for Dylan, and she would learn to live with it.

Still, her heart smiled when their dark heads popped into the bakery kitchen late on Monday morning when they stopped into filch snickerdoodle sandwich cookies on their way to the beach.

Dylan wrinkled his nose. "You've been making a lot of cinnamon stuff lately." But that didn't stop him from shoving half of it into his mouth on his first bite.

She ignored his comment. "Did you guys have a fun weekend?"

"Yeah! And guess what? Dad doesn't start another assignment until next Wednesday!" he almost shouted.

Luke clapped a hand on his shoulder. "I was thinking I would keep him during the day while you're at work, if that's okay."

"Sounds great," she said. "I'll let Mrs. Castro know you'll come get him after breakfast."

He cleared his throat. "I was thinking I'd come over when you need to leave for work and wait for him to wake up before we take off."

Dylan's eyes rounded. "I would get to sleep in? Yeah! Please, Mom?"

She shook her head. "I feel like I'm being ganged up on."

Luke's eyes grew anxious. "I'm sorry, I should have checked with you first."

"No! It's fine. I was kidding. It sounds like a great plan." She'd have to figure out how to brace herself for starting her day with an extra serving of Luke now, but it was worth it to see the delight on Dylan's face. She'd figure this out. "Have fun at the beach. Have him back by dinner?" she said to Luke, and he nodded agreement before they disappeared off to the sand.

When Luke reappeared a couple of hours after lunch, she glanced up in surprise from the frosting she was mixing. "Where's Dylan? Is something wrong?"

"No, sorry. No. We ran into the Batemans on the beach, and Cindy's keeping an eye on him for a few minutes."

She relaxed and returned to pouring cream into her mixer. "What's up?"

"I was wondering how you felt about me joining you guys for dinner."

"I don't think so."

"Wow. You didn't even hesitate."

She glanced up to catch the hurt on his face. "I'm sorry," she said. "I just don't want him getting mixed up again." And she couldn't take any extra servings of Luke. It was hard enough as it was. If she were a stronger woman, she'd have dialed back their together time much sooner.

"Would that be so bad?" he asked.

She paused, turned the mixer off, and turned to face him fully. "What?"

He shifted from foot to foot, a rare display of uncertainty. What was going on?

"Would it be so bad if Dylan thought we were together again?"

"Are you kidding me? You saw how confused he was getting before."

He sighed. "I'm not saying this right."

Now she was totally confused, so she didn't answer and waited for him to make more sense. He reached out and snagged one of her hands, tugging her toward him.

"What are you doing?" she asked, panicking when his

touch sent her pulse into overdrive. But she couldn't make herself pull away.

"This," he said, his voice low. He drew her against him and kissed her, his lips far more sure than his tone had been.

What was happening? But her mouth opened beneath his, and as he stole a taste of her, she groaned, and he held her tighter.

"I knew it wasn't my imagination," he whispered. "It's all still here." He bent to kiss her again, but she shoved him away.

"Stop it. I don't want this." *Liar.*

He didn't look any more convinced than her brain was. "The way we connect has always told the truth even when our words screwed it up." He reached out to run a finger across her cheekbone and smiled. "Let me be with you, Delilah. We're magic."

Where was this coming from? He'd made it clear that they could be civil as co-parents but that he couldn't ever forgive his lost years with Dylan. Why now? Why after they spent time apart and not when they'd been spending time together, all three of them—

Oh.

"Luke, you're turning into a great dad."

"Thanks." A pleased pink colored his cheeks even as he furrowed his brow. "But that's not what we're talking about here."

"Except that I think that it is. I think maybe you're panicking at this solo gig and you want the comfort of a wingman. Trust me," she said, holding up her hand when he started to protest. "I get it. I'm not even mad. But this was a bad idea. Maybe you should check on Dylan."

He looked as if he would argue again, but instead he turned his back to her and laced his fingers behind his head while he stared at the blank wall in front of him. Finally, he dropped his arms and headed for the door.

"You're right," he said before he slipped out. "This was a bad idea. We have to send him the right message. I'll drop him off at dinner, and you don't have to worry about me coming in."

She nodded. She'd never felt more miserable about being right, but she smiled at him to ease the awkwardness. "Thanks for being willing to work on all of this."

He shrugged. "Thanks for trusting me to. And I know I just said we don't want to send him mixed signals, but Dylan and I are finally planning a housewarming party at my place next Friday, and I hope you'll still come. There will be other people there, like the Batemans, so I don't think it'll be too confusing for him."

"Of course. What can I bring?"

"I don't know. You're the expert. We're pretty excited, so maybe something that tastes like happiness."

She shot him a sharp glance. It was an odd request, not the usual "chocolate cupcakes" kind of requests people made. But "tastes like happiness"? Did he know about her . . . gift? "I can do that."

For the next week and a half, Dylan nearly drove her crazy with his party planning, adding people to his list every day. Mr. Mennick from the toy store, his teacher, that one old guy down the street whose name they didn't know but who always waved while he watered his roses.

Thursday night before the party he was beside himself. "Text Mr. Dan please and tell him, okay, Mom? And tell him this address." And he rattled off an address that was not Luke's apartment.

"Wait, I thought this was at your dad's place."

He flushed. "Um, we're doing it at this place."

"That doesn't make any sense."

"It's just that I invited so many people that we couldn't fit them all in the apartment, so now we have to do it somewhere else."

She tried not to laugh. "Got it. All right, I'll give Dan the info."

When Luke walked in so she could leave for work the next morning, she couldn't resist teasing him. "I hear you had to move to a bigger location because Dylan got a little overexcited with his invites."

"Yeah. We're moving it to a park."

"So you're doing your housewarming not at your house?"

He held up his hands as if to say, *What are you going to do?*

"All right, I'll see you guys tonight."

He cocked his ear as if listening for Dylan, but the house was still. "I need this, Delilah. Tell me no if you don't too," he said, and he slid his hand into her hair. She knew all the reasons she should turn her head, step back, push him away, flat-out run. But she stayed.

The kiss was different than the ones they'd shared since he turned up again, and yet familiar. She knew it from before, from the first days after they'd met on the beach. It was a kiss full of lazy summer promise, and hope, and introduction, and rightness, and when he drew back and released her, her breath came out in a shudder.

"You have to stop that."

"Okay," he said, and then he kissed her again, long and deep, before he gently pushed her away and she walked out.

She tried to bake pure happiness, but apricot macarons took as much luck as skill to get them just so. They looked right, but they didn't taste like they should. She gave up after the third batch, knowing she would be useless until she baked the kiss out of her system, and Luke would just have to deal with sin-drenched eclairs.

With the eclairs out of the way and tempting her like another one of Luke's damn kisses, she set her mind to thinking about the party tonight and what it was for. Luke and Dylan had made a home together now too, and it made her happier than she could have ever thought to see them together. She had faith in Luke's commitment to Dylan's well-being. Everything else was details.

And then the happiness bubbled up in her as she thought of Dylan's excited phone calls with his dad and his contentment when he returned from their visits.

This time the apricot macarons were perfection.

Fourteen

*L*uke paced nervously, checking to see if Delilah had shown up yet. He'd made sure no one took her spot in the driveway, and Dylan had even painted a sign for her on a piece of old plywood: *Mom's spot.*

Finally, he spotted her car coming down the street. It slowed, hesitated in front of the house, kept going, eventually turning around at the end of the cul-de-sac. The car stopped again and pulled into the driveway.

"She's here, Dylan," he said. "Ready?"

"Ready, Dad. I'll get her! Go in the back."

He watched his son race out to the car and help his mom with one of the bakery boxes, his face lit up with a sneaky grin. Luke would have to work on the kid's poker face.

When they started toward the gate in the side fence, he hurried to his spot in the back, returning all the grins and high fives from the crowd already waiting. Man, he hoped she thought this was a good idea this time, because now two hearts were on the line. Then he thought about the kiss he'd stolen that morning and smiled.

This was right. He knew it.

He heard Dylan's chatter as they rounded the corner of the house. "You're never going to believe what a big surprise we pulled on you," Dylan said as she stopped in astonishment at the sight of just about anyone in town she and Dylan had ever known filling the backyard.

Several of them burst into laughter, and Roxy, grinning like mad, hurried forward to lift the treats from Delilah's arms and whisk them off to the covered tables Mrs. Castro had decorated.

"What's going on?" Delilah asked.

She looked adorable in a turquoise sundress and red sandals, bafflement on her face. "I thought you said you were doing this at the park."

"Dylan? You ready?"

"Ready, Dad!"

Dylan took Delilah's hand and drew her forward with him to Luke, who was waiting for them beside a potted citrus tree decorated with little white lights.

"Mom, this is our new house."

"Really?" she asked.

"Yes," Luke answered. "I'm here to stay, Delilah. I thought Dylan should have a yard and not a concrete balcony with apartment beige on his walls."

"It's great," she said, her face still confused as she noticed even more familiar faces.

"We have a proposal for you, Mom."

"Okay. Let's hear it."

Dylan slid his hand into Luke's and stared up at him with so much love in his eyes that Luke's throat closed up for a minute, and he couldn't get out his part.

"It's your line, Dad," Dylan said in a loud whisper, and a soft laugh rippled through the crowd.

"Dylan and I have decided we're the real deal," he said. "This thing he and I have, it's true love, and we're declaring it right now: we're a forever unit."

"Yeah!" Dylan shouted, and Delilah sniffled, tears trembling on the edges of her eyelashes, as their friends burst into applause and more laughter.

"I'm so, so happy for you guys," she said, kneeling to hug her son. He endured it for a moment before he wiggled out of it.

"It's not time for that yet, Mom. Stand up."

With even more confusion on her face, she did.

"Dylan and I are a unit, and we do love each other like crazy, but not just each other. We love you like crazy too," he said. Delilah gasped, and Dylan grinned up at her.

"I know you have some doubts about my feelings for you, and Dylan and I will give you all the time in the world to work through them, but I wanted you to see that I'm not confused, I'm not scared to do this alone, and I know exactly what I want. I want a family."

"Me too, Mom," Dylan said, but hurried to add, "but only when you're ready," before Luke could prompt him.

Luke grinned down at his son. Then, like they'd practiced a dozen times, they each went down on one knee, and a whole epidemic of sniffles broke out in the yard.

"Delilah Dawes, when you're ready, will you marry us?" Luke asked.

"Please?" Dylan added, and this time there was a full-blown sob from Delilah, who dropped to her knees again and showered their faces with kisses.

"That means yes, right, Mom?"

"It means yes," she said.

"Oh my," said cranky Miss Betty. But she wasn't watching them. She was staring down at a half-eaten creamy chocolate eclair from Delilah's baker box, her face half scandalized and half thrilled as she took another bite.

"What you'd make?" Luke asked as a line immediately began to form behind Miss Betty.

She covered Dylan's ears and whispered, "Don't worry about it. I'll serve you up some of your very own later."

And it was a good thing Luke was already on his knees, or the promise in her voice would have driven him there.

"I love you, Delilah Dawes."

"I love your more, Luke Romero."

"I love you most, Mom and Dad," Dylan said, peeling Delilah's hands from his ears.

And Luke knew Dylan believed it, but he also knew that no one's heart had ever been as full as his was at that moment with his family filling his arms.

PART TWO

The Art of Love

One

Roxy Randall hated her name all through elementary school. The boys would call her RR—or *Railroad*. As if that were clever. In high school, the RR morphed into Rated R, and the creeps all tried to hit on her. It didn't help that she was clumsy and tended to gravitate toward embarrassing situations, which earned her a lot of laughs. The wrong kind of laughs. It seemed she was ahead of her time, when hipsters and quirky sidekicks weren't quite yet cool. She was just a klutz who wore thrift-store clothing and too-big glasses.

In high school, she loved art and excelled in her art classes, but that only added to her reputation of being odd. She had hoped for a better life in college, but she only made it through half of a semester before dropping out.

Now, in her late twenties, Roxy wore contacts most of the time, and her clothing was splotched with paint nearly all of the time. She found that being an artist was the perfect

127

vocation for someone who was happier by herself. It sure beat the dating scene.

Painting almost always won out over any other activity. She could paint to music; she could paint to the sound of the crashing ocean waves outside her studio apartment. She could paint professionally. She could paint just for herself.

"Roxy, are you sure you aren't going deaf?"

The voice was familiar—sweet and cultured, but with an edge.

Roxy reached up to remove her earbuds, then realized she wasn't wearing any. She'd been putting in long shifts to get her latest mural job completed before the impending arrival of the Elliotts' first baby. They wanted the nursery to be a compilation of fairy tales so that their daughter could grow up believing she lived in Narnia.

Well, that was Roxy's opinion.

Roxy slid her gaze to the woman standing at the foot of the ladder.

Cheryl Elliott was a vision of perfection and could easily pose right now for a who's who feature in *Home and Gardens magazine.* Money was no object for the wife of the multi-millionaire computer software mogul, and their third, yes, third home was right here in Seashell Beach. Even though she sported her eight-month pregnant belly, every woman would envy Cheryl's slender figure.

Roxy had always been . . . curvy. Granted, she didn't run marathons, but she was on her feet a lot and very active, if painting could be considered an active profession. "I'm sorry," Roxy said, offering a nervous smile. "I didn't hear you. I must have been lost in Rapunzel's long hair." She motioned to the long, honey-colored locks she was currently painting.

Cheryl didn't laugh. But she did offer a patient smile— something that Roxy was well familiar with by now.

"We're going to a benefit dinner tonight at the Mariposa Hotel," Cheryl said. "We won't return until late, so you can just let yourself out. But go through the back door, and be sure to lock it behind you."

Most clients gave Roxy their house key—temporarily, of course. But not the Elliotts.

"Isn't Margo going to be here?" Roxy asked in an innocent voice. Margo was their maid, cook, or spy, or however one wanted to look at it.

"She's left for the evening," Cheryl said. "Her youngest son is graduating from high school."

"All right," Roxy said, looking back at her painting. The honey-gold color was working out better than expected. But it always took a while to get back into the groove once interrupted.

She could feel Cheryl still looking at her. So, with a silent sigh, Roxy looked back down at her current employer.

"There's one more thing," Cheryl said.

Cheryl Elliott was one of those women who had to have your full attention before she spoke.

"Yes?" Roxy prompted, even though she only wanted to grit her teeth.

"Don's brother, Mark, is in the backyard," she said. "He's our contractor, and we're having him put in a pool house. So he's here measuring out the location."

Roxy raised her brows and tried to look interested or impressed, or whatever people did when your extremely wealthy employer added yet another feature to their already dream mansion. Well, *third* dream mansion.

"And . . . does he have cooties or something?" Roxy asked before she could stop herself.

Cheryl wrinkled her nose, although there weren't really any wrinkles to be seen. "You have such an interesting sense

129

of humor," she said. "I just wanted you to be aware that Mark's on the grounds and that he's not some burglar."

Right. Because a burglar would be creeping around the Elliott estate at five in the afternoon.

"Thanks for letting me know," Roxy said. Unfortunately, she wasn't being paid by the hour for this mural, so it was a good time to get back to work. She had a new job starting on Monday, and since it was Saturday evening, she didn't have time to waste in chitchat.

Cheryl swept out of the room, and Roxy was more than happy to get back to work. She mixed up a bit more honey gold and set to painting Rapunzel's wavy curls for a child who wouldn't even be able to say *Rapunzel* for about three more years. Yet . . . even a fairytale girl doesn't like to be left half-finished.

Time sped by, and soon Roxy had to turn on all the lights. It was just after nine when she knew she needed *to* take a break and get a drink or she'd regret it later. She had the bad habit of working straight through mealtimes and paying for it later with a significant headache.

The house was so quiet, almost too quiet, that Roxy did start to feel a bit creeped out as she walked down the stairs to the kitchen. Earlier, she'd left her sack lunch in the refrigerator—bottom shelf, of course—right where she'd been instructed by the hovering Margo. It was a nice change not to have Margo waiting for her in the kitchen this time, eyeing her every movement and making sure a single crumb wasn't left behind.

The kitchen lights were all on, which was a bit strange, but nothing to think twice about.

Then Roxy heard a chair scrape across the floor, and she froze at the bottom of the stairs.

Had Margo returned after all?

Roxy's heart thumped hard until she remembered that Don's brother Mark was on the estate too. But a quick glance at the massive hanging clock above the stairwell told her hours had passed since the Elliotts had left. How long did a contractor need to measure out a pool house?

Her answer came moments later when she crept toward the kitchen and spied around the corner to see a man sitting at the counter on a barstool.

Apparently, it took a contractor over three hours to measure for a pool house.

At least, if she could assume that the man at the counter eating her lunch was Mark Elliott himself.

Roxy was, at first, speechless. Then angry. How dare he eat her food? She happened to know that the Elliotts' two refrigerators were filled with prepared meals—most of them of the gourmet type—yet this man had chosen her measly turkey sandwich and Greek yogurt. What man ate Greek yogurt?

She cleared her throat, to give him a bit of warning, then walked into the kitchen.

Mark turned around, seemingly a bit startled to have someone else in the house. He stood as if he wasn't sure if he should question her or introduce himself. For a moment, he said nothing, and it gave Roxy a chance to get a good look at him.

He didn't look like Don Elliott at all. Don was about six feet, lean, and blond, with a cleft chin. Don's dull blue eyes were a testament of how much time he spent working in front of a computer screen. Which Don essentially did. Roxy noticed these things—a blessing or a curse of the artist's eye.

This man was several inches taller than his brother. His face was squarer, and his eyes were deep brown, which complemented the dark sandy hair that looked like it was a few weeks overdue for a haircut, if Roxy were to go by the Elliott standard of perfection.

Although this man had the same slim build of his brother, Mark was more ... solid, manly. And although he wore a fitted T-shirt and everyday jeans, Roxy sensed they were still high quality. She'd never seen Don in anything but slacks and a nice button-down shirt, but Don wasn't the contractor in the family.

"Well," the man said, his brown eyes scanning her from head to foot. Roxy might have blushed, but she was quite sure he wasn't checking her out. From experience, she knew she had enough paint smudges on her that she looked more the part of an actor in Seussical than a freelance artist. "I'm not sure we've met," he continued.

"I'm working for Cheryl," she said, folding her arms. "And you're eating my dinner."

Two

ark tried not to laugh. He couldn't stop staring at the vision of the woman who'd just walked into his brother's kitchen. No, *vision* wasn't quite the right word. Mark was horrible with words—which was why he spent his days, and most nights, running his construction company.

She was more like an apparition of color. He guessed her to be about thirty years old and definitely unmarried. Oh yes, he could spot single women a mile away. Two miles on sunny days. They always had that look in their eyes—vulnerable and a bit wild, bordering on desperate. Maybe that wasn't entirely fair, but Mark had been on so many failed dates, one after another, so when he'd gotten into an argument with his brother about how Mark brought a different woman to every family event, Mark had decided to stop dating for a while. Don of course turned it into a challenge, and Mark had met the challenge and sworn off dating for a full twelve months. He was nearly eight months into that pledge, and he was beginning to understand that vulnerable/wild/desperate feeling, yet he was determined to stick out his pledge.

The woman in the entryway must be the artist that his sister-in-law had hired to paint their kid's nursery. It had been all that Cheryl talked about at the last family get-together. What was her name? He couldn't remember, but seeing the artist in person made him question Cheryl's choices. His sister-in-law was pretty much a control freak, and the fact that she was letting a woman like the apparition who stood in front of him even walk through her house told him that Cheryl's brain cells had been depleted with her pregnancy.

"Hi, I'm Mark," he said, extending his hand and purposely ignoring the fact that this woman claimed he'd eaten her dinner. The food was on *his* shelf, and Mark was sure that he remembered Cheryl saying she'd left him his usual sandwich.

Which happened to be a turkey sandwich. He'd grabbed the Greek yogurt because he'd always wanted to try it but hadn't dared buy it at the grocery store. One bite had convinced him that he didn't need to follow any food trend.

The artist woman actually took a step back, glancing at his hand with distaste. Huh. Was he really that off-putting? He must be losing his natural charm that women seemed to gravitate toward.

The artist's lashes were unusually long, but not the fake kind some women wore. And that brought his attention to the curve of her face and the way she was pursing her lips. And her eyes . . . All right, so her eyes were pretty. A sort of gray blue that Mark hadn't known existed.

But her hair was a riot of tangles—he didn't think it could be considered one of those messy buns that his last girlfriend had claimed was her favorite look. He had disagreed, but he and Julie had disagreed on pretty much everything. The artist's hair was . . . to be frank, pink. A dark pink at that.

It was only when he got past the shock of her pink hair that Mark noticed the paint blotches on her black shirt. Who wore black while painting? Her T-shirt was fitted, but Mark wasn't going to allow himself to notice her curves, nor the way her black jeans seemed custom-made for her.

Mark dropped his hand. "I'm Mark Elliott," he said. "I assume you're the muralist?"

The woman nodded, still keeping her arms crossed. Apparently she wasn't into handshakes.

"I, uh," he motioned to the kitchen counter, "are you sure that was your sandwich?"

She lifted a single brow. "Was it on the bottom shelf?"

"Yes," he said.

"Then it was mine," she said, her voice still a hard line. "And the yogurt."

"Ah," he said. "I was wondering why Cheryl would leave me yogurt."

The woman shook her head. "You had a whole refrigerator full of food to choose from, and you had to take my dinner."

She was truly upset, and Mark found it maddening—and adorable, which only made it more maddening. What were they in? First grade?

"Look, I'm sorry," Mark said, understanding that sometimes women, and men, were extra cranky when they were hungry. Perhaps this was the case here. Although, he wasn't quite sure why he cared so much about her mood—he didn't know her, and it wasn't like he was trying impress her or anything. "Cheryl usually leaves something for me to eat on the bottom shelf, so I just assumed . . ."

The woman's face relaxed, and Mark felt a twinge in his

chest. She really was pretty when her features softened—although it was still a bit difficult to get past the pink hair.

She exhaled and smoothed back a strand of hair from her face. "Is there any yogurt left, at least?"

Was she serious? Mark glanced over at the counter. He'd taken only one bite, but most people didn't share food with strangers. "I took a bite, but didn't care for it, so I can get you something else to eat."

She moved past him, walking toward the counter.

Mark caught a whiff of paint, but he liked the smell of paint, so it was sort of appealing. He really should smack his head on the wall or something. It was getting harder to remember why he'd banned himself from flirting and dating and all things female for a year.

"You're not really going to . . ." he started to say. She was.

The woman picked up the yogurt, grabbed a clean spoon from the nearby drawer, and started to eat it.

Well. He was speechless.

She finished off the yogurt faster than he'd ever seen anyone eat, which only made him feel guilty. Apparently she was starving.

He crossed to the refrigerator and pulled open the massive stainless steel door, determined to find something else for her to eat, something better than the used yogurt. An array of neatly organized food containers met his eyes. At least they were labeled, but they said things like "Fresh Kale" and "Raw Tofu."

"Like I said," the woman spoke behind him. "You ate my dinner."

He turned, nearly coming face-to-face with her. She was standing only a couple of feet away. It gave him a chance to notice the light freckles on her nose. Another lock of pink hair had escaped her "messy bun." He had the sudden urge to smooth it back, but he kept his hand by his side.

"It seems I owe you dinner," he said. "Do you like pizza?"

Her gray eyes widened. He could definitely see they were gray. Intriguing.

"Pizza? In *this* house?" she asked.

He laughed, and he was rewarded with a smile. His stomach flipped over when she smiled back. He stepped away from her and shut the refrigerator door.

"I'm in if you're in," he said. "They won't be home until late. What are the chances we can air everything out?"

"Where would we stash the pizza box?"

"I have a truck."

"Deal," she said, her gray eyes filling with amusement. She extended her hand.

Finally. Mark grasped her paint-spotted hand and shook it. "But I must know the name of my partner in crime."

She smiled again, and Mark's stomach did it again. Flipped.

"I'm Roxy."

Three

"I'm kind of a pepperoni guy," Mark said.

Roxy shook her head. Oh no. This guy wasn't going to dictate her dinner tonight, not after he'd ruined her first dinner. "Well, I'm sort of an everything girl."

His brows rose, and his brown eyes flashed with humor. "*Everything?*"

The way he said it made her skin feel hot. Mostly because of the way he kept looking at her. Like he was studying her intently. She wasn't used to guys really looking at her. They might check out her body, then give her a hard time about her name. But this guy didn't give her that type of vibe.

"Yep, everything," she said decisively. "And I think it's my choice anyway."

"You're right," Mark conceded. "How about we go half-and-half?"

Roxy sighed. "They'll still charge us the full combo price."

"I'm paying, remember?" he said.

139

Roxy smiled and leaned on the counter in front of her barstool while he stood on the other side of the counter, cell phone in hand. "Well, you can keep being 'pepperoni guy,' or you can be a little adventurous." She didn't know why she was teasing Mark. She'd never tease his brother, Don, or heaven forbid, Cheryl.

There was just something about the way Mark kept running a hand through his unkempt hair and fidgeting with his watch on his wrist that made her find this grown, definitely good-looking man fun to tease. He wasn't wearing a ring. Maybe contractors left them off due to job hazards, or maybe he wasn't married. Therefore, he was within the teasing limits.

"Is that what eating is to you? An adventure?" he asked.

"When someone else is paying."

He smiled and shook his head. "All right. Here it goes." He dialed on his cell, and when the line connected, he said, "I'd like to order a large pizza for delivery. Yes. That's the address. No, I'll buzz in the driver when he gets here. Uh, I want everything on it. Yep. Everything." He winked at Roxy. "Regular crust. Thirty minutes is fine."

When he hung up he looked at her. "You did want regular crust, right? Or do you have a preference—"

"Regular's just fine," she said with a shrug, and then she slid off the barstool. "I'll keep working until it comes."

Mark straightened as well. "Can I see?"

She paused. "The nursery?"

"Yeah." He crossed the kitchen before she could reply.

"Sure," she said. "Just don't touch the walls." Even though Cheryl had inspected her progress on a daily basis, it was unusual having someone else interested. Maybe Mark had kids and would hire her to paint a mural as well. So she happily led the way.

At the top of the stairs, she headed down the carpeted hallway until she reached the nursery suite.

"Here we are," she said, nudging the door open with her foot.

Mark came into the room behind her, and she tried not to notice his outdoorsy scent of pine and fresh air. It was probably the typical construction manager scent anyway. Or a really nice mosquito repellent. Nothing to think much about.

"Wow," Mark said. "This is great . . ."

His voice trailed off, and Roxy found herself looking at the room through another person's eyes. She'd left all the lights on, including the two custom lamps made of crystal. Why a baby room needed crystal lamps was beyond her. But they only added to the fairy tale ambiance. Spread across the walls was a collage of images ranging from Little Red Riding Hood to Rapunzel to Puss in Boots. She'd tried to paint them so one story transitioned into another.

She watched Mark walk around. He seemed to be admiring her work, for he was inspecting it rather thoroughly.

Suddenly, he turned to her, his brown eyes bright in the glow of the room. "This is amazing, Roxy."

She'd never heard her name quite spoken like that—with appreciation, and did she dare say awe? "Thank you," she said in what felt like a very small voice. "It's my job."

He turned toward the walls again and spent several more minutes looking at the painted figures.

This gave her plenty of time to do some studying of her own—of him. His shoulders were broad, and his T-shirt showed that he was in decent shape. Probably came with his profession of lifting things, measuring things, and transporting things. His hair was nice too. Unlike his brother's cropped hair, Mark's was a more natural length, even a bit on the long side. She'd noticed his hands earlier—lean and strong. It was just something that artists noticed about other people, because getting the hand proportions right was always tricky. Surprisingly, he had clean nails. Perhaps he was more of a paperwork guy and he had others do the harder labor.

And she definitely appreciated his height. Being five nine herself, she noticed taller guys. But again, that creep factor seemed to always kick in. Mark was different. She felt it. And she couldn't explain it. Maybe it was because he was the brother of one of her clients, so there wasn't that pickup factor involved when they met.

Of course, he'd been kind and generous—after he ate her dinner—yet maybe it was because he didn't see her as someone he found interesting in *that* way. He might be impressed with her mural, but now that she thought about it, it was probably because he had a contractor's eye.

Regardless, she couldn't keep admiring his backside, especially if he was married. She had to know. "Do you have kids, Mark? I do give referral discounts."

He turned again, and Roxy was reminded of how good-looking his face really was. She bit her lip, trying to keep a nonchalant expression on her face.

"Discounts to the old client or the new client?" he asked.

"Excuse me?"

He took a couple of steps so he was standing much closer to her.

She wanted to back up and lean forward at the same time.

"Would I get the discount or would my sister-in-law?" he asked, his gaze holding hers.

"Uh, both?" She couldn't think straight right now.

He nodded, then folded his arms, as if he were thinking about her offer. "Well, I'll keep that in mind if I ever do have kids."

"All right," she said quickly. "You'd want to discuss it with your wife anyway."

One side of his mouth lifted. "I'm not married, but if I were, I'd definitely discuss it with my wife."

She tried not to let the surprise or relief show on her face. So she turned toward the door. "I think I heard someone buzz in at the gate."

"You have really good hearing," Mark said in a dry voice.

She stepped into the hall and hurried down the stairs. The TV monitor in the kitchen showed a very empty driveway. "My mistake," she said as Mark came up behind her.

He chuckled and sat down at the counter. "Are you married, Roxy?" He looked over at her. He had the barest of smiles on his face, and he didn't sound like he was teasing her, but she wasn't entirely sure.

So she decided to keep things mellow and very, very platonic. "No."

He seemed to be waiting for something, perhaps more of an explanation. Then she understood. She rested her hands on her hips and narrowed her eyes.

"What?" she said. "You're not surprised, right?"

Four

Oh no, this wasn't how Mark intended the conversation to go. He had to backtrack, and fast. "You're not wearing a ring, that's all."

Roxy's face was flushed from either anger or something else. He wasn't sure.

"You're one of those guys, aren't you?" she said. Her voice had lost all of its earlier warmth.

"*Those* guys?" he asked. "Are you profiling me?"

She blew out a puff of air, and although it was probably an indicator of how annoyed she was, it was sort of endearing as well.

"You're what? Thirty-five? Not married, no kids . . . Are you divorced?" she asked.

Mark shook his head, wondering why he suddenly felt like he was sitting in an interrogation room with a fluorescent light buzzing overhead.

"Not divorced, then?" she continued. "Are you gay?"

He shook his head again. Now he was getting annoyed. "I'm straight, single, and not living at my mother's house."

"Which gives you the right to judge every single woman you meet, right?" she asked.

Mark raised his hands. "Whoa. I don't know what you're talking about."

"Be honest," Roxy said. "What did you think when you first saw me?" She came around the counter and stopped right next to him, looking down.

He couldn't bring himself to pull away from her even though she was invading his personal space. "I thought . . . Wow, her hair is really pink."

She seemed to hesitate at that, and he hoped it was a good thing.

She folded her arms and leaned her hip against the counter in front of him. "And?"

"And," he was feeling hot, "I could tell you were single."

Her gaze narrowed. Her eyes looked almost black when she did that. "How could you tell? Besides not wearing a ring—which I believe is completely normal for an artist in the middle of a painting job."

Mark rose to his feet. Now he towered over her, but she didn't back away or seem intimidated. "I can't explain it. I just know when a woman is single. It's not really any one specific thing . . . it's more of a vibe."

She blinked and looked away then. "Should I take that as a compliment or insult?" she asked in a quiet voice.

"Neither," Mark said. "It's just an observation." He couldn't stand it anymore. A strand of dark pink hair had fallen against her cheek. He smoothed it back from her face.

Her eyes widened, but she didn't move. In fact, she seemed to be holding her breath. Neither of them moved, but the warmth of the room concentrated between them.

"What's your real hair color?" he asked in the stillness of the moment.

One side of her mouth edged upward. "I don't remember."

"Really?" he asked, scanning the top of her head. He couldn't see any alternate colored roots. "How long have you been coloring your hair?"

"Since high school," she said, peering up at him.

He was finding it hard not to gaze back. Or to breathe in her scent. She did smell of paint, but there was something softer beneath. Something more like a sweet citrus. Another smell he didn't mind.

"What's your last name, Roxy?"

Panic flitted across her eyes. Mark hadn't expected that.

The buzz of the gate sounded on the intercom.

Neither of them moved for a moment.

"Pizza's here," Roxy finally said, straightening and crossing to the intercom pad. She pressed the open button.

On the monitor, the screen showed the gate opening and a car pulling through. When Roxy started for the front door, Mark followed and said, "I'm paying, remember?"

She said nothing but opened the door. The pizza delivery car had just pulled to a stop, and an older teenager climbed out. He gazed up at the house for a moment, his eyes wide, then he opened the back door of the car and lifted out a box.

Mark stepped out onto the porch to hand over money and accept the box.

Roxy took the box from his hands and lifted the lid. "Just to be sure they got it right."

"Is everything on it?" he asked as the pizza delivery guy drove away.

"Looks like it." She carried the box into the house, and Mark followed again.

He grabbed a couple of plates from the cupboard. By experience, he knew there were no paper products in his brother's household. So they'd have to make do with the everyday china.

Roxy lifted out a slice of pizza that looked like it weighed twice as much as her. She took a bite and closed her eyes, chewing as if it were manna from heaven.

Mark couldn't take his eyes off her. The women he took out to eat would pick at their green salads and take meager sips of their lemon water.

When Roxy took the second bite, Mark was still watching her, fascinated. He felt a strange satisfaction watching her enjoy her food. He found that he was grinning as she took the third bite.

Finally she seemed to wake up from her euphoria and met his gaze. "Still chicken?"

"Nope." Mark reached over and picked up his own slice. Without bothering to transfer it to the china plate, he closed his eyes and took a bite. He didn't really want to see the onions, peppers, mushrooms, pineapple, spinach, anchovies, and crumbly, white something before he bit into it. The strongest taste was the spicy meat, which was probably salami. Overall, it wasn't bad. He knew his stomach would pay for it later though. It preferred his usual turkey sandwich or regular pepperoni pizza.

When he opened his eyes, Mark found that Roxy was watching him, her eyebrows lifted in anticipation.

"So?" she prompted.

"Not as bad as I thought it would be," Mark admitted. "But, really, I'm afraid to digest it."

Roxy laughed, and he felt everything inside of him warm. Of course, that could be due to the peppers and onions.

"You have to at least finish one slice," she said when her laughter died. "*Without* picking anything off."

"Yes, ma'am."

"I'm a *miss*, not a ma'am."

Mark gazed at her. "You're what? Thirty or so? That's definitely *ma'am* territory, at least if I want to be respectful."

Her mouth fell open. "Now I really am offended."

"Why?" Mark said, grabbing a napkin and wiping his mouth. "How old are you?"

"Twenty-nine," she deadpanned.

He couldn't keep his smile tamped down. Nor his laughter.

Her face flushed, but he didn't feel guilty in the least. She pointedly ignored him and picked up another heavy-laden piece of pizza.

"When's your big three-O birthday?" he asked.

She shook her head and continued to chew.

Mark's phone buzzed, and he pulled it out of his back pocket. Roger Jensen was one of his more fastidious clients. Even though Mark had told him he'd be in first thing on Monday, the man kept texting and calling. Mark was surprised Roger had been silent for a couple of hours. He read the text: *I think there's a leak in the new bathroom. There's a lot of humidity in the air, and I can hear water dripping.*

Mark exhaled. He doubted there was a leak, but since it was after hours, he couldn't send one of his guys, so he'd have to go himself.

"Looks like I've got to go," he said. "Pesky client."

Roxy looked up as if she were startled he was still there. She'd just finished her second slice. Mark decided she must have a stomach made of steel. She slid the box toward him. "Take this. I've got to keep painting for a while, and I don't want to leave evidence around."

"I can put it in your car if you want," he said, although he hadn't seen an extra car in the driveway. Maybe she'd parked outside the gate. "I think you'll enjoy the leftovers much more than I would."

"I'll walk home when I finish," she said, blinking back at him.

He paused. "Tonight?"

She nodded, brushing the crumbs from the counter and into the palm of her hand.

"Is Don or Cheryl going to give you a ride?" he asked, picking up the box. He was going to dispose of it in the first Dumpster he came across.

"I'll be all right," she said. "I walk everywhere."

Mark couldn't just leave her stranded. His phone buzzed again. "How late will you be?"

"I'll be fine, really," she said. She pushed lightly against the pizza box. "Go take care of your client."

Still he hesitated. Surely Don would drive her home, wouldn't he?

"Why don't you put your number in my phone, and when I get done with checking things out at Roger's place, I'll see if you need a ride." He fished his phone out from his pocket and handed it to her.

She merely shook her head. "I don't have a cell phone, and I promise, I'll be fine. Seashell Beach is perfectly safe."

He swallowed. "You don't have a phone?"

"A cell phone," she corrected. "I have a landline, and between that and my email, I manage to get along just fine."

"What person doesn't have a cell phone?" he asked as his own phone buzzed yet again.

"A person who discovered that paint is a hazard to cell phones, and a person who has become tired of paying the deductible every few weeks for a new phone."

"Every few weeks?" Mark said, staring at her.

She grimaced. "Three times was enough." She moved past him. "I've really got to get back to work. I don't think Cheryl will like me painting in her house all night long."

She started up the steps and waved him off when he said he'd come back anyway.

Mark left through the front door, carrying the pizza box with him. Roxy was an enigma. She was extremely talented. She was stubborn. She was pretty in her own way. And she was growing on him. Too bad he was on dating hiatus, or he'd have to do something about her.

Five

oxy awakened in the bright sunlight. She shot up in bed. She must have overslept her alarm, because she'd told Cheryl she'd be back first thing in the morning. Even though it was a Sunday, there was no way she could have finished the mural last night. Not with the time detour of ordering pizza with Mark. After he left, she still felt distracted and had to take her time painting a mermaid in order to focus.

She checked the antique clock on her refinished bedside table. It was after 9:00 a.m. She was two hours behind what she'd planned. Roxy hurried to dress and brush her teeth. Then she grabbed a box of granola bars. It would have to suffice for both breakfast and lunch.

Exiting the bungalow that she'd bought a few years ago, she locked the door, then set off on the boardwalk. She waved at a few familiar faces as she went. But not a lot of people were up and about this early on a Sunday morning. Seashell Beach was a resort town, and the majority of the population was tourists—which meant late nights and lazy mornings.

Roxy headed away from the center of town and walked up the long hill that led to a collection of estates. The Elliotts' was at the very top, so Roxy counted the walk as her exercise for the day. At least she didn't have her paintbrush collection to carry with her up the hill. She'd be bringing it back down in a few hours though.

She didn't know if Mark ever returned to the house to look for her or offer her a ride back home. She left before any sign of his truck appeared. By the time Cheryl and Don returned, she was more than tired, so she said goodnight to them and left the house.

Now the morning sun greeted her, promising a warm, breezy day. When she reached the gate, she punched in the guest code, then walked through. Just walking up the driveway reminded her of Mark and the night before. The way he'd looked at her and teased her, but not in a mean or a cocky way. Most of the time he'd been genuinely interested, and then he'd been impressed with her art.

He seemed like a successful and positive person, but how was it that he was single and not even divorced at his age? The only real flaw she saw in him was his strong opinions, and that wasn't necessarily a flaw in most people's eyes. As she reached the front door, she wondered why Mark Elliott hadn't ever married. She supposed he could be a playboy type, but he hadn't given her that vibe either. If anything, he seemed the tiniest bit gun-shy.

Margo opened the door before Roxy could reach for the handle. She must have been watching on the monitor.

"Good morning," Roxy said in a bright voice.

Margo just nodded and stepped back to let Roxy in. Margo was an odd woman, and she didn't say much unless it was a reprimand. Well, Roxy must be starting the day off right. She walked through the main foyer, then up the stairs to the nursery. The door to the master suite was closed, and Roxy decided that meant Cheryl and her husband were still asleep. So Roxy determined to keep things as quiet as possible.

Time flew, as it usually did while she painted, and she finished the last section before noon.

She realized that the sounds in the house had come to life, but she'd worked through all of them. She was surprised Cheryl hadn't come in to check on her.

Roxy packed up her paints, then set her brushes in the cleaning kit. She'd soak them for twenty-four hours when she returned home. For now, she stood in the middle of the nursery and rotated, taking in the different fairytale scenes with a practiced eye. If she said so herself, it looked enchanting.

She gathered up the plastic drop covers and wadded them into a ball to throw away.

"Oh." Cheryl's voice startled Roxy. "You're finished?"

"I am," Roxy said, turning to face Cheryl.

As usual, the woman was dressed exquisitely. Her pale pink jogging suit hugged her body, yet made her pregnant belly look perky and cute.

"What do you think?" Roxy asked.

She appreciated that Cheryl walked around the room and looked at everything closely. She then turned to face Roxy. "It's lovely." The first real smile that Roxy had seen from Cheryl appeared.

And Roxy knew she could finally relax.

"Great, I'm so glad you like it," Roxy said.

Cheryl glanced at the paintbrush box Roxy was packing up. "Don can drive you back home since you don't have a car." There was a faint note of disdain in her voice, but Roxy decided to ignore it. After all, it was the first time Cheryl offered Roxy a ride anywhere. Perhaps it was fitting to have the offer on the last day of her job.

Tomorrow she'd be free and clear to start the mural at Delilah's Desserts.

Roxy's final act in the nursery was to take several pictures of the mural with her film camera. By the time she hauled her paint box downstairs and disposed of the painting tarps, Don had pulled one of his sports cars out of the massive five-car garage.

Roxy hesitated about where to put the paint box. She couldn't fathom setting it on the leather seat. So she kept the box on her lap, although the corners dug into her legs.

"Where to?" Don asked.

"Just down the main hill, then to the left where the row of older bungalows is along the boardwalk."

Don nodded and steered the car along the driveway.

Roxy had hardly spoken to Don—the painting job had been commissioned and watched over by his wife.

"I hope everything goes well with your upcoming baby," she said to fill the silence. The quiet between them wasn't exactly comfortable, although it wasn't like Roxy was obligated to do all the chatting.

Don nodded, and then as he exited through the estate gates, he suddenly said, "When we got home last night, Cheryl said the kitchen smelled like pizza."

Roxy opened her mouth, then shut it. She didn't know what to say exactly. Should she mention Mark or just the pizza?

Don chuckled. "Don't worry, your secret is safe. I told Cheryl that you must have left half your sandwich in the trash. I offered to dump it, and she went upstairs to bed." He met her gaze. "I smelled it too. It's not like I never eat pizza. Just not around Cheryl."

Don slowed the car. "But I don't think you'll be a pushover."

Roxy snapped her head to look at him. "A pushover for what?"

Don lifted a shoulder and smiled. He actually had a nice smile. Roxy just hadn't seen it much. In that moment, she could see the resemblance between Don and his brother. "You'll see."

Roxy felt her cheeks grow warm, and she didn't know if she wanted Don to keep talking or not. Her job at his home was finished, and she'd probably never see him, or Mark, again. They didn't move in the same social circles. Well, Roxy had no social circles, but still.

"Thank you for the ride," she said, popping the door open and trying to gracefully climb out of the sports car with her bulky paint box.

She carried her box to her front door, noticing that Don was gentleman enough to wait until she got her front door unlocked before pulling away from the curb. He could have helped carry the heavy box for her, but she truly didn't mind. She'd been on her own for so long that she never expected much from anyone.

A cat rubbed against her legs as she pushed the door open with her foot.

"Don't you dare come in," Roxy told the feline creature that was half pet, half stray. Roxy fed the thing, had even named her Cat, but cats and paint didn't mix well. So Cat had to stay outside no matter what.

But every so often, like today, Cat ignored Roxy's commands. Cat came inside with Roxy and leaped up on the armchair and began to lick herself. "There's more sun outside," Roxy protested. She set down the paint box on her refinished kitchen table. She redid it about once a year. It was currently red. "Look out there." She pointed through the doorway, but Cat ignored her completely. "There's an entire beach of sunshine. You don't need the small patch of sun on my chair."

Cat didn't even look at her.

Roxy sighed and locked the door. She'd kick the cat out of the house after her shower. Roxy didn't have a husband or children to come home to, so, for now, the cat was perfect company.

Six

ark pulled his truck in front of the old town hall building. It had been a children's discovery museum for a number of years, but with the new Mariposa Hotel and Resort, tourism was up and so was real estate. The value of the buildings on Main Street, including the old town hall, had skyrocketed, and the city was now selling it to a big-time investor. Apparently they'd move the children's museum to a location that wasn't on Main.

The investor had called Mark the week before to discuss the projected costs of renovating the building into office suites. All the suites would be leased out to companies, and conference rooms would be rented to business teams that were on retreats.

This morning was Mark's first chance to see the building. He hoped to have a bid to the investor by the end of the day. He hadn't been in this area of Main Street much. It was quaint, and most of the buildings and homes looked original to the town. He lived about twenty minutes up the coast in an older beach house that he was renovating in his spare time. When his brother had hired him to build the house in Seashell Beach a couple of years ago, Mark had fallen in love with the location, so he'd bought his own place. But he hadn't wanted to be too close to his brother.

Mark was a few minutes early for his meeting with the realtor, who'd be letting him into the building. So he walked around the building and noticed that the brickwork was all still in great shape. He might need to replace some of the concrete that made up the walkway between this building and the bank. Otherwise, the exterior was solid. He made notes on the legal pad he liked to sketch his ideas down on. Later he'd type everything onto an official bid sheet.

At the same time he reached the front of the building, an orange convertible driven by a woman with cropped blonde hair pulled up. And by the flash of her red nails and even brighter flash of her white smile when she saw him, Mark knew that this was the realtor, Brandy Livingston.

Brandy climbed out of her car, long legged and wearing a tight-fitting blue suit. She was pretty in a flashy sort of way, and she knew it. She was also definitely single. There had been quite a bit of flirting—on her end—during their phone conversation that morning.

"Mark Elliott," she said, her voice a breathless trill. "You look even better than your picture."

Mark's gut twisted as she approached. He'd let a website designer talk him into putting his picture on the home page of his construction company site. She'd said it would personalize the company. It also gave his clients an advantage over him because they knew what he looked like, so he was always the one in for a surprise. He supposed he could have looked up Brandy's name on the realtor website, but there had been no point.

"Nice to meet you." Mark stuck out his hand as she approached. She shook his hand warmly, and he couldn't help but think of how Roxy had refused the other night. Of course, once he got to know her more, that little detail hadn't bothered him in the least. If anything, it set her apart from women like Brandy.

Roxy was far from the norm, and Mark should know—he'd spent plenty of time thinking about her Saturday night, and even part of the time on Sunday. He was hoping this morning, a Monday no less, would clear his mind of all things Roxy. But, apparently, he was still thinking of her enough to compare the realtor to the artist.

Brandy released his hand, but then she touched his arm. "I'm so glad the investor decided to hire you. I couldn't recommend you highly enough."

Mark raised his brows. "I haven't done work for you, have I?" He'd certainly remember this woman.

She laughed. "Of course not. I've just heard good things about you from Cheryl."

"Oh, you know my sister-in-law?" he asked.

"We met a few months ago in the dentist's waiting room, and we just hit it off, you know?" she said. "Connected." She was still touching his arm.

"Great," Mark said, moving away from her so she'd drop her hand. "I'll be sure to thank Cheryl. Referrals are always welcome."

Brandy flashed a smile. "And you are most welcome." She actually puffed out her chest, as if Mark hadn't already noticed her cleavage.

Hopefully, Cheryl had also told Brandy about his dating hiatus. It would make things less awkward. Not that Mark thought Brandy was going to try to hit him up for a date; he knew she would. It was in the very air between them.

"So, did you bring the key?" he asked, moving a bit farther away from her. "I've only got a short time before I need to meet with another client." There. He'd let her know he was in a hurry.

"Of course," she said with a laugh. She dug into her purse and pulled out a key—kind of old-fashioned—then she strutted up the stairs, adding plenty of sway to her hips, to reach the double oak doors. Once the door was open, she turned around. "Come on in, Mark. I'll show you around."

Mark swallowed. He didn't want a tour. He had to be able to think and come up with ideas and calculate numbers. Mark followed Brandy inside, stepping into the wake of her strong, flowery perfume.

The entryway was set up as a reception area for purchasing tickets. This area could be renovated as a lobby, and office space would be on the second floor. Mark had already pulled the original blueprints and had the idea of putting in a few computer stations throughout the lobby. Sort of like a library, but less public. The hardwood floor was well worn, but it could possibly be restored without being replaced. Most everything from the museum had been taken out, although some features still remained, like the dual-sized water fountain on one wall and built-in bookcases that must have served as a reading corner. A wide staircase led to the second floor, and a sign remained at the base of the stairs that read: Small hands need to hold big hands to go up the stairs.

The windows were massive, letting in an incredible amount of light. That would be a big selling point. But then the walls drew Mark's eyes. The far wall to the right of the staircase was painted from top to bottom with a mural. It looked like a scene out of The Jungle Book. High grasses, vines, and a tangle of trees interspersed with children playing and reading.

Mark's heart thumped as he stared at the mural. It would have to come down, or be painted over . . . whatever one did to get rid of a mural. And he had an idea of who painted it.

"Isn't it charming?" Brandy said, cutting into his thoughts. "Too bad it doesn't fit the investor's plans."

"Who—who painted it?" he asked. Even as he spoke, he decided it was an odd question. But he had to know.

"Oh, Roxy, of course," Brandy said, her voice high and bright. "She's like our own little hometown artist. You should see the upstairs. This mural's just a starting point."

Mark's heart sank. "Is she painting new ones for the new museum?"

Brandy shrugged. "I have no idea. I'm not all that close with her, even though we did go to high school together."

This caught Mark's interest. "Really? Did she paint a lot in high school?"

The realtor tilted her head as if she were thinking back. "I don't know. Like I said, we weren't really friends. I was a cheerleader and all."

Mark could've guessed that himself.

Brandy gave a shrug. "She was . . . quiet. Come on," she said, another smile flashing across her face. "I'll show you the upstairs."

Seven

Mark followed the realtor up the stairs of the old building, noting that they creaked quite a bit. That would have to be fixed. On the second story, the long corridor stretched in two different directions. The half dozen rooms must have each held different exhibits and activities for the kids. And true to Brandy's pronouncement, each room contained a different mural.

He stopped and stared at the one of the universe. The entire room was part of the mural, even the ceiling. No matter which way he turned, there were the galaxies, stars, planets, asteroids, and more. He could imagine the kids entering this room for the first time and feeling like they were in outer space.

His stomach felt like he'd swallowed a rock. All of this would have to come down. He couldn't imagine the investor would agree to keep up a mural of kids playing in a jungle or of a farm with a red barn and happy farm animals.

Mark found that he was more looking at the details of the

paintings than making a professional assessment of what needed to be done to convert the rooms into office space.

"So what do you think?" Brandy asked.

He'd almost forgotten that she was in the building. "I—" He blinked. "It might take me a bit to complete the bid."

"Right," Brandy said. "Well, you have my number." She gave him the tiniest of nudges as if she were hinting that perhaps he should call for reasons other than business ones. "Cheryl told me you recently moved to the area. I'm happy to show you around Seashell Beach."

She waited for his response. In truth, he knew what the polite thing to say would be, but he wasn't typical, no matter what Roxy might have accused him of.

"Look, Brandy, I appreciate the offer," he started. "But I'm on sort of a break from dating."

Her eyes widened, and her cheeks flushed.

He rushed on. "Not that you were implying, but I know how an innocent invitation might lead to, uh, other expectations."

Her cheeks were definitely red now, and not in the pretty way that Roxy had blushed. Brandy was angry. She opened her mouth, ready to retort, but no sound came out. Finally, she snapped her mouth shut and turned away.

Mark listened to the sound of her heels clicking all the way down the creaky stairs and across the entry. The door slammed, and Mark flinched. Well then. So much for being direct and honest. But it was better than the alternative.

"Back to work," Mark muttered to himself. Two hours later, he'd completed what should have been a one-hour job. All he could think about the whole time was how Roxy would react if she knew what was about to happen to her artwork. And there was no way Mark would be the one to inform her.

He climbed back into his truck and rolled down the windows to let the fresh sea air inside. By now it was midmorning, and tourists were roaming Main Street, buying coffee and bagels. About half a block down, a sign caught his eye. It was a bakery shop on Tangerine Street. Delilah's Desserts. Mark's stomach grumbled as he thought about the delicious food that might be inside.

He'd told his brother that he'd get the supplies ordered for the pool house today so he could start in the next couple of days, but a detour for breakfast wouldn't put him behind.

So Mark climbed back out of his truck, deciding he didn't need to try and do a U-turn on the increasingly busy street. He walked to the corner opposite of the bakery, where there was a crosswalk, and while he was waiting for a break in the traffic, he saw her. Her.

Roxy.

Mark blinked a few times and refocused. She wore a pair of cutoffs that showed tanned legs and a tie-dyed tank. She wheeled a large box on some sort of a luggage cart. The woman had platinum-blonde hair, not pink. It wasn't her. Roxy had dark pink hair.

The light changed, and the tourists crossed the street without him because Mark was rooted to the ground. The woman reminded him so much of Roxy. Her walk, her posture, the way determination seemed to ooze from her. The woman reached up and smoothed back a strand of hair that had escaped whatever contraption she'd pulled her hair back into.

Roxy? Mark stepped off the curb as the light turned yellow, earning him a couple of honks by the time he reached the middle of the street. Mark snapped out of his distracted thoughts and hurried the rest of the way as another angry horn blared. For a tourist town, the tourists were sure impatient on their supposed vacations. When he reached the sidewalk, the woman had disappeared inside the bakery—the same one he'd been headed toward.

Mark took a couple of deep breaths, his heart hammering. Probably from crossing an intersection at the wrong moment. Surely he wasn't so caught up in seeing a Roxy lookalike that he'd practically run into oncoming traffic. Surely not.

Besides, if he'd seen Roxy, it wouldn't be a good idea to seek her out. He'd have to tell her about the murals he was going to have to paint over, and then he'd spend the next few days thinking about her again.

"Welcome to Delilah's," a woman called out from behind a long glass display case. Her dark hair was pulled back from her face. She had pretty hazel eyes, and although she smiled at him, she also seemed to be intensely scrutinizing him. Without waiting for him to return her greeting, she turned back to the line of customers. All of them looked like tourists.

Mark got in line, because really, he'd probably have to stand in line wherever he went this time of morning. Plus, the place smelled heavenly, and his stomach did another pinching grumble.

The platinum-blonde woman was nowhere to be seen. Maybe she was one of the bakers and worked in the back room. He dismissed his foolish street crossing from his mind and focused on the handwritten menu on a dark brown chalkboard hanging on the wall above one of the glass displays. He was impressed with the variety—everything from cannoli, cupcakes, sugar cookies and sweet bread, and it looked like the menu changed often.

Everything looked good, and he could eat anything at this point. Based on the number of people in line and no remaining tables, he'd be eating in his truck anyway. No problem. He had to get the bid on the office suite project typed up and get the pool house order in.

Then the blonde woman appeared from the back room. She wore an apron, but instead of saying Delilah's Desserts or something, it had paint splotches on it. She smiled at the woman who'd greeted him earlier.

"So glad you could make it today," the baker said, giving the blonde woman a hug.

Mark stared because he'd bet his life that the woman was Roxy. Blonde hair and all.

"I finished the nursery mural sooner than planned," the blonde woman said. "Yesterday afternoon, in fact. So I'm all ready to set up."

The baker grinned. "You'll have to scoot over a table for the drop cloth, but the wall has already been scrubbed down."

"Great," the blonde said, her gray eyes shifting toward the wall in question. Just beyond Mark. Her gaze stopped on him, moved past, then returned. Her mouth fell open.

She recognized him. She closed her mouth and gave him a small smile before she returned her focus to her friend.

Mark couldn't quite make out what else they said to each other because the man in line in front of him answered a phone call. Despite that, Mark willed his pulse to return to normal. He felt rather warm. Sure, the bakery was probably warmer than outside, but he was ridiculously uncomfortable all of a sudden.

He lost sight of Roxy for a moment when it was his turn to order. He had no hesitation ordering two cannoli and a coffee. After he paid the cashier, he glanced around again. Roxy had spread a tarp on the floor in front of one of the walls. She was mixing up paint on an oval palette. He wondered why she was painting while there were customers in the store. But as he watched, he realized it was something interesting for them to watch. Roxy perched on a metal stepstool and began to make quick strokes across the bare wall. The kids in the place seemed fascinated as she outlined what looked to be a fairy or a pixie holding a tray with a giant cupcake.

Mark wandered a little closer, taking a sip of his coffee, then taking a bite of his first cannoli.

With the fairy outlined, next she painted what appeared to be a platter of cupcakes.

Mark felt like one of the kids, just standing there watching, as others came in and out of the shop. Eventually, a table opened, and he sat down, finished with his dessert, but still sipped on his coffee. He hadn't dared interrupt Roxy's work, but he also sensed that she knew he was there, watching.

He replied to a couple of texts that came in from a newer client, but mostly he just watched Roxy. She'd kicked off her sandals and now stood on tiptoe to fill in the fairy's strands of hair.

Over an hour passed, and the bakery had mostly emptied. Only a couple of the tables were filled.

Roxy stepped down from the ladder and took a few steps back. "What do you think?" she said.

Mark realized she was talking to him.

He rose from his chair and came to stand right next to her. "I like it," he said simply.

Roxy gave a small nod, but she smiled. He smiled too.

"Did you get home all right the other night?" he asked.

"I'm here, aren't I?" Her tone was light. Soft.

"You are here," Mark agreed. "And you're blonde."

She touched her hair and turned to face him. "Do you like it?"

He looked at her. Gray eyes. Long eyelashes. Freckled nose. Rosy lips. A strand of hair edging her eye. He brushed it out of the way. "I do like it."

"Better than pink?" she asked.

This he considered. "Pink stands out more. But it wasn't bad. I don't mind the blonde though."

Eight

oxy tilted her head, looking at Mark. She couldn't believe he was at Delilah's Desserts, of all places. He was dressed a little nicer this morning. Instead of a T-shirt, he wore a short-sleeve button-down and khaki pants. His brown eyes seemed lighter in the bakery, and his hair was less messy.

He'd been watching her paint for more than an hour. Didn't he have a job to do somewhere, building something? She was flattered, to say the least, but she also wasn't about to let herself get any hopes up. So what if he was good-looking, interesting, sometimes charming, and well . . . sort of hard to ignore? So what if he liked her hair?

"What brings you here?" she asked. "I didn't think you lived in this area."

"I don't exactly," he said, and there seemed to be hesitation in his voice when he spoke next. "I'm working on a bid for renovating the former children's museum that used to be the old town hall."

173

She'd heard that the children's museum was moving, and she could only hope that whatever happened to the building, the new owners would keep her murals. She'd spent weeks painting them. "I heard they were moving the children's museum."

"Yeah." Mark's reluctance was plain.

"So, who's buying the building?"

"It's an investor," Mark said in a slow voice. "The place will be turned into office suites."

Roxy nodded, letting the information sink in. "Will they be offices for say, child therapists?"

"I don't think so, Roxy," he said.

She loved it when he said her name, but she wasn't loving it now. "So the murals will get painted over?"

At least there was sincere regret in his voice when he said, "It looks like it. I haven't put in my renovation bid yet, but I don't really see a way around it."

She turned to look at the beginnings of her mural on the bakery wall. "I suppose something like that was bound to happen at some point. I mean, even with the nursery at Cheryl's place, she'll want to redecorate someday."

Mark didn't say anything for a moment, but she felt his gaze on her. When she'd completed the murals in the children's museum, a local journalist had written up an article about her and published pictures of her standing next to the murals. She'd felt like a town celebrity for weeks after that. She'd even gone on a couple of dates with the journalist—Tom was his name. But she was just a stepping stone onto something bigger. When he'd gotten hired at a larger paper in LA, they eventually lost contact.

Tom had been the last guy she'd dated, and that was over three years ago. Had it really been that long ago?

"I have an idea," Mark said.

His voice broke her out of her growing self-pity. She looked over at him, curious.

"What if you do a photoshoot?" he continued. "Bring in a professional photographer to take pictures of the murals, and you could turn them into huge posters."

"Posters?" She wasn't sure if she should be insulted or appreciate that he was making a suggestion.

"Look," he continued. "I know you can't ever duplicate those murals and that they'll be lost forever when they're painted over. But you could use the images in marketing your services. You could even make more posters, maybe postcards, and sell them."

Roxy didn't know if she should be horrified or laugh at his suggestion. "I don't do commercial work. It sort of defeats the purpose of my career."

Mark didn't seem deterred by her pronouncement. "Whether or not you decide to sell posters or postcards, you should at least do the photo shoot. Save those original murals in at least one format."

She nodded. Mark was right, but what if he did have influence with the investor? What if he could talk the man into keeping the murals?

"Maybe a photo shoot is a good idea," she hedged. If anything, she'd be kept in the loop of when the renovation would be taking place. It had nothing to do with the fact that it would also keep her in contact with Mark.

"So," Mark said, nodding toward the sketched-out mural on the bakery wall. "Are you doing the whole wall?"

"Oh, no," Roxy said. "Delilah just wants some splashes here and there. She's going to put a couple of small kids' tables in this corner, and she thought a fairy figure carrying a dessert tray would be fun."

"Do you paint anything else besides fairytale creatures?" he asked.

She turned to him in surprise, then realized where he was coming from. If he'd seen only the murals at the children's museum and in Cheryl's house, then he might think that. "I do realistic art as well."

His eyes connected with hers. "I'd love to see your other work sometime." He wore a half smile on his face.

She stared at him for a moment, and then she put her hands on her hips. "Really? So, is this a date?"

"No," he said very quickly. His eyes narrowed. "Don talked to you, didn't he?"

"Maybe," Roxy said, grinning at him. "I think it's commendable, by the way. Sounds like something I would do."

His eyes narrowed further, as if he were trying to decide if she was making fun of him.

"Come over sometime, and I'll show you my portfolios." She pointed out the window. "Turn at the end of Tangerine Street right before the boardwalk. My bungalow has a yellow door."

He looked surprised—maybe that she'd agreed or that she'd invited him to her house. Or maybe he had expected her to rattle off a professional website.

"All right," he said, his eyebrows lifting. "I can give you my cell—"

"No, it's okay," Roxy cut in. "I'm home most nights. Painting is better done in the natural light of day." She hoped she hadn't alluded to the fact that she had no life outside of painting. It was too late for that now. "By the way," she continued, "the desserts here are delicious."

She stepped away from him, indicating her break was over. Picking up the paintbrush she'd left on the palette, she swirled on more color and with the palette in one hand climbed the stepladder.

She could feel Mark still watching her. Perhaps he expected a formal goodbye, a thanks-for-coming, or a nice-to-see-you-again. Nope.

"Would you like anything to go?" Delilah's voice sailed across the bakery, and Roxy smiled to herself.

Mark stuttered out a polite, "No, thank you," then he said, more directly to Roxy, "I might take you up on that offer."

"Sounds good to me," Roxy said without turning. She could feel him hesitate, and then the sound of the door jangled as he walked outside.

She released the breath she hadn't realized she'd been holding. She really had to come up with some deep flaws for Mark. He was way too easy on the eyes and almost as easy on the heart.

"Who was that?" Delilah asked, coming to stand by the stepladder.

"Mark Elliott," Roxy said in a matter-of-fact voice. "He's Don Elliott's brother."

"Wow." Delilah peered up at her, her brows raised in question. "He'd better be single."

"He's single," Roxy said. "Too single, in fact. Never been married or anything. Not a commitment guy, it appears. In fact, he's on a year-long dating hiatus."

Delilah laughed, and Roxy found herself smiling. It was ridiculous.

"Sounds like something out of a chick flick," Delilah said, shaking her head.

"Yeah, well, I think it's just for attention," Roxy said as she filled in the violet ruffles that edged the fairy's dress.

A customer came in, and Delilah greeted them. Then she turned back to Roxy. "How's that?"

"I don't know all the family dynamics, but his brother's like a multimillionaire, Cheryl's a trophy wife, and now they're about to have their first baby," Roxy said, making her strokes broader so they'd give a flowy feeling to the fairy skirt. "It seems that Mark is doing everything he can do to be opposite of his brother."

"Hmm," Delilah said. "You might be right. Did you get all of this from the psychology class you failed in college?"

"Funny," Roxy said, pointing the paintbrush at her friend. She saw Delilah only when she came in to buy something, but the baker was the closest thing to a friend that Roxy had in this town. Maybe it was because she didn't know Roxy's last name or her history in high school.

"It's obvious he's very interested in you," Delilah said, stepping out of the way of Roxy's paintbrush.

"Too bad he's on a dating hiatus," Roxy said sarcastically. "As if he'd ever be interested in me. I'm practically a cat lady."

"Only a stray cat, so you're not beyond saving yet," Delilah said.

A family came into the bakery, meaning things were about to get a lot more busy.

"Go help your customers," Roxy said. "You're distracting me." She smiled as Delilah laughed again, then made her way over to the counter.

Roxy returned her focus to painting, but she couldn't get Delilah's words out of her mind. Was Mark really interested in her? She exhaled. It would be just her luck to attract a guy who couldn't date in the first place.

The next few hours sped by as Roxy painted. Delilah had wanted her painting while customers were coming in and out of the store so they could watch as well. About once an hour, Roxy had quite the crowd watching. She also handed out four business cards to potential clients. Win-win.

Nine

Mark drummed his fingers on the armrest of the chair he had situated on his newly sanded deck. He'd refinished the deck chair as well, and it was now a glossy sandalwood color. The ocean was gray this evening. The sunshine of the afternoon had been covered by heavy, dark clouds.

Mark had no doubt that it was raining over the ocean, and it was only a matter of time before the rain reached his beach house. He'd turned in the renovation bid to the investor and had already been sent an approval. Work would start as soon as he got the order in and the laborers scheduled.

The pool house supplies would be delivered to Don's tomorrow morning, and Mark already had an eight-man crew booked for the job. And he'd exchanged emails with several other clients who were looking at either home renovations or building upgrades. Business was good.

So why did he feel unsettled? Usually approaching storms made him want to hibernate and wait it out. Maybe

THE ART OF LOVE

warm up a freezer dinner, watch an old cowboy movie on cable. But he kept thinking about the color of Roxy's hair and how she'd given him that impish smile when she first saw him in the bakery. And . . . how she'd invited him to her bungalow.

Mark took a long drink from the water bottle in his nondrumming hand. She'd probably be home now. The lighting was far from good with the approaching storm. He wondered if she'd had dinner yet. Maybe she wouldn't mind if he grabbed something and brought it over. It wouldn't really be a date, would it?

This dating hiatus had started out as an argument between him and his brother. Don had called Mark out and told him that he was a serial dater—a menace to society. Mark had said he'd prove him wrong. He wouldn't date anyone for six months.

Don had taken on Mark's challenge and said he'd take Mark skydiving if he could last nine months. Mark had laughed and said he could last an entire year, that it would actually be refreshing not to have to worry about the next male-female encounter. Don had stuck out his hand, and they'd shaken on it.

It wasn't that Mark couldn't pay for a skydiving trip on his own, but it was being challenged by his brother that had spurred him on. Yes, it might seem juvenile to some people that Mark had made a silly bet and felt like he had to prove something, but to Don, he did have to prove something.

Mark had tried calling his brother twice that day to find out what exactly he'd said to Roxy about Mark's dating hiatus. But Don's secretary had said he was slammed with meetings.

"Even multimillionaires have to eat," Mark muttered. He fished his cell phone from the side table next to his chair and called his brother yet again.

"Mark, I was just thinking about you," Don said in a cheery voice when he answered.

"Probably because I called you twice today," Mark said.

"Yeah, today was crazy," Don said. "Is everything ready to go for the pool house?"

"We start tomorrow."

"Great," Don said. "I don't want to have your crew and all the pounding noise when we have a newborn in the house."

"We'll be done before then," Mark promised. "But that's not the only thing I'm calling about. What did you say to Roxy the other day?"

Don chuckled. "I knew it. You're interested."

"I'm interested in what's being said about me behind my back."

Don only laughed again. "Have you called her yet?"

No, not technically. "I don't have her phone number."

"That shouldn't stop my brother," Don said, lowering his voice. "Hey, I've got to go. Just know that I only said good things about you, and that I might have spilled the beans on your dating hiatus. But I figured that wasn't exactly a secret anyway and that you're going to break it."

"Why would you think I'm going to break it?" Mark asked. "Only four months left to go."

Don just laughed and hung up.

The first raindrop hit the deck, then another. The rain came faster, its plopping sound urging him to go, go, go. Mark rose from the chair and went in through the sliding glass door. He set down his water bottle and picked up his truck keys. Moments later, he was driving down the coastal highway, his windshield wipers turned on.

By the time he got to the bungalow with the yellow door, the beaches were empty of tourists, all of them taking cover during the storm. In one hand, Mark carried a large paper sack with takeout from The Fortune Café, a local Chinese restaurant. With his free hand, Mark knocked on the yellow door, hoping that Roxy liked Chinese.

Light glowed from a window, so Mark took that as a good sign.

Soon the door opened, and Roxy stood there.

"What in the—get in here," she said, grasping his arm and tugging him inside.

Okay, so he was drenched. Between the walk from the restaurant back to his truck and the walk to the bungalow, he'd been rained on quite a bit.

"I hope you like Chinese," he said, holding up the bag. The bag had miraculously remained mostly dry.

Roxy looked at the bag, then back up to him. She started laughing.

Mark set the bag on the floor while she continued to laugh and shrugged off his jacket and hung it on the doorknob. That got rid of some of the moisture. Next, he took off his shoes, then his socks, which were quite damp.

Roxy picked up the sack from the floor. "Make yourself at home," she said in a teasing voice. As if he hadn't already removed his shoes and socks. "I do in fact like Chinese, and we can eat in my morning room."

"Morning room?" Mark echoed. He didn't need any more encouragement to follow her through the bungalow. No lights were on anywhere else in the place. She stopped at a bay window alcove where the gray light of the evening poured in. There was a table and two chairs. The windows were huge, and through the rain-speckled glass was a view of the ocean much like the one he had.

"Yes," Roxy said, setting the Chinese food on the surprisingly clean table.

Mark had expected everything inside her bungalow to be a bit ratty and paint splattered. But so far, he hadn't seen any paint splatters, and the place was spotless. The furniture was older but refinished, and that he could appreciate. He wondered if she'd done it herself.

"This room captures the sun in the morning, and it gives me inspiration for my work." She lifted her shoulder. "I'm watching the storm pass over."

Right now the morning room was a bit gloomy, but it was gothic gloomy.

The room brightened momentarily as lightning streaked across the sky. "It looks like a pretty good storm," Mark commented.

Roxy unwrapped the chopsticks and handed a pair over to Mark. "Which is why you decided to come over?"

"The storm has nothing to do with it," he said, stepping closer. Roxy had changed her clothes again from earlier. She wore a flowy white shirt with some embroidery lining the neckline and orange capri pants that looked like they were well-worn and well loved. She was barefoot like him. Her blonde hair was pulled into a knot at the back of her head, and more than one section had fallen out of the knot.

"I was hoping to see your portfolio," he continued, and he took another step since she hadn't moved. "You did invite me, you know."

"Yeah, but I didn't exactly think you'd show up," Roxy said. "And not tonight. I mean, I just saw you this morning."

"You don't like Chinese food?" he said.

She smirked. "This is an obvious bribe."

"Hmm." He couldn't take his eyes off her. She smelled like fresh laundry and something else, maybe oranges. "I'm just a curious guy."

She rested her hands on her hips. "You're also flirting."

Mark raised his eyebrows. One point to Roxy for being blunt. He was flirting, but he couldn't seem to help it. "Is that terrible?" he asked.

"Your brother was right," Roxy said. "You don't like women who are pushovers."

"He said that?" Mark asked. Where was she going with this? Why did she have to be so tempting? He couldn't date her, but could he kiss her?

"The more I give you a hard time, the more you seem to come around," Roxy said, her voice softening. "And you're standing really close to me."

"Yeah, I am," Mark said, reaching up to smooth back her hair, but he didn't drop his hand this time. Instead, he cupped her cheek and leaned down.

She didn't move, didn't back away.

So Mark took that as a good sign. He closed the distance and kissed her.

Still, she didn't move, didn't kiss him back. The rain pelting the windows and their breathing were the only sounds in the morning room. He slid his hand to her neck, pulling her closer, hoping for some reciprocation as he kissed her again.

When it came, he didn't know why he'd doubted in the first place. There was definitely interest on both sides, and for all her teasing, perhaps he should have expected her hesitation. All of that fled though when she kissed him back, grasping his upper arms and tugging him closer.

She tasted sweet, and he could feel the pounding of her heart mirror his own as their bodies pressed together. For him, it had been a long time since he kissed another woman, but he didn't remember feeling quite this invested back then. He wanted to slow time down, savor every second of this kiss, and remember the feel of her warm skin beneath his hands.

The way her breathing had increased and the way she clung to him as if he were the center of her universe.

"Mark," she whispered, breaking away from the kiss. "You're cheating."

He laughed and lifted her up against him so that she had to wrap her arms about his neck. His mouth found hers again, and he slowly spun until she was backed up against the table. He lowered her, and she released the tiniest of moans, which only made him want to deepen the kiss. His pounding pulse was growing erratic, and he knew he had to put some space between them.

"Roxy," he said, against her mouth.

"Hmmm?" she breathed.

He lifted his head, but the gray vastness in her eyes when they blinked open to gaze at him only propelled him to lean forward and kiss each eyelid.

"That tickles," she said, but she didn't loosen her hold on him.

He settled his hands at her waist and breathed in all of her. His brother had just won their bet, because Mark had no intention of staying away from Roxy.

Ten

Mark's hands felt like they were burning the skin where they rested on Roxy's hips. He'd kissed her, really kissed her, and he was still kissing her. He abandoned her mouth, and now his mouth was trailing kisses along her jaw, then her neck.

Goose pimples broke out on Roxy's skin at the warmth of Mark's breath, the touch of his mouth, exploring. Lightning flashed outside, brightening the walls, but it only made Mark pull her closer.

She'd been surprised to see him at her doorstep, in the rain, no less. But her heart had started thumping the moment she'd opened the door, and she knew he was definitely interested. His kisses were certainly proving that as well. Delilah had been right.

Wasn't he on a dating hiatus? Unless he didn't count this as a date. She certainly did—and she didn't do hookups. "Mark," she said, sliding her hands from behind his neck to his chest. "Mark."

He lifted his head, his brown eyes appearing darker in the gray light of the storm.

"I don't do hookups," she said.

He stared at her for a moment, then he leaned in and kissed the edge of her mouth. "Good, I don't either."

"What's going on here, then?" she pressed. "I mean, you're on a dating hiatus, yet"—she motioned between the two of them—"this is happening."

Mark drew away, but only slightly. His hands were still securely on her hips, anchoring her against him. "About that hiatus," he began. "It was more of a challenge than anything. Don will be happy that he beat me yet again."

"It was between you and your brother?" she asked.

"Yeah," he said, sliding his hands behind her back, and she knew she would become lost in kissing him again.

But she wanted answers. "Why do it in the first place?"

He stilled, holding her gaze. "Don thought I was too flakey with women. That I couldn't commit to anything or to any one person."

"So the solution was to not date at all?" she asked. She rested her hands on his upper arms. Construction work definitely had its advantages on a man's physique.

"It was more of a battle of wills against each other," he said. "If I won, he was going to take me skydiving. If he won, he'd get bragging rights."

"So, now what?" she asked.

"Has anyone ever told you that you're very direct?" Mark asked, his mouth lifting in a smile.

"Not really," Roxy said, sliding her hands down his arms and pulling his hands from her waist. "I'm not exactly typical."

He let her remove his hands, but then he linked their fingers together. "I noticed that."

She bit her lip.

"What's wrong?" he asked.

She took a deep breath. "I haven't told you my last name."

He looked confused for a second, then he grinned. "So . . . tell me."

This wasn't a laughing matter. "The food is probably cold." She turned from him and opened one of the containers, then peered inside.

"Roxy," Mark said, grabbing her wrist and pulling her toward him. "What's your last name?"

"I—it's dumb."

"Your last name is dumb?" The surprise in his voice was plain.

She blinked up at him. Why did he have to be so appealing? "No, I mean, yes, and I was teased a lot about it."

He touched her chin and lifted it so that she had to look at him. "Do you think I'm going to give you a hard time about your last name?"

She looked away, feeling sheepish. He dropped his hand but didn't move away. Now that she was making it into a big deal, it would be a big deal. She was twenty-nine, and it was time to get over the RR initials she had no control over. When she couldn't bring herself to say anything, he said, "Do you want me to guess?"

She snapped her gaze back to him. "Guess?"

"Sure," he said in a casual tone. "Guessing games are fun, right?" He picked up a pair of chopsticks and unwrapped them. Then he opened one of the containers and used the chopsticks to lift out a piece of sweet-and-sour chicken. He popped it into his mouth, chewed, swallowed, and then said, "Johnson."

"No," she said, drawing her eyebrows together. "What, are you going to guess all night?"

191

"If I have to," he said with a wink.

Her heart pitter-pattered like the rain outside.

He held out the container of sweet-and-sour chicken toward her. "This is really good, do you want to try it?"

She took it from him and dug in her chopsticks. She popped one into her mouth. It was good. He picked up another container with something beefy inside and started eating that. He seemed comfortable in her morning room and didn't seem bothered that they'd been kissing just a short time ago. He acted like everything was normal and they'd known each other for a long time.

After a moment, he said, "Jackson?"

"No," she said, hiding the small smile that was beginning to grow.

He sank onto one of the chairs and took a couple more bites of the beef dish. "Richards? Roxy Richards?"

He was actually close. "No."

Mark looked over at her. "Can you give me a hint?"

She exhaled. Mark was interesting, and she was attracted to him. He was a really good kisser as well, and those hands . . . If they were actually going to start dating, it would be weird if he didn't know her last name. "It starts with an R."

"Ah, so I was close," he said simply. He didn't comment on the double Rs.

She took another bite of the chicken. It either was the best sweet-and-sour chicken she'd ever had or she was really hungry.

"Can I get a drink?" he asked.

"Sure," Roxy said, starting to stand up.

"I'll grab it." Mark was on his feet first, so Roxy shrugged.

"You know where the kitchen is." For some reason, she was fine with him in her house. She didn't feel the need to follow him or point things out.

He returned a short time later carrying two water bottles. "Thanks," she said as he set one in front of her.

He took a long pull of the water before he said, "Ricardo?"

Roxy nearly spit out her water with a laugh. "Do I look like a Ricardo?"

Mark shrugged and grinned. "You could be one-quarter or something." He sat down and opened another container of food.

She just shook her head. "You aren't too great at this game."

"Then give me another hint, or else . . ." He looked over at her with a significant look.

As if she knew what that meant. "Or else what?"

He reached over and hooked his fingers around the back of her chair. Then he dragged it toward him. He kissed her again.

She let her eyes close and warmth travel all over her body as he kissed her.

"Reynolds," he said, pulling away.

She opened her eyes. His intense gaze sent goose pimples across her skin. "Randall," she said.

"Roxy Randall," Mark said in a slow voice. She waited for a joke, for him to tease, but instead he said, "Will you go out with me tomorrow?"

She felt like grinning, but she refrained. "What about the deal with your brother?"

"Hmm, I'm pretty sure it's already off."

A streak of lightning arced across the sky outside, followed by the boom of thunder. It was loud enough that it made Roxy flinch. Then the house went completely silent. No hum of the refrigerator. The ceiling fan stopped.

She looked around the room. "Do you think the lightning struck something?"

"I'll check," Mark said, pushing back his chair and standing.

"Wait," Roxy said, standing as well. "What are you going to do?"

"Check the fuse box first and see if I can reset it," he said. "If that doesn't work, I'll look around outside."

Roxy looked toward the windows. The rain hadn't let up at all, and it was nearly dark. For all she knew, the electricity was out along the whole street. "I'll show you where the fuse box is."

Mark followed her to the short hallway that led to the bedroom. Embedded into the wall was the fuse box. He turned on his cell phone flashlight, then opened the thin metal door. He flipped all of the switches, but nothing happened.

When Mark turned, he said, "I'll see if the neighbors have power."

Roxy walked with him to the front door. He pulled it open only to be greeted by a gusty wind and cold rain.

Roxy stuck her head out of the door for a few seconds and looked down the row of bungalows. All of them were dark. "The power's out on the whole street," she said above the wind and rain.

Mark pulled the door shut and turned toward her. "Do you know the city emergency number? I need to let them know."

"Sure," Roxy said. "I have a list of numbers on the fridge." They walked into the kitchen, and Mark called the city offices. No one answered, but he left a message.

Then he turned to Roxy. "I don't want to leave you here alone, without electricity." He paused. "I can sleep on the couch."

"I'll be fine, really," Roxy said just as another bolt of lightning struck, hitting somewhere close if the next boom of thunder was any indication. She flinched again, then gave a nervous laugh. "I'm not usually this jumpy."

Mark linked their fingers together. "My offer still stands."

As if to answer, another streak of lightning flashed outside. Having Mark stay on the couch might not be such a bad idea, and he wouldn't have to drive home in the storm. She took a deep breath. "Okay."

Eleven

Mark blinked his eyes open in the early morning light. It took him a moment to remember where he was. The blue walls and sound of a distant wind chime were unfamiliar to him.

Roxy. Mark sat up, wincing at the ache in his neck. He'd slept on her couch, and although it had been much too small for any sort of comfort, he'd been determined to be the perfect gentleman.

The hum of the refrigerator told him that the electricity had come back on. He stood from the couch. His mouth was paper dry, and more than his neck ached now. Walking into the kitchen, he found it empty. So he grabbed a water bottle from the fridge and drank most of it down.

Next, he went to the morning room. The early morning light made the place glow, and with the ocean view through the windows, the place could have easily been a postcard image. The portfolios she'd shown him by flashlight last night were still on the table.

197

There were no sounds other than his footsteps. No smell of coffee. Was she still asleep? Mark walked quietly down the hallway and nudged the bedroom door open. The bed was made and the room was empty.

"Roxy?" No answer.

He turned back and walked to the couch. Sometime during the night, she'd put a blanket on him. So he folded it up and looked around. No note. Nothing.

Did artists start work this early in the morning? Yesterday, when he'd seen her arrive at Delilah's Bakery, it had been midmorning.

The front door opened, and Mark turned to see Roxy enter. She carried a sack with her.

"You're awake," she said with a hesitant smile.

"I'm awake," he repeated. Morning Roxy was even sexier than daytime Roxy. She wore leggings, jogging shoes, and a tank shirt. She held out the sack she carried.

"Bagels."

"And coffee?" he asked.

"I can make tea."

He hid a groan. "All right."

She walked into the kitchen, practically ignoring him. Would it be too presumptive for him to expect a kiss in greeting? He shook his head. He hadn't ever acted this puppy eyed with anyone else he dated.

Mark leaned against the doorframe as Roxy filled a teapot with water. It was quite enjoyable to watch the movements of her lithe body.

"Do you have some ibuprofen?" he asked.

She pointed to a cupboard, so he crossed the kitchen and found the medicine. He drank the last of his water bottle with it.

"Did you sleep well?" she asked, setting the teapot on the stove and turning on the burner.

"Eventually," he said.

She turned to look at him. "Eventually?"

"It was kind of hard to keep to myself, knowing you were down the hall."

She blinked, then her cheeks flushed. "You're flirting again."

He gave her a half smile. "I am. Is it working?"

She folded her arms across her chest. "It depends on what you're trying to accomplish."

Stepping forward, he moved close to her. He placed his hands on her shoulders. "I was hoping you'd go out with me tonight."

She tilted her head, thinking. Or maybe she was giving him a hard time. It was hard to tell exactly.

"Food will be involved," he said, moving even closer. She smelled like lemons. How did she do that?

She leaned into him, and he didn't hesitate. He kissed her, and as she wrapped her arms about his neck, he wished he could take the day off and stay right here.

When Roxy drew away, she said, "I'm pretty booked this week. I'm finishing up at the bakery today, and then I have a playhouse to do at another mansion."

"Hmm," Mark said. "I could bring you food."

She lowered her hands to his chest. "Funny." Then she stepped out of his arms and moved toward the teapot as it started to whistle.

"Maybe this weekend," she said, turning off the element.

"All right," Mark said in a slow voice. This weekend—as in Friday, Saturday, or Sunday? "What's the best way to get ahold of you?"

She lifted a shoulder. "Just stop by." She took down two

mugs from the cupboard and poured hot water into them.

Was she blowing him off? She was being sort of maddening. "Which night?"

She looked over at him, her gray eyes unreadable. "Any night I'm here."

Okay, fair enough. She wanted to be a little elusive; he could give her that. She'd seemed to enjoy kissing him at least. He could work on the rest. Because apparently he was all in, and for the first time in his life, he was a bit unsure of himself.

They drank tea and ate bagels together, watching the sun spill its orange and gold rays across the ocean. Roxy told him about the client who had built a playhouse for his three-year-old, and Mark found he was fascinated with the details Roxy had noticed. He also found that he couldn't stop watching her.

When he asked her about her former boyfriends, she just shrugged and said, "No one is worth mentioning. They were all short-lived relationships."

This should have been a red-flag, but in truth, he figured that maybe, like him, she was busy and picky.

When Mark left her bungalow that morning, he had a hard time focusing on his pending projects. First, he headed over to Don's place to make sure he was there when the building supplies arrived and to double-check the order. His lead project manager had already texted to say that the crew would be there in about ten minutes.

Things were running smoothly so far, which gave Mark a moment to wonder if Roxy would think he was being too pushy if he bought her a cell phone. It had been only twenty minutes since he'd seen her, and already he wanted to call or text her. He released a sigh as he pulled through the gates of his brother's estate.

He parked and called the delivery company. They were only a few minutes out, so he was pleased with that. He covered up a huge yawn. He figured he'd gotten about two or three hours of sleep total last night. Between the rain and the lightning and being in the same space as Roxy, he couldn't get his mind to shut off. The front door opened, and both Don and Cheryl came out.

Mark's heart sank. First because Cheryl had that determined look on her face, and second because he wasn't exactly looking forward to Don's gloating when Mark confessed that he was dating someone.

Mark climbed out of the truck. "The delivery should be here in a few minutes," Mark said as his brother came down the porch steps.

"Great." Don nodded. "I'll try to get out a little early today to check on everything." He kissed Cheryl on the cheek, then walked along the driveway to the massive garage that housed several sports cars.

"How are you doing, Cheryl?" Mark asked, feeling a bit uncomfortable when he was faced with his sister-in-law alone. She was so . . . perfect. And she had that knowing look in her eyes all of the time.

"As well as can be expected," Cheryl said with a sigh.

Mark didn't ask her to elaborate.

"We're having a barbecue on Saturday, and we're inviting you," she said. "Don's inviting his executive team, and I'll invite a few friends as well. We'd love for you to come."

When Mark didn't answer right away, Cheryl continued, "You'll make some great contacts—these executives have plenty of money, and their wives are always redecorating."

"I'm not an interior designer," Mark deadpanned.

Cheryl smiled. "Of course not, but a lead is a lead. What do you say?"

Saturdays were usually filled with client projects, but the upcoming weekend was slower than usual. "What time?"

"About five," Cheryl said, touching his arm. "See you then."

She turned before he could say anything else and walked back up the stairs.

Mark was still standing in the driveway when Don pulled out in a yellow sports car. He waved as he passed.

If Mark had known how crappy the rest of the week would turn out, he would have climbed back into his truck and driven back home.

As it was, he didn't see Roxy until Friday night.

He'd been swamped because one of the crewmen had become sick, and the investor on the old children's museum wanted the renovation timeline cut in half. So it was after 9:00 p.m. when Mark pulled up to Roxy's bungalow.

Her lights were on, and that was the best thing that Mark had seen all day.

When he knocked on the yellow door, his heart hammered along with his knock. It had been several days, and he was feeling like it had been weeks since he'd seen her.

She opened the door, and he couldn't help but smile. She looked like she'd just gotten out of the shower. Her hair was still blonde, and it hung in damp curls against her shoulders.

"I was wondering if you'd show up," she said.

"You need a cell phone," he said. "I can't just keep driving by. And you don't answer your house phone."

She smiled. "Maybe I want you to drive by."

Mark leaned toward her. "I'm hoping you want to stay in tonight. I'm exhausted."

"Order pizza or something?" she asked.

"Anything."

She opened the door, and he practically tumbled inside. They ordered pizza and spent a couple of hours together sitting on the couch as they talked about their childhoods.

Mark felt like he was revealing a lot more than Roxy, but he was content just to be in her company. He convinced her to do a photo shoot of her murals in the children's museum and to possibly photograph other murals she had around town as well. She could decide what to do with the pictures later. Mark couldn't remember a time when he'd just sat on a woman's couch and talked for hours. On the downside, they didn't kiss nearly enough, but he had a feeling he didn't want to do anything to push her away. And moving too fast might do that. He even asked her to the barbecue at his brother's house.

Just before 11:00 p.m., she said, "I've got a crazy day tomorrow that starts really early." She rose from where they were sitting on the couch and tugged his hand.

He stood up next to her, and she led him to the front door.

"How early?" he asked.

She laughed, opening the door. "Do you want me to come with you to the barbecue or not?"

He pulled her against him. "I do." He kissed her neck, and she let him for a moment, seeming to melt against him, and then she pushed him the rest of the way out the door.

When the yellow door closed to separate them, Mark exhaled. He was falling in love with her. The trouble was, she didn't seem as affected. Sure, she acted as if she liked him, and, well, she seemed to enjoy spending time with him. But she hadn't instigated getting together. She'd left it all up to him.

He shoved his hands into his pockets and walked to the truck. At least she'd agreed to come to the barbecue with him tomorrow. He'd give Don a heads-up a few minutes before he arrived so his brother wouldn't be totally shocked.

Twelve

oxy had exactly forty minutes before Mark would arrive at her place to pick her up. She hurried to pack her paints, store her brushes in their jars of turpentine, and then lock the playhouse so the kid wouldn't get into her stuff. One more day on the project and she'd be done. If she didn't have the barbecue plans with Mark, she might have tried to push herself to finish today. It would be nice to have an entire day off work.

She half jogged the ten minutes to Delilah's Desserts, where Roxy had ordered a dozen cupcakes to take to the barbecue. Then she hurried the rest of the way to her bungalow. The nice thing about jobs in Seashell Beach was that she didn't have to take a bus. The closer she got to home, the more she realized how nervous she was.

Mark's invitation to the barbecue might seem like a simple thing, but for her, it wasn't. What she'd neglected to tell Mark was that she'd never been on more than two dates

205

with a guy. Ever. The couple of evenings they'd spent together were more than she'd ever spent with another man.

The barbecue this evening would more than double that time spent. Not only was this nearly a third date, it was at Mark's brother's house. It wasn't exactly a family function, but it would definitely put their relationship in the public sphere. When Mark had come over the night before, she'd tried to act casual, relaxed, and like their growing relationship wasn't causing her to stress out every minute of every day. But today, she'd noticed it in the small things. She'd messed up on some of her basic illustrating and mixed the wrong colors a couple of times.

She liked Mark. More than liked him, which made her worry. He hadn't made a joke about her double initials, but now she realized that was just something she used to hide behind. Her reluctance about getting to know a man and developing a real relationship with him wasn't about the fear of him teasing her or not asking her on a second or third date.

She was afraid that she'd open up, show her real self, and then be rejected. How did someone recover from that? Whatever autonomy and self-confidence she had now would all but disappear. Since high school she'd worked hard to build up her immune system to hurtful sayings and suggestive teasing about being the odd girl, the clumsy girl. So now, if she let down her guard and let Mark fully in, she was taking a huge risk.

Of getting her heart, and subsequently her psyche, trampled on.

Roxy reached home, put the cupcakes in the refrigerator, and then hurried in the shower. She wouldn't have time to dry wet hair, so she opted not to wash it. Once she was out of the shower, she faced her closet. She didn't have too many nice outfits, and nothing would compare to whatever Cheryl would be wearing.

So Roxy made the logical choice and picked out a pale pink sundress that fell to just above her knees. She'd purposely worn some old tennis shoes to her job today so she wouldn't have to scratch paint off her toes. This allowed her to look decent in a pair of comfortable sandals.

Roxy spent a few extra minutes on her makeup and then combed through her hair. She was already getting tired of the blonde. Checking the clock, she saw she still had a good ten minutes. Just enough to add a few streaks of color.

She sorted through the coloring tubes in her bathroom, picked a turquoise, and then pulled on a pair of latex gloves. Five minutes later, she had pale turquoise streaks in her hair. Next, she twisted her hair into a knot and let a few of the turquoise strands dangle down the side of her face. The only thing left to put on were her silver earrings.

Staying busy helped with her nerves, and so she'd gotten carried away organizing her cupboards. When she finally started getting ready, she had less time than she thought. Just as she put in her earrings, someone knocked at the door.

She glanced one more time in the mirror, then walked to the front door.

The first thing that Roxy noticed was that Mark hadn't shaved—which turned out to be a nice look on him. He was also carrying flowers—a variety of several colors.

"Hi," Mark said, scanning her from head to toe.

The nerves were back, and Roxy's skin heated up. He smelled great. And looked great. He wore jeans that fit perfectly and a pressed shirt with the sleeves rolled up. When he leaned down and kissed her cheek while resting his hand casually on her waist, Roxy forgot to breathe.

"Thanks for the flowers," she managed to say. "I'll just put them in a vase."

Mark followed her inside, making Roxy even more aware of him. Her bungalow felt different when he was there.

"How's the playhouse mural going?" Mark asked.

"Great," she said, filling a vase with water.

Mark unwrapped the flowers and handed them over to her.

She arranged them in the vase, added a little more water, then carried the vase to the morning room and put the flowers on the table. It made the room look pretty. When she returned to the kitchen, Mark was leaning against the counter, watching her. "Blue, huh?"

Roxy touched her hair. "Turquoise, actually."

Mark's mouth lifted into a half smile. "What's your record?"

"For what?" she asked, stepping past him and opening the refrigerator door to lift out the cupcake box.

"For keeping your hair the same color."

Roxy shrugged. "Maybe a few weeks."

Mark raised his hand and ran his fingers along one of the turquoise strands.

He was really close, and he was really distracting.

"I could color your hair, you know," she said.

He lifted his brows.

"Cupcakes," she said, holding up the box. "I hope Cheryl will approve."

Mark glanced at the box. "She'll approve." He moved closer. "I can carry the box."

The box wasn't heavy, of course, but Roxy relinquished it to Mark. She was feeling even more nervous now than she had before.

He grasped her hand and linked their fingers. "Are you all right?"

She looked up at him. "What did your brother say?"

"He doesn't know yet," Mark said, tugging her close. "I was going to tell him, but then I decided that you're going to be a surprise."

"Do you think that's a good thing?" she asked, feeling breathless both at Mark's revelation and his closeness.

"He'll get a good laugh out of it."

"What about Cheryl?" Roxy said. "She's sort of perfect, and Don said—"

Mark leaned down the rest of the way and brushed his lips against hers. "Let's not worry about everyone else. We'll eat some good food, and then we can leave."

She nodded, her heart hammering. "All right."

They left the bungalow and climbed into Mark's truck. By the time they reached the Elliott estate, several cars were already parked. A hired parking valet shuffled them into a golf cart that would take them to the far side of the estate.

"There's a bit of construction going on in the backyard," Mark said, settling next to Roxy in the second row of the golf cart, "so the barbecue is by the gazebo."

Roxy hadn't seen the entire estate, but it was clear that all of it was gorgeous.

The golf cart driver took them to a garden arch that led through a line of hedges.

Mark lifted the lid of the cupcake box. "These look really good," he said. "Mind if I steal one?"

Roxy laughed nervously. "Dessert before dinner? Sure."

He winked at her and lifted out a cupcake. It was gone in just a few bites.

When the golf cart stopped, Mark climbed out, and Roxy followed. They walked beneath the arch, which was twined with rose vines, and arrived at an open space dotted with stone benches and fountains. Several food tables had been set up in the gazebo, and beyond that sat three giant grills. Smoke and steam rose from the grills, scenting the air with spicy scents.

On the edge of the lawn, an old-fashioned band stand had been set up, and the band members were playing a mellow tune.

Hand in hand, Mark and Roxy walked to the gazebo, where Mark set down the cupcake box.

Don, who was standing near one of the grills—not actually grilling, just talking to someone in a chef's apron—spotted them first.

"Mark," he called out and hurried over to them. He looked at Roxy, then did a double take. Mark held her hand, making it obvious that they were together on a date. "Hi, Roxy. Welcome." Don's gaze went back to Mark. "I didn't know you were bringing . . . a date."

"I guess I don't need to introduce her," Mark said with a laugh.

But Don didn't even crack a smile. Roxy's heart raced. Was she really so pathetic that Mark's brother would think poorly of him for dating her?

"You won the bet," Mark continued, as if he was oblivious to the pale shade that Don's face had turned.

The man looked positively sick. Perhaps it had nothing to do with Roxy at all.

Then Cheryl was there, as if she'd floated down from the sky. She wore a pale blue, flowy pantsuit. It made her crystal-blue eyes seem twice as large.

"Oh, I didn't know that Don invited you, Roxy," Cheryl said, her tone stiff and glaringly polite.

Roxy smiled, her stomach feeling like it was slowly turning inside out.

Mark was talking to Don, so Roxy was left on her own.

"Well, uh, Mark invited me," Roxy said.

Cheryl's eyes narrowed for the slightest moment.

Then Cheryl noticed that Roxy was holding Mark's hand. The woman's face went pink.

Pink.

Roxy felt mortified.

"Great," Cheryl said. "I hope you enjoy yourself, and thanks for . . . ." She glanced at the cupcake box on the table. The rectangle cardboard box stood out among the crystal platters arranged with finger foods.

"They're cupcakes from Delilah's Desserts," Roxy said. "I didn't know if you had food assignments."

"No food assignments," Cheryl said, her voice sounding strangely distant. "I always have our parties catered."

Roxy really had no idea how to reply to that. Another woman's voice cut in.

"Mark, is that you?"

Roxy turned at the same time Mark did. Her mouth nearly fell open, but she pressed her lips together instead. One of her high-school classmates was walking directly toward them. Brandy Livingston. She was a realtor now—one couldn't miss the advertising Brandy did with her giant smile plastered all over—but apparently she knew Mark?

Roxy glanced about the place, wishing that she could be anywhere doing anything else. Brandy had been one of those girls in high school. Popular and never afraid of giving Roxy a hard time behind everyone's backs. Roxy had seen her about the town a couple of times but had always managed to avoid running directly into her.

Now, Brandy looked like a life-size Barbie doll, and Roxy guessed that most everything she was looking at was either enhanced or fake.

"I didn't know you'd be here," Brandy oozed, coming closer and smiling widely.

Out of the corner of her eye, Roxy saw Cheryl smile—like the Cheshire cat.

Then Roxy knew. Brandy was the woman that Cheryl was trying to set Mark up with.

"I'm so glad you were able to make it, Brandy," Cheryl said, stepping forward and air-kissing the woman.

"Mark has spoken so highly of you," Cheryl said. "He says you've been a dream to work with."

Roxy stared. She knew she was being rude, but she couldn't help it. When did Mark and Brandy work together? It wasn't really any of her business, but out of all the women in the entire province of Seashell Beach, why did Brandy have to set her sights on Mark?

It was obvious from the way that Brandy ogled Mark that she was very, very interested. Had they dated in the past?

That thought made her realize Mark had released her hand. He held out his hand to Brandy, and she slowly shook it. Then they both sort of hugged. Roxy looked away. So were they more than acquaintances? Roxy wasn't sure if it was her imagination, but Brandy's cheeks had flushed.

This was a setup. Don's reaction, then Cheryl's... They'd invited Brandy to spend time with Mark.

Roxy swallowed back her mortification. She was the third wheel here. Mark was no longer holding her hand, but was talking to Brandy about the renovation of the children's museum. And then it made sense. Brandy must be the realtor on the project, which meant that they'd had plenty of interaction. And Mark was acting very attentive to her, listening to every word and keeping his gaze solely on Brandy.

If Roxy had known that Brandy would be here, Roxy wouldn't have come. Just seeing the woman brought back a flood of memories from high school, and none of them were pleasant.

She felt forgotten, but it was an emotion she'd become used to. She moved to the food tables and opened the cupcake box. Lifting them out, she set them on a platter that had some extra room. She was about to pick up one herself and take a bite, because why not? She might as well enjoy the food if her date was going to have intense chats with other women.

"Roxy? Is that really you?"

Roxy lowered the cupcake without taking a bite. She turned to see that Brandy was walking toward her, eyes wide.

"Oh my gosh," Brandy cooed. "I didn't recognize you at first. Roxy Randall—who would have thought? After all these years." Brandy's eagle-eyed gaze assessed Roxy's appearance in a few seconds flat. "You look . . . the same."

Roxy felt like stuffing two cupcakes in her mouth.

Mark was following Brandy, a half smile on his face—the one that Roxy had found adorable. But now it was focused on Brandy.

"Hi," Roxy said, giving a half wave. "I'll be right back." She turned and crossed the gazebo to the other side, where she hurried down the couple of steps and practically ran out of the garden area.

Thirteen

"Now, I guess she forgot something," Brandy said, turning her sharp blue eyes upon Mark.

He watched Roxy hurry around a few tables. Maybe she had to use the ladies' room? He wasn't sure how everything was set up. But Brandy was watching him closely, so he didn't want to appear too interested in Roxy.

Brandy was a nice woman too. Who would have thought that this barbecue event would have so many nice-looking women in attendance?

"Oh, I love these cupcakes," Brandy said, her voice cutting into Mark's perusal of the other guests. She rejoined him, holding two cupcakes. "Want one?" she teased.

"Sure," Mark said. It looked like the grills were working hard to produce the main dish, but there was no sign of platters of meat yet. He took one of the cupcakes and bit into it, not mentioning he'd already eaten one on the way.

Brandy took smaller, more delicate bites.

By the time they'd finished eating, she'd looped her arm

through his. "Oh, there's my boss," she said. "Paul Studly." She laughed. "Isn't that the best name? I tease him all the time."

Mark chuckled. Paul Studly was quite the name, but the man looked like it hadn't set him back any. He was obviously successful, and he was standing in a circle of people, having captured everyone's attention with some story he was telling.

"Come on, honey," Brandy said, tugging gently on his arm while she simultaneously brushed against him. Her blouse was smooth and silky, and she smelled quite nice.

Mark tried to remember why he'd felt put off by her when he'd first met her. Brandy was friendly, and there was nothing wrong with that. She also had a great smile. She'd called him "honey," which was normally a red flag for him, but he found he really didn't mind. It seemed to fit her personality.

"Paul," Brandy sang out.

The man turned and smiled. Brandy introduced Mark, and then he shook hands with a few other women in the circle. Wow. He didn't know Seashell Beach had so many gorgeous women. He had a hard time deciding which one he should ask for numbers. Although it would be rude to do so in front of Brandy. And speaking of women, where had Roxy gone? He glanced around for a few seconds, but he didn't see her.

"Mark," Brandy said, rising up on her tiptoes so that she could whisper in his ear, "should we dance?"

"Sure," Mark said. He definitely wanted to dance with Brandy. The band had started playing something slow, and a few other couples swayed to the music. He walked her to where the other couples danced and pulled her into his arms.

Brandy looped her arms around his neck and nestled close, as if she'd been waiting for this exact moment.

Across the lawn, Mark caught his brother watching him. Don looked upset, which only confused Mark. Hadn't Cheryl hinted that she wanted him to pay some attention to Brandy?

Well, here he was, dancing with her. Not that he was complaining.

Brandy was a great dancer, she smelled great, and, well, she was easy on the eyes.

The next couple of hours passed, and Mark ate another cupcake, mingled with the other guests, and danced another time with Brandy and with a couple of other women as well. He didn't know why he'd ever let Don talk him into taking that bet. Although he didn't know where Roxy had gone, and he hoped she was all right, Mark was more than enjoying himself.

By the time the guests started to leave, Mark was beginning to get more and more worried about Roxy. What if she'd been sick? He had called her home number at one point, but there had been no answer. Maybe she'd told him she had to leave early and he'd just forgotten.

Brandy gave him a lingering hug goodbye and made him promise to call her the next day. He readily agreed. Crossing the lawn to where Don was talking to another guest, Mark broke in and thanked his brother for such a great time and excellent barbecue.

Don told him goodbye, but he had a strange look on his face. No matter, because Cheryl was all smiles, and she even hugged Mark. A rare event.

Once in his truck, Mark called Roxy's number again. No answer still.

Maybe she was mad about the attention he'd paid to Brandy, but Roxy hadn't even been around when he'd danced with Brandy. So that wasn't it. He thought about stopping at her place, but if she wasn't answering her phone, then maybe she'd gone to bed early.

So, Mark continued home, and exhaustion overtook him after such a long week. He fell asleep before he knew it.

When Mark awoke some hours later, it was still dark. He laid in bed and listened for a moment, wondering why he'd awakened so early. His mind replayed the events at the barbecue, and suddenly he sat up in bed.

Roxy.

He'd been a complete and utter jerk.

How could he have even danced with Brandy, let alone promise to call her? How could he have been flirting with so many women all night when the only woman he'd wanted to be with had left? Why didn't he go after her?

His mind had been caught up in Brandy of all people. How did that happen? It was like the moment they arrived at the barbecue, he lost all his common sense.

Mark checked his cell to see that it was just after 4:00 a.m. He couldn't very well go over to Roxy's house right now and knock on the door to apologize. He'd have to apologize again for waking her up.

Then Mark saw that he had a text alert. It must have come in after he'd gone to sleep. The text was from Don: *I know that Cheryl is happy that you spent so much time with Brandy at the barbecue, but I expected more from you, bro.*

Mark reread the words. They were like daggers because his brother was right. Mark groaned and flopped back down on the bed, squeezing his eyes shut. How could he have been such an idiot? He'd known that Roxy was nervous about showing up as a couple, and then Mark had to go and prove her right.

Eventually Mark fell into a half sleep, only to be awakened a few hours later when his cell phone rang.

It was Don. Mark answered right away.

"Mark," Cheryl's voice oozed into the phone, "I hoped you'd be awake by now. Hey, look, I'm so glad you and Brandy hit it off. I'd like to invite both of you to a brunch at the

Mariposa Hotel this morning. You know, make it more of a group thing so that there's not a lot of pressure and expectation."

Mark said nothing for a moment. He literally didn't know how to respond. The hole he'd dug himself into last night was deeper than he thought. But he had to get out of it. Even a semblance of a date with Brandy would take him down a path he didn't want.

"I'm sorry, Cheryl," he began, trying to formulate his reply as he spoke. "I wasn't myself last night. In fact, I was exceptionally rude to Roxy, who I brought as my date."

Cheryl gave a light laugh. "Roxy is a talented artist, I'll give you that. But the two of you aren't really in the same sphere."

Mark stiffened. "What do you mean by that?"

Another light laugh. "Oh, Brandy filled me in last night. I guess Roxy was an odd duck in high school, and she hasn't really changed. I mean, she looked like she was wearing a twenty-year-old hand-me-down last night. With what I paid her and what I'm sure other clients pay her, she could at least wear something decent to an exclusive barbecue."

Mark was completely flabbergasted. Roxy had looked pretty—no, beautiful. And she had a natural beauty that women like Brandy and Cheryl could never buy from a bottle or surgeon.

"I guess in high school she used to go barefoot half the time," Cheryl continued, as if she were sharing some juicy gossip with someone who cared. "She was called down to the principal's office more than once because of it. Brandy nicknamed her Shoeless Roxy."

Mark didn't care to hear anything more from Cheryl, or Brandy, for that matter. "Give Brandy my apologies, Cheryl," he said in a firm voice. "I won't make it today. Roxy and I have plans. And by the way, we are dating. At least, I hope we still are. And I'd appreciate it if you and your friends would stop acting like you're in middle school."

Without waiting for Cheryl's reply, Mark hung up. Don would be calling him soon, probably to demand an apology to Cheryl.

It seemed that Mark had a lot of apologizing to do. But first he showered, then climbed in his truck to drive to the nearest florist.

Fourteen

*R*oxy surveyed her appearance in the mirror. She'd dyed every bit of her hair a coal black. It looked good with the red ribbon headband—maybe a bit Snow-Whitish, but that was all right. She didn't want any trace of the night before left on her person.

She'd been tempted to burn the sundress, but instead she dyed it to a dark blue and hung it behind the bungalow to dry.

It had been a busy Sunday morning, and Roxy had decided to take the complete day off from painting. With the exception of dying her hair and clothing, she wasn't going to paint. At all. She knew once she started, she'd have to think about the way Mark had looked at Brandy at the barbecue.

She couldn't face Brandy and the memories her mere presence stirred. Brandy had been the instigator of more than one of Roxy's nicknames in high school. So Roxy had left the barbecue. Not immediately though. She'd hovered in one part of the garden for several moments, long enough to see that Mark wasn't even missing her, that he was totally into Brandy.

Roxy could only guess what happened next. In fact, they might still be together. Mark was a grown, gorgeous man, and Brandy was a skilled seducer. Roxy could think of a few of her own nicknames she could give Brandy.

But it didn't matter. Mark was interested in Brandy, which meant Roxy was completely out of the picture. Why should she be surprised? It was just another week in her life of dashed hopes and crushed dreams. All right, so she was being a bit melodramatic. But she'd allow herself this day of pouting.

She left the bathroom, red hair ribbon in place, and opened up the back door. At least the day was beautiful. The blue sky was vast, and a slight breeze kept the sun from being too hot.

A meow came from her left, and Roxy looked over to see Cat.

"Hello there," she said, bending down to scratch the scruffy thing's head. It had taken months for Cat to allow Roxy the pleasure of touching her.

"Want to go for a walk?" Roxy asked.

The cat sat on her haunches and began licking herself.

"Well, then," Roxy said. "I'll just be down the beach a ways if you change your mind." She continued down the back steps and shoved her hands into her shorts pockets as she walked barefoot through the sand.

She had nothing to complain about, not really. She didn't have to endure a breakup after a long relationship. She lived in a beautiful coastal town. Her job was her passion. And she had a cat. Apparently Cat had changed her mind; she was trotting after Roxy.

Roxy didn't dare say anything or bring attention to the fact that the cat was being friendlier than usual. It might ruin everything.

Out here in the open, with the wind pushing through her

black hair and the waves crashing just a few feet away, her dismay over Mark seemed such a small thing. Here was an entire world full of people, full of problems, but also full of beauty. Losing a man who she'd only met a week ago wasn't really a big deal in the scheme of things.

Her eyes burned with tears anyway. Best to get the crying out of the way so she could return home feeling renewed.

If Mark was the type of man to be so easily distracted by another woman, then she didn't want to be involved with him anyway. No matter how charming he was. Or had been. She was pretty sure that he'd called her, possibly more than once. But she hadn't answered her phone. There was no voice mail left anyway.

Roxy slowed as she passed by an eight- or nine-year-old boy digging a giant hole at the water's edge. His mom sat a few feet away, reading a book. The boy was covered in sand, and he was so focused on his task that he didn't even notice Roxy walking by. It made her smile to see his determination.

"Look, Mom!" the boy called out. "I'm almost to China."

His mother laughed, but not in a teasing way. In a loving way. "You're doing a great job," she simply said.

Roxy walked on, glancing behind her. Cat had sauntered off, spooked by the incoming waves. Apparently the cat didn't want to get too close to the water.

A couple of teen boys were throwing a football back and forth. When a group of teen girls walked by, going in the opposite direction of Roxy, the boys stopped to watch them.

Roxy had never been noticed like that. Not in high school, not in college. She walked on. It didn't matter. She loved a lot of things about her life. Roxy brushed at the moisture on her cheeks, although the wind had dried most of it.

She'd be fine. Tomorrow, if not the next day, she'd be back to normal.

Up ahead, a man walked, holding the hand of a woman. For a brief instant, Roxy was reminded of Mark. The man was tall and had medium-brown hair, but he was too thin. Mark had broader shoulders. And the woman the man walked with was pregnant, probably his wife.

They meandered slowly together, talking and laughing.

Roxy's heart twisted. She turned her face toward the wind, letting the breeze brush over her face, and she inhaled the sea air. A screech of gulls caught her attention as two birds seemed to fight over the same morsel floating in the ocean. The gulls broke apart, and one of them flew away. The second gull remained floating on the water, content to have won the battle.

It was like that in life, she realized. Sometimes you won, sometimes you lost.

Roxy realized she'd walked a lot farther than she'd intended, and she was just below Delilah's Desserts. She decided to grab a quick treat since she hadn't had any of the cupcakes she'd bought the night before. But then she remembered she didn't have any money with her. Not that Delilah wouldn't spot her a treat, but Roxy decided she'd head home.

Once she reached the bungalow, she saw Cat lurking under the back porch.

"There you are," she said. "I was wondering where you'd gone."

The cat made a small meow, but she didn't budge from her position beneath the porch.

Roxy opened the back door to her bungalow, and immediately she knew something was different.

The place smelled different, for one thing. And on the

table in the morning room sat several vases filled with flowers. She didn't dare move. She'd left the door unlocked . . .

Roxy glanced toward the living room, her heart pounding. Another vase of flowers was on the coffee table.

"Hello?" she said. It came out more as a whisper.

Something clanked in the kitchen, and Roxy backed toward the door.

"Who's there?" she called out, much louder this time.

Everything was silent. Then she heard footsteps.

"Roxy," a man said.

She yelped, reacting to the sound, before realizing she recognized Mark's voice.

He came around the corner, and Roxy's breath left her.

He was carrying another vase of flowers. When he saw the panic in her eyes, he said, "Sorry, I was hoping to get out of here before you returned."

Still, she couldn't speak.

"I . . ." He crossed to the table and set down the flowers he was carrying. Then he waved his hand at the display of flowers covering her bungalow. "I owe you an apology." He took a card out of his pocket. "I was going to leave this, but—" He scrubbed his hand through his hair.

Roxy exhaled. "You just walked in here?"

At least he had the decency to look sheepish, and he was going red in the face.

Roxy folded her arms. Cat meowed behind her, picking this moment to rub against Roxy's legs and walk into the house. Then she walked right up to Mark like they were friends.

Mark eyed the cat as it rubbed against his leg too.

"Since I'm here, I guess I'll just forget the card and talk to you in person." He took a deep breath and pocketed the card.

Roxy held out her hand. "I want to read the card first."

225

She wasn't going to let him get away with anything, especially with him breaking into her place and all.

Mark's brows lifted, but he handed over the card. Roxy was careful not to touch his hand as she took it from him.

The message inside was very short.

Dear Roxy,

Hoping for a second chance.

Mark

"There's not much to it," she said, turning it over as if to look for a continuing message.

"I thought the flowers would help too," Mark said, gesturing again to them.

He had brought quite a lot of flowers. If Roxy were to guess, there were at least ten dozen roses. And then she noticed a bakery box.

"Cupcakes?" she asked, walking toward the table. She lifted the lid at the same time Mark said, "Yes."

"But here's the thing," he continued. "Those cupcakes have been doctored."

Roxy snapped her gaze to his. "What do you mean?"

He walked closer to her, tentatively. Cat followed. "Remember how I ate one on the way to the barbecue?" he asked.

Roxy nodded. Did he feel guilty about eating a cupcake in advance? It was hard for her to think clearly because of all the flowers and his note asking for a second chance . . .

"I ate two more at the barbecue," he continued.

"Mark," she said, holding up her hand as if she could stop his advance. "It's all right. You didn't need to replace the cupcakes. They were for the guests, and, well, you were a guest too."

"No, that's not what I'm trying to say," he said.

He stood only a couple of feet away from her now and

was looking down at her with such intensity that Roxy had a hard time breathing.

"There was something in the cupcakes that made me go a little crazy," he said in a low voice.

He seemed so serious that Roxy felt like smiling. Instead, she said, "What do you mean?"

"I don't know exactly," he said with an exhale. "Maybe they had high doses of sugar or something else more nefarious. Whatever was in those cupcakes made me act like . . . a lovesick teenage boy."

Roxy stared at him, trying not to laugh. Was he serious? "You're kidding."

"I'm not." There was no quirk of the mouth, no amusement in his eyes. He opened the lid of the cupcake box and lifted out one. "Try it. See what happens."

Roxy scoffed and folded her arms. "No thanks."

"I know it sounds crazy to say this," Mark said, still holding the cupcake out to her. "But I can't come up with any other explanation."

Roxy shook her head. Maybe it was better she found out that Mark had a loose screw now rather than later. "You owe me no explanation, Mark. I get it. You like Brandy. End of story." She waved her hand. "All of this was really sweet though. We can still be cordial to each other—don't worry about me."

"I don't like Brandy," Mark said, his tone emphatic. "I didn't like her before I even met you. We talked on the phone a few times about business, and even then she annoyed me. When I met her at the old children's museum, yes, I thought she was nice-looking in an extremely high-maintenance way, but not my type at all."

Mark set down the cupcake on the table and turned to look out the window. "Even before I made the stupid bet with my brother, I wouldn't have dated someone like Brandy. I can spot fake a mile away." He glanced over at her.

Roxy still refused to give him the benefit of the doubt.

"I'm here for one reason," he continued. This time he turned to face her again. "I'm tired of women like Brandy. I'm tired of fake. I'm tired of trendy."

"You were still a jerk last night," Roxy said. It just slipped out. The best thing she could do was show him the door, but something in his eyes kept her rooted to the floor.

"I know—but it wasn't *me*," Mark said. "At least not me in my right mind. I know it sounds crazy, but those cupcakes are laced with something."

Roxy picked up the cupcake that Mark had left on the table. The white frosting looked delicious. She took a bite, chewed, and swallowed.

"Nope," she said. "Nothing."

"You need to eat the whole thing, or maybe three," Mark said. Finally there was lightness to his tone, but he was still serious.

"I'm not going to eat three cupcakes so that you can prove your really crazy point," Roxy said, setting it down. "So you're really not into Brandy?"

Fifteen

"I'm not interested in Brandy. At all. Or any other woman," Mark said. Roxy was finally softening. A good sign. There was really no excuse for his behavior last night, but he had felt a bit off, like he was in an alternate reality. What else could make Brandy desirable to him?

Even through whatever haze his mind had been in, he'd still kept thinking about Roxy and wondering where she'd gone. That had to count for something.

Was her suddenly black hair an indication of something? He'd never known any woman to change hair color as often as Roxy did. "I'm interested only in you, Roxy Randall," he said in a low voice.

She was wavering, and he hoped that meant she'd be able to trust him. That would be the most valuable thing he could have from her.

"Does Brandy know you're not interested in her?" she asked.

"Cheryl called this morning trying to set us up for a brunch date. After making it clear to Cheryl that I wasn't interested in her friend, I called up Brandy too." He saw her stiffen. "Brandy sounded put out, and I don't blame her because of the way I acted last night. But I made it very, very clear."

Roxy was watching him closely. "Did you tell her about the cupcakes?"

"No, I didn't think she'd believe me. Plus it might've insulted her more."

"Hmm, smart lady," Roxy said.

Mark took a tentative step toward Roxy. When she didn't move away, he took another step closer. "I think you're pretty smart."

The edges of her mouth twitched. She blinked her eyes up at him, still not moving away. He took it as a good sign.

"What else do you think?" she asked.

Another step and he slid his arms about her waist. She didn't flinch or pull away. "I think you're talented." She smelled like the sea breeze and warm sunshine.

"And?" she prompted.

"And . . . I think you smell nice," he said, leaning down to breathe her in, hoping she'd let him kiss her.

Her gray eyes were steady on his, and finally a smile tugged her mouth upward. "That's all?"

"You're beautiful, Roxy Randall," Mark said, scanning her face, the light dusting of freckles, and her pale pink lips. "And I want there to be an *us*, if you're okay with that."

A moment passed, then two. "I'm okay with that," she whispered.

He'd never felt so relieved in his life. Did this mean she accepted his apology? He had one more thing to try. He closed the distance between them and brushed his mouth against hers, lightly, to test her reaction. She tasted of sun and salt.

She closed her eyes, so he kissed her again. Her arms came around his neck, and she pressed her body against him. Her mouth was warm, accepting, and he knew he could easily get lost in her and lose all track of time.

When she broke away, she kept her arms around his neck. "I have my own confession to make."

He couldn't be more curious. Whatever it was, it couldn't be worse than his flirting with Brandy at the barbecue. "What's your secret?"

"I haven't had a boyfriend before," she whispered. "Like ever. I've only been on a handful of dates. They were all disasters. I was reconciled to being a cat lady the rest of my life, even though the only cat I have isn't really mine and pretty much likes you better than me."

As if to confirm Roxy's statement, said cat brushed against his legs.

Mark knew that Roxy was almost thirty, so it was surprising she hadn't been in a relationship. But he couldn't come up with any real complaint. He supposed that the bullying that had happened to her in high school had some long-term consequences. "So you're saying you want me to be your boyfriend?"

She blushed a bright red, and he laughed. Then he kissed her again, because she let him. And because she fit perfectly against him, and he couldn't seem to get enough of her.

"I don't mind being your first boyfriend," he said when they broke apart again.

Her face was still pink. "I don't know if I should forgive you or if I should kick you out though. I mean, I'm not exactly experienced in relationships."

"Are you asking my opinion?" he asked. "I'm happy to give it, you know."

She shrugged.

Mark took that as a yes. "I think you should forgive me. Don't kick me out. And let's order pizza. We can have cupcakes for dessert."

She stared at him for a second, and he thought he might have gone too far. Then she started to laugh. She pulled him tightly against her, and he lifted her up off the ground, spinning slowly.

"That sounds good to me," she said in a breathless voice. "But you can only eat the cupcakes in my presence."

He set her down and released her, then cradled her face with both hands. "Deal," he said and kissed her forehead. Mark ran his fingers down the sides of her neck to where her pulse beat rapidly. He moved his hands behind her shoulders and pulled her close.

She nestled against him, and he didn't know which he liked better: kissing her on a sunny day or kissing her during a rainstorm.

"I like the black hair," he murmured into her hair.

She sighed. "I like you too, Mark. And by the way, I do forgive you."

PART THREE

Much Ado about Cupcakes

One

How do you eat an elephant?
One bite at a time.
How do you become vegan?
Don't eat the elephant.
—*No Cheat Days*, KC Casey

*K*C glanced at her watch before taking a sip of her lemon-infused water.

"Is your date late, KC?" Cái asked as he refilled her water glass from his pitcher. He owned the Fortune Café and was one of KC's favorite people on all of Tangerine Street because his restaurant offered some of the best vegan options she'd ever tasted.

"No. He's not late. And he's also not my date."

Cái raised an eyebrow. "Then why do you look so . . ."

"So?"

He raised a shoulder to match the eyebrow. "I don't

know, exactly. You've got your hair up in a golden bun like some Greek goddess. It feels like it means something—like you are a woman about to meet up with destiny."

She grinned. "Well, then you got it right at the same time you got it wrong. I'm meeting with a journalist from *Vegan Zen* magazine. And they only interview people who have finally made it."

"Ah. I see. This is about your book, then?"

She nodded and felt a deep rush of pride and gratitude for the turn her life had taken. Her new book, *No Cheat Days*, had not only recently hit the *New York Times* bestseller list, but her agent had informed her it had sold foreign rights in nine different countries, and there were more courting them every day. And *Vegan Zen* magazine was so much more than just a magazine. They were the hub of all things health and nutrition for the world. They did retreats and conferences, their YouTube channel gave recipes and instructions for yoga and fitness routines, and they connected people together. *Vegan Zen* was a game changer.

She had never planned on so much abundance in her life. Sure, she kept her hands open and accepting at all times, but even she could not have seen this. So if she looked like a woman about to meet with destiny, how could she debate the fact?

The interviewer wasn't late and couldn't be faulted with the fact that she'd shown up early. But she did worry for the briefest of moments when her watch showed the time clicking over from noon to 12:01. When it clicked over to 12:04, she feared she'd maybe written the time down wrong.

The door to the restaurant opened, and she recognized the man she'd been waiting for immediately. Everyone in the vegan health industry knew Michael Arturo. Knew and sighed over. Michael kept his dark hair long enough to fall into his eyes but not wild and out of control like some people in the industry expected. Stereotypes thrived in the vegan world. Not everyone wore dreads and went barefoot through the forest while chaining themselves to trees. In fact, most didn't. Most were like her, like Michael. Just everyday people living everyday lives. Some might even go as far as to call them normal.

Though, as she watched Michael hold the door open for someone else to exit through before he entered, she knew normal wasn't the right word for him. She'd read nearly all his articles. She knew behind that beautiful face was a mind to match.

KC automatically stood, as if Michael's gravity pulled her to her feet.

Cái snort-laughed, forcing her to pry her eyes from Michael to see what Cái found so funny. "That was an unconvincing beginning to a nondate. I think you might be meeting with my version of destiny after all."

"Cái!" she scolded. She hoped Michael hadn't overheard him.

Cái chuckled again but stepped back and made his way to the front counter as KC stepped forward to greet Michael. She put her hand out and smiled. "Michael! It's such a pleasure to meet you finally!"

"KC Casey. The pleasure is all mine." He took her extended hand, gave it a squeeze, and used it to pull her toward him in an almost embrace as he dropped a glancing kiss on her cheek.

The place where his lips grazed her cheek burned, and she blinked in surprise at the intimate gesture. Not that she should have been surprised. It seemed a good third of the people she'd met in both the vegan and publishing industry, both male and female, handed out cheek kisses like they were coconut sprinkles: healthy and sweet and harmless. It was just one of those cultural norms she was going to have to force herself to get used to. Though she'd thought she was used to it. It hadn't bothered her from her agent, from her publisher, from the book designer, or from half the vegan chefs she'd been able to meet at places like Veg Fest.

And it wasn't that it bothered her now with Michael. Bothered wasn't the right word. It flustered her and set her off balance. Maybe because she'd been thinking about how handsome he was or because she'd been remembering all the rumors she'd heard of Michael Arturo from all of her friends when she met up with them at yoga retreats. He was the man who stayed on the radar of every woman who met him and even most of those who had seen only pictures.

She forced a smile and hoped he didn't notice the heat in her face. He didn't seem to notice. Michael had already stepped safely back out of her personal space and was pulling his messenger bag off his shoulder and removing his jacket to drape over the back of his chair.

Did it make her a female chauvinist to have been ogling him when he walked in? Did it make her a female chauvinist to continue to ogle him through his every movement even though he was right in front of her and likely noticed?

Probably.

What a waste of her liberal arts education regarding equality and double standards.

She sat down, feeling properly self-chastised. This was business, not anything else.

As if to punctuate her thoughts, Michael removed a slim laptop from his bag and settled it onto the table between them.

"KC Casey. KC Casey . . ." He drew the words out long and slow and grinned at her. "I love saying your name. It's unique and interesting. To start out the interview, would you mind sharing what your initials stand for?"

All interviews she'd had so far in her career and all lists of questions she received on Instagram, YouTube, Facebook, and every other social media platform began with this one. She tilted her head, gave him a wide, toothy smile, but didn't answer.

"I'm going to take that as a nonverbal no to my question. Fair enough." He typed something into his laptop.

She hoped his words would be favorable. His assessment of her would affect the way millions of people viewed her.

"So . . . Seashell Beach?"

"It's the place where peace and joy meet up to tango," she said.

His fingers stopped on the keyboard as he glanced up long enough to grace her with a grin. "That's a perfect endorsement. Almost makes me want to move."

"There's always room for one more in Seashell Beach," she said. "And if my endorsement doesn't convince you, the food might. How about we order lunch first and do the interview while we wait?"

"Right. Food. Sorry. I was just so excited to meet you that I forgot we were in a restaurant."

Cái must have heard the comment because he tossed a glare from the front counter over to where they sat. He gratefully didn't say anything. Cái was an incredibly opinionated man and could get pretty persnickety if he felt anyone was dissing on his beloved restaurant. For KC, the comment was nothing more than high praise. He was excited to meet her?

High praise indeed.

Taking her advice, Michael perused the menu before

making a quick selection, placing his order with the waiter, and diving right back into interviewer mode.

The guy was seriously all work and no play.

They went through all the usual questions, the ones almost all interviewers asked her. She liked that because those answers were rehearsed and comfortable.

He typed as they talked. He hardly looked at his laptop as he maintained complete engagement in their conversation. She shifted uncomfortably as he kept his eyes on her and continued hammering on the keyboard with his fingers. Did he never need to look at his hands or his screen?

She always did. That visual verification of her words going down accurately was why it took her so long to get her book written. If she'd had his superpower of typing, the book would have been done in less than a month.

He allowed a break when the food came, sighed happily over the perfection of his Mediterranean salad, and went right back to the interview once he'd pounded down his food.

"So, here's the big one," he said. "Why veganism? What brought you to this ridiculously rigid lifestyle structure?"

She'd had the question before. It's like asking a newlywed how she met her husband. Everyone wanted to know the path that led to the destination. But no one had ever called it rigid before—certainly not ridiculously rigid with that tone of scorn. At least none of her interviewers ever had. A lot of haters existed in the world who didn't understand the lifestyle choice, but her interviewers were always people who were part of the lifestyle, and none of them had ever used the term rigid, with all the negative implications that came with it.

That one term changed the question for her—enough that she felt disinclined to give a straight answer. "What about you?" she asked instead of answering. "What brought you to this 'ridiculously rigid' lifestyle choice?" She air quoted the words *ridiculously rigid* and couldn't keep the defensiveness from her tone. That was her number-one worst flaw: she was far too transparent. If someone got her hackles up, they knew it immediately.

He blinked, and his fingers froze on the keys, an audible addition to the sudden awkward turn in the interview. "I don't think anyone has ever asked me that before."

She didn't respond. She simply waited for him to answer.

He studied her for a long time before continuing. "I'm not actually vegan."

Her mouth fell open in surprise. "What? But everything you write, all the articles on healthy lifestyles?"

"I'm mostly vegan. But I indulge in honey and some dairy products. Occasionally, I will eat chicken or fish if my body really craves such things. And, if you've really read all my articles, then you know I've never stated allegiance to a strict dietary preference. In fact, in my bio, it states my food preference as mostly vegetarian."

"But your bio is so tongue-in-cheek . . . *mostly vegetarian* sounded more like you were trying to make a joke." She stopped herself to keep from protesting because, now that she thought about it, why would he be making a joke about such a thing? "Okay. You've never declared an allegiance. I just assumed . . ." The words felt lame to say out loud. Assumptions were made by the uneducated.

"Most people assume, so don't worry about it. I really do believe in the health benefits of many of the dietary choices made by vegans. But I also believe in moderation, balance, and listening to your body." He shrugged. "My editor hates that I won't go fully vegan. He'd even settle for me pretending to be vegan, but I refuse to represent myself as something that I'm not. He often accuses my morality of getting in the way of better editorial opportunities, but I refuse to allow the public to believe something about me that isn't true. I'm not a full vegan and don't have any intention of becoming one."

She felt disappointment so profound tears welled up in her eyes. He'd been one of her heroes in the plant-based diet cause, and now, here she was listening to him give her a view of him she had never considered. She swallowed her disappointment and lifted her chin slightly. "So why are you writing for an industry you don't want to participate in? Is it just a paycheck to you?" She kept her voice low, soft, nonjudgmental. No one was ever swayed to any cause by judgment. But she had to ask the question. She had to know why he sat at the table across from her if he didn't believe it the way she did.

He leaned back in his chair, watching her closely as he shook his head. "No. It is absolutely not just a paycheck. I'm here because I believe in being healthy. My family was all morbidly obese. My parents both died in their fifties, which is far too young, especially with all the modern medicine that allows most people to live well into their eighties without experiencing any real break in their health. I'm the oldest of three children and was just starting college when my parents passed four months apart from each other. My sister and brother were both in high school, and I had to quit school altogether so I could go back home, take care of them, and settle the affairs of the household in a way that didn't leave my siblings homeless and unprotected."

KC suddenly felt guilty for being defensive, guilty for asking him such a personal question—even though he'd asked her that same question just a moment before. She shook her head and opened her mouth to apologize for being so . . . what? Callous? Intrusive? Easily offended?

But as he kept talking, she closed her mouth again. His story drew her in, and she wanted him to finish it.

"Anyway, after the funeral, I went upstairs to my parents' room and stood in front of the full-length mirror looking at myself in the suit that I'd almost already outgrown even though it was pretty new. I realized I was well on my way to the same gravesite. So were my brother and sister. We grew up on steak and potatoes and ice cream and cakes. The idea of a glass of water as a beverage was so foreign to us, we never would have considered it. We didn't know how to eat any other way. But I knew I could learn how. Since I was suddenly in charge of the meals for my family, I started finding heart-healthy recipes and changed the way we all ate. When I finally went back to school, I obtained my doctorate in nutritional studies, became an expert, had a knack for writing, and here I am."

"And your brother and sister?" KC asked.

"My brother is still on the path to a heart attack. He really resented that I was trying to parent him. He rebelled a lot and felt like I was being disrespectful to my parents by saying the way they trained us to eat was bad. My sister is healthy, happy, married, and still using the recipes I taught her when she was in high school. Now, if we die from heart disease, at least I'll know I did what I could to prevent it."

He fell silent, reminding KC that she had been snippy and should likely make amends for that in some way. "I'm sorry," she said finally. "I didn't mean to pry." She folded her hands in front of her. "My story is sort of similar. My journey to veganism started when I was thirteen and my mom came home from her annual checkup with a breast cancer diagnosis. Since my dad was already gone, she was determined not to leave me as an orphan. The cancer scare loomed over us like

Everest, and we dove headfirst into a plant-based lifestyle that changed everything about us and how we viewed the world."

"And your mom?"

"She survived. She got a clean bill of health as cancer-free nearly a year later." KC didn't tell him the rest, didn't tell him that though she didn't end up an orphan in her teen years, her early twenties hadn't been so kind. The cancer didn't get her mom, but the drunk driver had.

"That's wonderful!" he said in response to the cancer survival. She smiled and tried not to think about the sadder ending to her story. She didn't offer the sadder ending to many people. It still affected her too much, still felt so insanely personal. She figured it would likely always feel that way.

Her mother's memory had become a sacred refuge in her own mind. It was a place where no one else was allowed access.

Except . . . someone who lost both his parents, who might actually understand her emotionally, sat in front of her. He was a man she'd respected for years. She wanted to let him into her life, to see more than other interviewers saw.

"My father died very young, too," she said.

She'd already told him this. But he didn't know the story behind the fact.

"How old was he?"

She swirled her finger over the rim of her water glass. "Twenty-eight. It was a drug-related death. So not necessarily because of eating habits, but certainly because of lifestyle choices that affect health."

"I'm sorry to hear that." Michael looked sorry, too. It pricked up emotions in her that made tears threaten to fall again—emotions she didn't know she even had.

She tamped them down and shrugged. "It was a long time ago. And I never really knew him. That wound doesn't really hurt any more than the Revolutionary War hurts the British. It's just history."

Michael laughed. "I like the way you say things."

Her face warmed with the compliment. The compliment from one of the best minds in her industry. And *he'd* given it to *her*. "I like the way you say things as well. I've read everything you've written."

"I doubt that."

"No, really. Everything."

He grinned, his fingers no longer anywhere near his keyboard, which made her feel like she'd won something, though she wasn't sure exactly what. He leaned in closer to her, and—she couldn't help it—she leaned in, too. "So how did you get ahold of my journals?"

She laughed. "You keep a diary?"

"Not a diary. A journal. It's totally different."

"Maybe. The difference between a journal and a diary all depends on if the cover has a picture of a sparkling unicorn on it or not."

He just smiled.

"So? Does it?"

"Does it? Does it what?"

"Have a sparkling unicorn on it?"

He leaned in even more, close enough she could see the bits of green in his brown eyes. "I'm only going to say that I expect you to respect my life choices."

She burst out laughing, and he grinned in a way that showed he was pleased with the turn of the conversation. They had breached the wall of professionalism to arrive somewhere friendly and companionable.

When Cái showed up twenty minutes later with a plate bearing two fortune cookies, KC shook her head. "Not for me today, Cái."

"They're the vegan ones." He smiled wide, as if offering her something sinful while trying to make it look innocent.

"I love that you work so hard to take care of me. But it's the last Friday of the month."

Cái nodded. "So it is. I'm sorry I forgot." His gaze slid to Michael, and his lips quirked upward into a smirk. "It appears you don't really need these anyway. You're already on your way." Cái left with a little bow, taking his plate of cookies with him.

Michael looked like he might say something but closed his mouth instead. KC was relieved he hadn't asked her to explain. Cái felt his cookies were magical, and he never missed a chance to play matchmaker with them. The fact that he left them alone without trying to make a love match meant he'd entirely misread the situation. If she'd had to explain to Michael about magic cookies making a couple out of them, what would his interview of her look like in print?

Wanting to return the conversation to something less mortifying, she asked more about his siblings, where they lived, what they did for jobs, if they were still close.

He answered all her questions, and he even closed the lid on his laptop and turned his full attention to her. By the time she looked at a clock, she realized another half hour had passed in which they had just been two people learning about each other, not an interviewer and interviewee. They'd become something more.

Whatever it was they'd become, disappointment flooded her when he looked at his watch, blinked in surprise, and leaped into action to collect the bill, pay, and leave—all while apologizing that he had set up another appointment in San Diego for a different interview since he was already so far south for the day.

She moved with a calculated slowness as he packed his

computer away in its case. She didn't want their lunch to come to an end but could think of nothing else to detain him, and she certainly didn't want to make him late.

KC considered asking him if he wanted to get dinner later or take a private tour of all that Tangerine Street had to offer, but all of his rushed movements—the way he tapped his fingers as he waited for the server to return with his credit card, the way his leg bounced as if keeping time with the seconds ticking by—acted as barriers to further plans. She had his email address. Maybe she could invite him back when the next book released. Maybe.

Maybe not.

KC wasn't that girl. She wasn't the girl who pursued men like some desperate, insecure excuse for a human.

But Michael Arturo wasn't just any guy. He was intelligent conversation, good humor, and handsome company. She could even overlook the fact that he wasn't fully vegan.

With that in mind, she decided she would call him as soon as her next book came out and another interview might be deemed appropriate. At least, she would if this first interview turned out favorable, though she didn't feel any fear of it being anything but favorable.

As they stood, made their way out the front door, and then turned to face each other to make their goodbyes, KC expected another cheek kiss and felt a little disgruntled when he held out his hand to her instead. A kiss to a stranger and a handshake to a friend?

He gave her hand a squeeze before releasing it. "Goodbye, KC. It was a pleasure to meet you. You are everything everyone says you are. Not one of those self-righteous vegans."

Again with the mixed signals about how he felt regarding the lifestyle. "What exactly is a self-righteous vegan?"

"You've got to know what I mean. The kind who judge everyone for what they eat and who make a point of telling everyone about every bite of food they're eating and down-talking all those who don't choose to be vegan. From the answers you gave for the interview, you're not judging anyone else for their choices. You're happy if they join you in the lifestyle, but you're willing to love them if they don't. You're the friendly neighborhood vegan. The kind people like no matter what lifestyle choice they make for themselves. There's also the kind who claim veganism and then smother their rolls with butter and don't bother to notice that the roll was made with eggs and dairy products. They do this all while snubbing others who ordered the burger. You're refreshing because you are neither type. It's nice to meet people like you." He cocked his head to the side and squinted as if trying to see her better. "Are we still friends?"

The question came as a surprise after such a shower of compliments. "Why would you ask such a thing?"

"I did confess I have an appetite for more than plants."

She laughed. "Of course we're still friends. Like you said, I don't judge. I just feel dumb for assuming."

He laughed and then grimaced. "I better go. It looks bad when I'm late. But I promise for days to come, I will regret leaving you. Goodbye, KC Casey." He flashed her a smile that made her glad she was standing still. If she'd been in motion when struck by the full force of that smile, she would definitely have stumbled.

"Goodbye, Michael Arturo."

He walked away to where he parked his car a few doors down. KC didn't do the proper thing by turning her own way. She watched him all the way until he was in his car with the door closed and with his sunglasses on. He waved at her through his rearview mirror, making her realize she'd been staring. Only then did she move down Tangerine Street going the opposite direction. She had plans of her own today, and none of those plans included standing around staring at beautiful men all day.

Two

In the zombie apocalypse,
you don't have to run fast.
You just have to run faster than your neighbor.
—"Top Ten Reasons to Stay Fit," Michael Arturo

Michael grinned when KC Casey finally turned away from where she'd been watching him. He was used to women staring at him, and she'd checked him out pretty thoroughly when he first entered the restaurant, but it felt different at the end. It felt that she'd been looking at all of him, not just his surface. And, if he was honest with himself, he had wanted to spend the day staring at her, too. KC was a very pretty woman. That natural blonde hair looked like spun gold. But it wasn't until after the time spent talking with her that she became someone he considered stunning. Funny how getting to know a person could do that to you.

He had loved every minute of his lunch with KC Casey. Well, not every minute. There had been that glitch where the waiter offered them fortune cookies and then took them away after KC had declined the offer. The waiter didn't even give Michael a chance to decline or accept the cookie. He just took the treat away. Who offered cookies and then took them away like that? Only a timeshare salesman would do something so heartless.

Michael had felt sullen about not getting a cookie, but he didn't want to make a scene. What would she think of him if he threw a tantrum over something as lame as a cookie in the middle of a working lunch date?

Working lunch date.

So which was it?

Work? Date? Or was it that weird in between that was merely lunch? Michael wasn't really sure. It had definitely started as work, but something about her, this woman with the future shining brightly in front of her, was attractive.

Not just attractive. Intriguing.

And he hadn't missed the fact that she didn't flinch too much when he'd called veganism ridiculous. Sure, she stiffened slightly, and she even nipped back, but most people handled it with far less grace. He found you could learn a lot about a person in an interview if you poked at the things they felt were sacred. He never poked too hard or too deep, but just enough to gauge a person's true depth. A shallow person fell apart and babbled on and on about how hard their journey had been and how no one understood them. An insecure person didn't simply nip back, they bit back with jaws fully engaged. A person less devoted to their ideals became crazy defensive. But a secure person who genuinely believed in their cause acted as KC had acted. They defended without getting defensive.

And when he told her he wasn't actually a vegan, she hadn't gone Southern preacher on him to convert him to the cause. He'd never told any of his interviewees about his personal choices before. Granted, none of them had ever asked before either, but still . . . he liked that KC was a woman of principles who lived her life honestly and let others do the same. Honesty in a person was a refreshing break from the full-of-themselves superstars of the food industry.

And it was *attractive*.

He sighed. If only that lunch could have gone a little longer. He'd thought himself so efficient and clever with his time when he made the second appointment, but now he felt nothing except deep regret. He sighed again as he turned off of Tangerine Street to face the punishment of his own efficiency.

His phone's ringing yanked him from his own wallowing, and he hit the answer button on his steering wheel. "Michael here," he answered.

"Hey, Mike, yeah, I know we were supposed to do that interview thing for your magazine dealy, but I'm afraid I'm going to have to cancel."

It was his next appointment, Nathan Fredericks. Michael rolled his eyes a little at the flippant way Nathan called the interview a thing and the magazine a dealy, but rejoiced in the news of a cancellation, even if it was entirely unprofessional.

He wasn't too far from where he'd left KC. Maybe he could still catch her and ask for a tour of the town or something, anything that would extend the conversation a little while. He needed to know if time spent with KC Casey was something he ought to pursue. And the only way to know that was to spend some more time with her.

He went back to his original parking spot, grateful it was still available since tourists seemed to come from everywhere to enjoy Tangerine Street for the day. He felt doubly lucky when he realized that, by moving his car and parking it again, he restarted his two-hour parking time limit. No parking ticket.

He jumped out of his car, pressed the fob to lock it up, and hurried in the direction he'd last seen KC go. He walked the boardwalk, peering into the windows of every shop he passed to make sure he didn't accidentally miss her. He didn't bother peeking into the deli because it was nothing but meat and cheese, and in no real-world scenario would a staunch vegan ever go into such a place without a good reason.

As he continued up the street, he almost didn't bother looking into the window of Delilah's Desserts either. But the bright, inviting window pulled his gaze to the interior of the shop, and he stopped in his tracks. KC stood at the counter, pointing to a confection in the display case and then smiling as the woman behind the counter removed the confection and placed it into a bag. KC paid for her purchase and left the bakery. He raised his hand to wave, but she didn't see him standing at the window. She seemed focused and intent in her every movement. Her determined demeanor made him falter, and the greeting he'd been about to utter stuck in his throat.

She actually looked unhappy.

In a flash of genius, Michael decided to go in, grab a cupcake and chase her down. They could share a confection, maybe she would cry on his shoulder over whatever made her unhappy, and he'd get a chance for a second date.

Did the lunch count as a date?

Maybe. It would depend on how the rest of the afternoon played out.

He ducked into Delilah's Desserts and went to the front counter, where a pretty brunette smiled and offered a greeting. Her name tag said Delilah. She must be the owner.

"Hi there," he said, smiling back. "What are your vegan options for cupcakes?"

She furrowed her brow and gave a half grin like he must have been crazy. "Vegan options? Honey, this is a bakery, not a health-food store. We don't take shortcuts with our flavors. We have no vegan options."

Michael froze. His mouth hung open until he remembered to snap it shut. "But your last customer . . ."

"KC?"

"Right. KC Casey just bought a cupcake here, didn't she?"

Delilah nodded. "Every month on the last Friday. A person could make a calendar around her."

"Right."

Michael stared at the woman for a few seconds longer before she prompted, "Can I get you something?"

"No. No thanks." He hurried out of the shop. And stared down the direction KC had gone. The author of *No Cheat Days* got a nonvegan cupcake on the last Friday of every month? What could such information possibly mean? He remembered when she declined the vegan fortune cookies, she'd told the waiter it was the last Friday of the month like it was supposed to mean something, and the waiter, apparently, knew what that meant.

But Michael felt completely in the dark. And angry. He felt angry, too. Angry because he'd just finished complimenting her on being exactly what she seemed to be. He'd complimented her on being open and honest and nonjudgmental. But of course, she wouldn't judge a nonvegan because she apparently was a nonvegan on occasion. He felt like she lied to him, and though it shouldn't have mattered since he'd just met the woman . . . it totally mattered. Michael believed in honesty, in being true to the person you really were, in not making excuses. Even though he didn't love that his brother ate like he'd made a personal commitment to the fast-track to a heart attack, Michael respected that his brother never pretended to be anything that he wasn't.

Michael shook his head to clear the thoughts of betrayal. What if there was a perfectly good explanation for her buying a nonvegan cupcake? Buying something nonvegan didn't mean she'd betrayed her professed beliefs. Maybe she was buying it for someone else. It's not like he'd seen her eating it or anything.

He turned and hurried in the direction she'd gone. He had to know that cupcake's ultimate fate. He continued to check in windows, this time not being so blinded with admiration for her that he skipped anything that might be questionable. "I'm being stupid," he muttered aloud as he peeked into an antique store through the door window. Could following her like a crazed man be considered stalking?

Maybe.

But that didn't deter him in his purpose, even if he wasn't sure what that purpose might actually be. Was it to catch her doing something wrong in the eyes of her adoring public? Or was it to prove that she was everything she had told him, everything he believed about her, everything he wanted to take out on a date or two, or three, or a lot?

But he couldn't date a woman who'd hoodwinked an entire demographic into believing she was something she wasn't. Not only would it be professional suicide for him to have a personal relationship with such a person when she got caught—and she would eventually be caught and outed—but a guy could never trust a woman who used deception to earn a quick buck.

He passed by all kinds of shops: jewelry stores, dress

shops, even a hat store where the door sign claimed that all hats were custom-designed and handmade.

"You make a lousy excuse for an investigative journalist, Arturo," he muttered when he feared he'd lost KC's trail. But even as the words left him, he caught sight of her turning down a side alley between buildings that led to the oceanfront. Trying not to be seen and hoping she didn't call the police and file for a restraining order if she did catch him spying on her, he flattened himself against the wall and tried to look casual to any passersby while he waited for her to clear the alley so he could follow her.

He almost wished she were the sort of woman who wore heels so he could hear more easily when her feet left the boardwalk for the sand, but her flat sneakers were silent. He waited an extra minute or so just in case and then glanced around the corner. Her cream-colored skirt swished around the corner, making him glad he'd waited as long as he had. He'd almost jumped into the alley too soon.

Shooting a look around the street to make sure no one paid attention to his more-than-suspicious behavior, Michael ducked into the alley. A quick glance at the beach at the end of the alley revealed his mark. She'd tugged off her shoes and had them in her hand swinging at her side as she made her way alongside a derelict wood fence that probably once marked property lines or maybe kept litter from traveling too far, but now only added ambiance and charm. At the end of the fence, she disappeared behind a high rise in the sand.

Michael kept his distance, figuring she couldn't get too far away out in the open range of a beach. He was so intent on watching the spot where he'd last seen her, he nearly tripped on an old red bike someone had parked alongside the fence. He cursed the owner and bikes on beaches in general and continued to where he could finally see over the rise in the sand.

KC sat on a bench bolted down on a small cement slab. She stared out at the ocean. The bag from the pastry shop sat unopened next to her.

Was she waiting for someone?

As much as he hated the idea of her waiting for someone just in case that someone might be male, he hated the idea of her not waiting for someone even more because that would mean she was a phony. He would rather find out she was unavailable than discover she was a phony.

Maybe she was one of those weird vegans. He'd met one guy who craved nonvegan food and so fed his dog all the food he craved rather than eat it himself. Maybe KC planned on feeding the seagulls with it.

And while Michael thought that was pretty strange, that would also be better than discovering she'd lied to him and the rest of the industry regarding her ideals.

She took a deep breath, placed her hand over the bag, and without even looking down at it, slid her fingers along the crease of the fold, so the bag opened. She lifted the cupcake out and brought it in front of her face, where he could no longer see it from his vantage point. When she pulled it away, a big bite was gone.

Michael growled low under his breath. He finally met a girl he was interested in, and she turned out to be a fraud. She probably had an eating disorder of some sort on top of this deception. How she could feel okay writing a book with the title *No Cheat Days* while giving herself a monthly, and maybe more than monthly, cheat day completely eluded him. Didn't anyone have integrity anymore?

He turned and made his way back down the alley to the

boardwalk. At least he'd figured it out before he got too involved this time. He'd had several relationships that hadn't come with any warnings or signs of trouble, but they had ended in deception on the woman's part, and he was glad to not get involved in another one.

At least that's what he told himself as he thumped down the boardwalk, harrumphing at the Delilah's Desserts sign as he passed. Telling himself and believing himself weren't the same thing at all, however.

Because the fact remained that she had looked beautiful out in the full light of sunshine with her hair lifting up off her neck in the ocean breeze.

The fact remained that hers had been one of the best conversations he'd had in months, if not years.

The fact remained that his attraction to her only served to increase his irritation with her. Why did she have to be a faker? She'd even had the nerve to accuse him of writing to the industry just for a paycheck. And she'd sounded so sincere when she'd made the accusation that he actually found it adorable at the time. Now? Now, nothing seemed adorable. At least he found out now that she ran along the shallow side of sincerity before he went beyond a simple professional interview.

He halted just a few feet from his car.

The interview.

What was he supposed to do about the interview?

He certainly couldn't print the interview he had intended originally. The words written on his laptop showered KC Casey with glittering praise. He'd be a total liar if he went to press with such an article, and it would put a blemish on him professionally when the truth came out about her.

His pulse spiked as a new thought formed. While it would hurt him professionally to write well of her and then have her outed as a fraud, it would boost him professionally to be the one calling her out.

"I can't do that. I'm not a snake," he said out loud, and he stepped up to his car. He wasn't sure what exempted KC from the truth. He'd exposed other people in the past. He shook his head as he got in. No. He wouldn't be the whistleblower with KC Casey. Someone would do it eventually, but that someone would not be him. He'd written those kind of exposé articles before. He was good at getting people to talk, to tell things they didn't necessarily want the world to know. He was good at writing articles that drilled to the truth.

For reasons Michael didn't want to examine too closely, he couldn't do that to KC.

As he turned the key and pulled out onto the road, he decided he just wouldn't do the article at all. He would chalk up the whole interview as good practice and leave it at that. He had a dozen ideas that could easily fill the slot set aside for the *No Cheat Days* interview, and all of those ideas would be better because they would be honest. Sure, his editor would be miffed, but Andy would get over it. Andy always did when he felt Michael took an overly moralistic approach to his writing.

Michael felt better having made the decision to dump the interview. At least that's what he told himself.

Too bad what he told himself and what he actually felt were so completely different.

Three

A vegan diet is not about despairing over what you can't eat.
It's about discovering all the amazing plant-based options
that you can!
—*No Cheat Days*, KC Casey

*K*C checked the *Vegan Zen* website for the tenth time
that day. Her interview should have been released
already. She'd been surprised when it hadn't shown
up in the last weekly issue but figured it probably had to work
its way through the schedule. That meant it would be released
with this newest issue. The new week usually didn't go live
until after ten at night, but she kept checking anyway.

She'd had dozens of interviews and hadn't obsessed over
any of them, but this one couldn't be helped. This was the big
interview, in the biggest magazine, the one most widely read
in her industry, the one that mattered to anyone who was
anyone. This interview would open the door for many more
companies to approach her as an ambassador or an influencer.

She told herself that these were the reasons making her unable to stop obsessing, but the truth was that she needed to know what Michael thought of her. She didn't just want to know, she needed it like plants needed sunlight for photosynthesis. She knew if he wrote a favorable review filled with light and happiness, she would be able to turn that light into usable energy. She would finally get the guts up to call him and ask him out.

If the review wasn't favorable, she wouldn't call. She didn't think about the fact that an unfavorable review would likely make her shrivel and die because she wouldn't shrivel and die. She might want to, but she wouldn't.

Her mother's illness taught her that much.

Bad things might happen, not even necessarily bad things, but merely unfavorable things, and when they did, strong women did not allow themselves to shrivel and die. They might allow a moment in time to mourn and to consider, but they always got back up and faced the day. They looked for the good opportunities still waiting for them.

With that in mind, KC pushed her chair back from the desk and left her apartment to go for a walk. She hoped a walk would be good for her. She'd been feeling out of sorts ever since the interview. Well, not since the interview. She felt great immediately after the interview. It was as she walked home from having her last Friday of the month with Mom that she felt . . . off. It was like some sort of weight or sadness or anxiety had settled over her shoulders, and she couldn't quite shake it loose.

She'd never had that happen to her before. She'd always come back from getting her Friday cupcake at Delilah's Desserts feeling refreshed, calm, peaceful, even downright euphoric sometimes.

But this time, she felt like ... well, she couldn't even describe it except to call it off.

The only thing that happened any differently from normal that day was the interview. The interview with a man she could not stop thinking about. He was the reason she felt so unsettled. He had to be. It had been three weeks since the interview, and her stomach had felt like a taffy pull that whole time.

Why could that interview not be posted already?

If he'd posted it, she could comment on it or maybe send him a casual text letting him know how much she liked what he'd done with the information given. She might ask him to meet her for a quick lunch to bounce ideas off of him for her next book. She might do any number of things that would allow her the chance to be with him again. If only the interview would go live, she would know what to do next.

From the little house she rented, it was a half mile to Tangerine Street, and just beyond that lay the beach. At the beach, her walk turned into a run. She moved to where the sand was packed down by the surf so she wasn't slogging through loose sand with every step. KC didn't mind when her running shoes met up with foamy waves. She kept her pace even. The shoes were old and cracked from the salt water abuse, but that was the price you paid to not zigzag all over the place to avoid the waves.

Usually a walk or a run made her feel better, but since her interview, nothing made her feel better. It was like someone had stuffed her heart with nothing but sawdust.

Sadness and sawdust.

Though none of that made any sense, it was how she felt emotionally, and it was killing her. Those sensitivities were not like her at all. Melancholy feelings came from other people, not from KC.

She ran harder, pumping her frustration and ache out through her extremities. She had assumed that when she was done four miles later, she would feel better, but nothing changed. She checked her phone again to see if the article had posted yet. Nothing changed there, either.

Head hanging, KC trudged home. Sadness and sawdust. There was no other way to describe it.

The next day, *Vegan Zen* had all the new articles up on its site. None of them were of her interview, though Michael Arturo had a new article on ethics and full disclosure in the health industry that she really enjoyed. It was a repurposing of the exposé he'd done on the Jog through the Fog Blog. The woman who owned the blog, Becky Webster, had the online persona of a seasoned runner. She claimed to have run marathons and triathlons and was making a lot of money every month as an ambassador for several companies. Michael's interview with her led him to the discovery that she never ran. It wasn't just that she never participated in a triathlon or marathon, but that she literally never ran. She was discovered when an outsider secretly filmed her doing her Mile-a-Day Snapchat, which she did to help motivate her fans. The film was sent to Michael, who did his own research into her activities and then blew the lid off the fact that she was a fraud. She ran while she filmed her Snapchat, then ground to a halt as soon as she turned the camera off. The industry devoured her whole when they found out.

Michael's most recent article dug a little deeper into the importance of being honest with your fans and with the people and companies you represent.

KC enjoyed the recap. A lot of frauds existed in the world. Off the top of her head, she could cite a dozen companies that made claims that weren't true regarding their products or of people who claimed their rock-solid abs came from exercise and training but were actually helped along by various phar-maceuticals. But she had the feeling he didn't mean any of those things. She had the feeling he was speaking to her directly, which made no sense at all. There was just something about the article that didn't exactly sit right with her.

He used the phrase, "Don't say *No Cheat Days* when you don't mean it." He'd even capitalized it and italicized it like he would a book title.

The comment felt directed at her because of the title of her book. That was really the only thing that could connect her to his remark. It's not like she ever had cheat days, which was why she felt okay giving such a title to her book.

Even her once-a-month cupcake had nothing to do with a desire to cheat on her lifestyle choices. It had everything to do with her desire to keep a tradition started in love all those years ago. Besides, the cupcake had always been accounted for in her diet. There was no cheat about it. She was very clear about that sort of thing in her book. If people knew what they couldn't live without, then they needed to account for those things in their food schedule. The cupcake was a calculated part of her life. Who was Michael to assume that scheduling something counted as a cheat? If it was planned for, it definitely wasn't a cheat; it was part of the plan. KC took a deep breath to keep herself from getting worked up over the one-sided argument based on assumptions she fought in her own mind. It wasn't like Michael knew about her cupcake. She was sure she hadn't said anything that would have given him any reason to get suspicious.

But his remark in his article took bites of her security and confidence with every passing thought she gave it.

She ordered takeout for lunch from the Fortune Café and determined to not think about it by spending her day working on her next book. When she picked up her takeout order, Cái stood behind the counter. She reached to take the food from him, but he didn't release it immediately. He stared at her over the white paper bag and frowned. "You've eaten something that doesn't agree with you."

She tried to smile. "No. I haven't eaten anything at all yet today except a smoothie for breakfast hours ago. That's why I'm here. At least that's why if you'll surrender my order to me."

His frown deepened, but he let go of the bag. "Food magic is tricky. It affects people differently. It's taking much, much longer to leave your system than it does for others. Be careful with what you eat."

KC finally did smile, and it actually felt genuine for the first time in weeks. "In my lifestyle, I'm always careful what I eat."

He waved her comment away with his frown still intact. "You know what I mean."

KC had no idea what he meant but took the bag anyway and jogged back to her house. Since she planned on working all day at the computer, her outing to get lunch might be the only exercise she'd get in the day.

She settled into work and tried to forget about the interview that still hadn't appeared on her computer screen.

Except she couldn't forget.

It was like he'd called her out for something in his article. The whole thing felt very personal.

So she did the only thing she could think of to eliminate her anxiety. She wrote him an email expressing all the ways she had enjoyed his article, all the ways in which she agreed with him. She kept it so positive, she didn't even point out the typo in the second to last paragraph. He didn't need to know about that. Besides, chances were good she had typos in the email she sent to him. People in glass houses shouldn't throw rocks.

With the email sent, KC felt certain she'd be able to move on with her day. Except she couldn't. Now, instead of her checking the website, she was checking her email for his response.

He never responded. All that day and late into the night, her inbox filled with emails from her editor, her publicist, a few of her friends, social media notifications, and a few spam emails offering to save her money on her mortgage.

The next morning was more of the same. She responded to her friends' emails and to her editor and to her publicist. She hit the send-receive button on her email in between each response in the hope that she would finally receive an email from Michael.

By midafternoon, she'd had enough.

She dialed his phone number. Instead of wondering what he was thinking and wondering if he was mad at her for some unknown reason, she would talk to him and ask him outright.

He didn't answer his phone.

KC grunted when his cheery voice recording identified him as Michael Arturo with *Vegan Zen* and invited her to leave a message so he could get "right back" with her.

After the beep, she said, "Hello Michael, This is KC Casey. I loved your article today in *Vegan Zen*. I just wanted to discuss a few things with you. It's kind of important, so if you could call me back, that would be great. Thanks."

She hit the button to end the call feeling more dissatisfied than she had before she dialed his number.

Stupid man.

She growled at herself. Insulting him didn't change anything. Working on her book proved pointless, since she'd deleted every single word she'd written that day and even deleted several she'd written the day previous. Mediation made her ornery. Exercise exhausted her. Nothing could distract her from the missing article on *Vegan Zen*'s page.

She couldn't wallow any further since she was the instructor for the evening yoga class at the gym. It didn't matter how she felt. She had to paste on a smile and help others breathe away their stress. "Maybe breathing away stress will work for me, too."

She arrived at the gym, greeted the yoga class, and threw herself heart and soul into her session.

At least she did until her phone rang while she was leading the class through the uttanasana pose. If it hadn't been for the light that flashed from where she'd left the phone on the bench next to her so she could keep track of the time, she would never have noticed the call coming in.

Ignore it, she thought. What were the chances Michael actually returned her call? And even if he did, now was not the time to answer. No matter who was on the other end of that number, her focus and responsibility were to the room and the people who were in the room with her. Be present, she thought, and she decided to repeat her thought aloud for everyone.

After all, it was good advice. And if vocalizing helped her ignore the fact that the call hadn't gone to voicemail and that the caller hadn't hung up, yet, all the better.

"Do you need to get that, KC?" The whispered question came from Alison, who had been coming to yoga classes from the very beginning of KC's career and who taught the class on days when KC couldn't be there.

KC widened her eyes and gave her head a small shake as if to admonish Alison for calling attention to the blinking light.

Alison moved out of the uttanasana position, scooted KC

to the side, and took over as instructor. "If it's enough to distract you right now when nothing ever distracts you, then it's enough for you to give your full attention to it," she whispered as she shooed KC away from the front.

Aside from a few curious glances, no one seemed to mind the change of the guard, so KC swept up her phone and quietly exited the room. Before she could hit the answer button, the ringing stopped. She grunted when she confirmed that the call had come from Michael. She hoped he would leave a message.

He didn't.

He called back.

She answered almost immediately and then chastised herself for looking like she was waiting around for him to call back. She was waiting, but she didn't want to look like it.

"Hey KC, this is Michael, how are you doing?"

His voice shivered right through her. "Michael, hi. I'm well. How are you?" She covered her eyes with her hand and shook her head. Could she sound any more stilted and unnatural?

"I am also well. I got your message and decided to call back and see what you might need."

"Oh. Yes. I called." KC walked farther from the yoga room even though she knew the glass was too thick for sound to carry through. It was bad enough she left the class; she didn't want to continue to act as a disruption. "I just wanted to get an idea of when you thought the interview would be going live. I want to make sure to give it a shout out on social media and support *Vegan Zen* in any way I can."

He was silent for several seconds, long enough to make KC wonder if they'd become disconnected.

"Right. The interview," he said slowly. "I have some more work that needs to be done on it. I'm actually going to be in town next week. Maybe we could get together?"

KC exhaled a silent breath of relief. He wanted to get together. He couldn't be mad at her for something if he wanted to see her. She was getting paranoid. She smiled even though he couldn't see it. "I'd love to get together." She tried not to analyze the deeper meaning of those words but pushed forward. "What day? What time?"

Again there was a pause before he answered. Maybe the phones were experiencing a delay in response. "I'll be in at the end of next week. I was thinking we could spend the day together on Friday. The last day of the month."

"Friday? Yes, Friday works. Lunch or dinner?"

"Let's go the whole day. I would love to see how a day in the life of KC Casey works."

"All day?" KC felt her smile slip into a frown. "The thirty-first?"

"Yep. On the last Friday of the month. "

KC's frown deepened. Was that a touch of smug satisfaction in his voice? Over what? What could he possibly feel smug about? Gah! She was overthinking everything—like she had been for three weeks. It was time to stop being paranoid and get out of the funk that threatened to topple her entirely.

She was on top of the world doing what she loved, being who she wanted, and helping others do and be the same. This weird, overwhelming sadness had reached its end. She would allow it no more power over her life.

She liked this guy and wanted to get to know him better. It didn't matter what day he wanted to meet. "That sounds great," she said.

"Wonderful," he said, though the word sounded strained and a little less than wonderful.

Stop it, KC. Stop trying to sabotage this, she thought. "Great. Should we meet at noon somewhere?"

"How about I pick you up for an early-morning run on the beach? In my interview with you, you mentioned you liked jogging at sunrise. The sun is up this time of year at 5:46. I looked it up. I could come get you by 5:30. Does that sound okay?"

KC almost choked on the idea. "So early?" It wasn't that she never got up early—she usually woke up with the sun for some sort of exercise, just like she'd told him during the interview—but a sunrise run was definitely a date activity. Either that or a photo shoot. Since he wasn't bringing a photographer, he had to like her enough to want to spend time with her that way. There was no other explanation.

"Early bird gets the worm," he said.

"Worms." She laughed. "One of the top ten reasons to be vegan. It allows you to get up early without having to have a gross breakfast."

He didn't laugh like she expected him to do at her reference to his infamous top-ten lists. She figured maybe he was nervous. Spending a day with her went far beyond professional duty. It might have been hard for him to ask her when a day together was so much more like a date than a work meeting. Maybe actual dating made him uncomfortable. Maybe he was one of those shy types who hid everything in work.

"Well," she said when the conversation had sunk too far into the chasm of awkward silence. "I guess I'll see you then?"

"I'll see you then," he confirmed. The line disconnected immediately.

KC didn't return to the yoga class. Instead she sat on a bench in the locker room and contemplated the conversation. She tasted it on all sides, trying to discern what the whole thing really meant.

The warmth and friendliness in his tone from before had been absent during the call, but he wanted to see her. All day. He had expressly requested her for all day on the last day of the month. He stressed that part: the last day of the month. Not just any last day. The last Friday.

To her, those words had meaning, but did he know that?

He might have an inkling of it. She had turned down the fortune cookies from Cái with the excuse of it being the last day of the month. Cái had been good friends with KC's mom. He knew what that day meant to her. But Michael wouldn't know.

Would he?

She frowned, hating how that facial expression seemed to have taken over her face lately, and moved slowly as she dressed and considered all the ways Michael might know what the last Friday of each month meant to her.

"Gah!" she said aloud, and she shut her locker. She didn't know what information he had or didn't have and gave herself permission to not care. She only knew she liked him, had enjoyed talking to him, and wanted to see him again. Everything she knew about Michael Arturo was good.

Armed with that knowledge, she tied her shoes and went home determined to look forward to her day with the one man she could not stop thinking about.

Four

The gym is full of annoying people.
Hit the trails, not the treadmills.
—"Top Ten Reasons to Take Your Workout to the
Outdoors," Michael Arturo

"Happy now?" Michael asked when he hit end on the call and flung the phone to the couch.

Michael's editor raised a dark, bushy eyebrow at the phone. It had landed close enough to him that he probably knew Michael had used restraint in not throwing it at him directly. "Michael," Andy said, "this is not about my being happy. This is about you. You've let this girl get under your skin like I've never seen before. She's thrown you off your game. You've become broody and ranty instead of clever and charming. You're a columnist, not a rock star. You don't get to brood."

Michael wished he had his phone back so he could make

273

better use of his aim. "And you think spending the day with her is going to fix me?"

Andy shrugged. "Maybe. Maybe not. But it'll at least get it all out in the open. You'll get the chance to confront her, and I'll get my writer back and a good story out of it as well."

"There might not be a story."

Andy pushed himself up off the couch and tugged his arms through the sleeves of his jacket. "Of course there's a story. What you mean to say is that there might not be a good story, which would be too bad. Either way, I think shadowing her for a day could be interesting. If nothing else, you can write a story about how vegans thrive, or maybe you'll decide you like her after all and get a kiss goodnight. Who knows? Regardless, this will be good for you."

"You mean it'll be good for you," Michael countered.

"I certainly hope so. It depends on if you're willing to write the story you get. You said she has some pretty suspicious ritualistic behaviors. Go figure out what they all are. The game's afoot. Get the story."

Michael rolled his eyes. "Stop binge-watching Sherlock Holmes. Nothing is afoot. There is no game."

Andy laughed. "You are so tense! She really has gotten to you, which is just fascinating and makes this a total game—a spectator sport from my vantage point." When Andy noticed Michael wasn't laughing, he said, "Seriously man, stop fretting. I hate it when you overanalyze your moral ground and start fretting."

"I think I'm going to call her back and cancel," Michael said, even though the idea of calling her back made him feel slightly ill. If he called her back, he'd have to talk to her again. Talking to her was his kryptonite.

Andy stuck out a warning finger. "If you do, then I'll have to fire you."

The threat to be fired came almost as often as Michael's threats to quit. "If you fire me, then I'll tell everyone why, and they'll know you're a snake, preying on the weaknesses of others."

"If you tell everyone I prey on weaknesses, then you'll have to explain that the no-cheat author is actually a cheater, thus exploiting that same weakness, which is what you're really trying to avoid here. You might as well do it my way and keep your job."

"Andy . . ." Michael didn't even try to keep the tired out of voice.

"You're fretting again," Andy said with a laugh. "Thanks for the poker. I'll pay up next round."

"Bring enough to pay for the next round, too, since you can't seem to ever win."

"I'm getting better," Andy insisted.

"If it makes you feel better to say so."

"It does." And with that, Andy left so Michael could fret in peace.

Though his fretting was anything but peaceful.

That woman did not know when to leave well enough alone. She called. He could not believe she'd actually had the nerve to call. He'd been startled when she'd written and had expected some snide bit of counterattack regarding his article. But rather than be insulted by his article, she'd declared that she'd loved it. She showered him with praise for being so honest and showing the importance of integrity and ethics in the work environment.

She missed the entire point of his article by being willfully clueless of the fact that the whole thing had been aimed at her. He fumed over her email for several hours until the real bomb dropped with her phone call.

He'd actually almost answered at first because he hadn't

looked to see who was calling until just before his finger swiped right to answer. He was grateful for quick reflexes that allowed him to snatch his hand away before he was forced into a conversation he just wasn't ready for.

If Andy hadn't been present for the whole thing, Michael would never have called back. He might have even blocked the number. But Andy had been intrigued by Michael's response to the call and demanded to hear the whole story. Once he had the story, Andy wanted all of it. And he wanted it for the magazine.

Why did she have to call? Didn't she see how that article was for her?

She had to have seen. KC Casey was not a stupid woman. He'd laid it on thick enough, she would have had to be in a coma to miss the references to her.

But her calling him was his undoing. Her calling while Andy was a witness made everything so much worse.

It was her voice. Michael couldn't help that his stupid, traitor heart flipped a little when he heard her voice. That heart flip was the ultimate reason he called her back even though Andy probably thought the call back was due to his goading. Once Michael heard her voice on his voicemail, he knew he had to see her again, confront her personally, and get her out of his system once and for all.

He really hoped it would work that way. He'd been on two dates since he'd met KC. With every word of conversation, he ended up comparing those other two women with KC. They both fell short.

Which was what made her calling him so maddening.

How was he supposed to forget he ever met her if she wouldn't get out of his headspace?

But hearing her voice again reminded him of why he had felt attracted in the first place. And it made him soften the fiendish villain he'd set her up as in his mind. She wasn't a fiendish villain. She was a just an ordinary woman doing ordinary things. Ordinary women, and men, too, for that matter, cheated on their dietary habits all the time. And really, the cheating on the diet part wasn't a big deal. It wasn't like he was a vegan with some sort of moral dilemma with eating things that weren't plant-based. What was a big deal was that she'd set herself up as someone who didn't do those things. She preached one thing to her rather extensive group of followers and then did something else. She was sponsored by companies who expected her to be honest.

He had wanted her to be more than ordinary.

But she wasn't.

So what?

If they didn't work in the same industry, he'd overlook the flaw and ask her on a real date regardless. But they did work in the same industry. Dating her would be a professional scandal.

Sadly, it was a professional scandal that Andy wanted.

Andy wanted to set up a sting operation where Michael followed KC around all day and got photos of the big cheat. Andy even planned on running the article under the title "The Big Cheat Day."

"No, Andy," Michael had said.

But Andy still believed such an article was in his future.

It wasn't. It never would be.

Would it?

No.

"So what am I proving to myself by spending Friday with her?" he wondered aloud. He wasn't proving anything to himself. And by agreeing to spend the day with her, he all but confirmed to Andy that there would be a story.

While Michael had been talking to KC on the phone,

Andy looked up the hours for Delilah's Desserts and scribbled a quick note to Michael to make sure he was with KC before the bakery opened and after it closed again.

The whole plan was stupid. How devoted to this ritual was she? Would she really go through with it while he was with her? He felt like he was missing information—information he couldn't ask for outright.

"If I was a real investigative journalist, I'd get background information," he said to his empty living room. That decided everything. He would have a go at real journalism. It was time to get to know Tangerine Street and its occupants a little better.

The next morning found him strolling along Tangerine Street trying not to look as guilty as he felt for invading KC's personal territory. Wasn't it bad enough that he planned on spending the day with her on Friday? Did he really need to shake down her neighbors for information?

He walked past Delilah's Desserts several times before deciding he looked like he was staking out the place for a later robbery. The owner might call the police if he didn't just go in.

He opened the door and breathed deeply of the sweet, comforting scents of baked goods and frostings. Well, if nothing else, he was going to indulge and get himself a cupcake. If the vegan could have one, the mostly vegetarian should be able to as well.

"The vegan?" he said to himself. Had he really just referred to her as the vegan?

"Excuse me?" The woman behind the counter said. She had apparently heard him muttering to himself and assumed he was addressing her.

"Oh nothing, just talking to myself."

She gave him a look that seemed to say, There's a

medication for that, buddy. But what she actually said was, "Let me know if I can help you with anything."

He nodded that he would and then turned his attention to peruse the glass cases, intrigued by the many colors and swirls and perfection of confection.

"What would you recommend?" he finally asked when he realized how daunting a task picking something out might be and how much more daunting it would be to get the baker to open up and talk to him. Asking for her help was the only way he could think to start a genuine conversation that could lead the way to other topics.

"That really depends on you. It depends on if you're a sweet, spicy, or sour kind of guy, and it depends a lot on what's going on in your day. From the look on your face, I suggest you get something with chocolate in it."

Michael gave a startled laugh. "Chocolate? Why? What look is on my face?"

She lifted a shoulder in a half shrug. "You just look like a guy who needs a boost for the day he has ahead. Chocolate is the stuff that feeds the soul."

"And my soul needs feeding?"

She nodded. "You should get two. And maybe share one. Sharing feeds the soul, too." She gave a half smile to go with her half shrug.

"Well, the only person I want to share with I won't be seeing until tomorrow." He tried to look like he was contemplating her advice when he said, "Hey, you probably know her. You could tell me what she likes best, and I can have a cupcake ready for her when I see her tomorrow."

"Who is she?"

"KC Casey."

Delilah frowned the tiniest bit, a barely-there crease between her eyebrows. "You probably shouldn't get her anything. Cupcakes can be pretty personal. She can come get her own."

He flashed her his most disarming smile, the one that made most women sigh. "But you did just tell me to share."

"KC is a little different. She'll want to get her own. She only comes in once a month. And it isn't something she does with anyone else."

Michael kept his lips up in a friendly smile. Of course the vegan didn't cheat on her lifestyle with anyone else. Witnesses would be a problem for her entire career. KC catered to a tough crowd. If any of them caught a whiff of her reality, they would skewer her like tempeh and roast her on the grill.

What he said to Delilah was, "Once a month, huh? You'd have to have pretty intense willpower to resist such a temptation for all the rest of the month."

Delilah leaned against the back side of her display case. "I sometimes think it takes more willpower for her to come in than it would take for her to stay away. She's a vegan. I'm a violation of her very existence since I don't have vegan options." Delilah's frown deepened as she focused her gaze on Michael as if seeing him for the first time. "But you know all that already, don't you? Weren't you in here the other day?"

Caught.

Michael nodded casually as if her remembering him didn't make him feel sick to his stomach. "Yes. I'm not vegan, though. I just wanted to impress her by buying her something she would approve of and appreciate. I'm seeing her tomorrow. You don't think she'd appreciate a gift from here?"

Delilah seemed to believe that he was taking KC on a date, because she didn't throw him out immediately. And, in a way, wasn't it a date? A tricky, underhanded, sneaky sort of date that made him not like himself very much. He hadn't felt this way when he'd busted the jogger blogger. Delilah kept talking, so he chose to focus on her and what she said over the anxiety of his own conscience.

"She wouldn't appreciate you buying her anything from my shop." Delilah began organizing the cupcakes inside the display case. "Like I said, it's personal to her ... almost a religious kind of personal."

"Sounds serious," he said, hoping such a statement encouraged her to continue. He was careful to also focus on the cupcakes, trying to look like he was choosing one instead of cataloging her every word.

"Yeah. It's a tradition her mom started when she found out she was sick. It started before I ever took over the bakery. KC is pretty devoted to the tradition, almost like it's a spiritual cleansing. It's sweet, really, that she wants to honor the memory of her mother that way. We do what we can to keep our loved ones with us."

"Wait. Her mom passed away?"

Delilah tilted her head as if trying to look at him better, her dark brown ponytail swung down over her shoulder. "Aren't you friends? I thought you knew her."

"I am her friend," Michael said, not feeling like the kind of guy who was anyone's friend at the moment. "She told me her mom survived her cancer."

"Her mom did survive the cancer." Delilah then turned her back on him, as if she'd decided she was done with the conversation.

"But you just said she passed away," he persisted, refusing to be shut down by this skinny baker. Why was he even listening to her? Everyone knew a skinny baker couldn't be trusted.

"If you want to know anything else, I suggest you ask her." Delilah turned back to him, but now her entire demeanor, which had been open and friendly, was closed and wary. "In the meantime, is there anything I can help you with as far as baked goods?"

She was apparently done with answering his questions. He had the sneaking suspicion that if he asked about anything that wasn't directly related to frosting and flavors, she'd throw him out of the place.

"I'll take something with chocolate," he said, trying to get back on her good side.

Michael felt a stab of shame as Delilah went through the various chocolate options. *Aren't you friends? I thought you knew her*, Delilah had said to him. He wasn't being a friend as he shook down the local baker for background information. And now he felt a little lost as to what he should do next. Delilah seemed to think the transgression of KC's monthly visit to the bakery was a cleansing. In his line of work, this was a word he knew well, but usually, it was in reference to a juice fast or some other kind of vegetable and fruit detox. He'd never heard of a cleansing that came with cupcakes—though he could see the appeal of such a thing.

Delilah cleared her throat to indicate she was done giving him options; he now had to make a choice.

He took the one with the most chocolate ingredients—the one she called Death by Chocolate—figuring she would approve of his choice, and he felt glad to see that she did seem to approve.

As she prepped the cupcake to leave the bakery, he laughed at himself for actually wanting the approval of this skinny baker who had enough moxie to shut him down when she felt he'd gone too far.

Michael imagined Delilah made an incredibly loyal and formidable friend. She was definitely the woman you wanted on your side instead of marching to war against you.

"Here you are," Delilah said, handing over a bag that probably represented his entire suggested daily caloric intake.

"Thanks." He hesitated before leaving, wanting to try to leave on a friendly note so she knew he didn't mean any harm to KC, but he thought better of it because he wasn't sure what he meant or didn't mean. "Thanks," he said again, then left the shop.

Once back out on the street, Michael wasn't sure what he was supposed to do next. Should he go to the gym where she did yoga classes? He looked both ways as if he was a child checking for traffic before crossing the street. He finally chose to go in the direction that was familiar to him. He went to the Fortune Café. That waiter guy knew about KC's last Friday of the month habit.

The entire conversation with Delilah had gone in a direction that had surprised Michael. KC's mother had died. The cupcake thing was a tradition started by her mom. And her mom was gone.

That was the information that surprised him the most. Their first meeting together had been charming and open. He felt a degree of hurt over the fact that KC hadn't shared this detail about her life. And then he chided himself for being so childish. Did he deserve to know such an intimate detail? After all, wasn't he the guy pounding the pavement to dig up information regarding KC's habits?

But that was different. At the time of their first meeting, he wasn't guilty of anything. He'd been completely open with her about his parents passing away. Didn't such open honesty deserve some return? Weren't emotional exchanges of that sort the kind of thing solid relationships were built on?

Michael stopped on the boardwalk in front of a local handmade jewelry store and took several deep breaths as he stared into the window without really seeing anything. Solid relationships? Where had that thought come from? Michael had already decided he didn't want a solid relationship with a woman who didn't just cheat on her lifestyle choices, but also cheated on her fandom. Didn't her faithful followers deserve her being faithful?

But her mother was gone.

That information changed a lot for him. Her mother's health was the reason KC Casey became a vegan in the first place. This cheat seemed to stem from the same reason.

While Michael didn't understand how both of those things could come from the same place, he understood the emotions behind them. He realized KC's cheat might be far less than it appeared and far more. While staring into the jewelry shop window with the words Spy Glass Jewelry stenciled on the glass, Michael absently removed the cupcake from the bag and took a bite.

Three bites later, he understood why the cupcake was called Death by Chocolate. It was easily the richest, most decadent thing he'd ever eaten, but any death it might cause was blissfully painless. He squinted to see better into the shop window and spied a pendant hanging on a long silver chain. The pendant was a small diamond sunburst embedded into what looked like a silver teardrop.

The setting was beautiful and made his eyes sting with tears he forced back with rapid blinking. He took a fourth bite of the cupcake and felt awash with emotions of love and longing—emotions he hadn't remembered since his parents had died. The longer he stood still and silent staring at the pendant, with the light bouncing off the many facets of the diamond and the teardrop, the more deeply he felt he understood KC's position, the more he felt KC needed a necklace that showed the light shining in spite of the lingering pain. He went inside.

The woman behind the counter had a small light focused in on where she worked over a jewelry setting with a pair of impossibly tiny pliers.

"Hello?" Michael said.

"I'll be just a moment," the woman said. "Feel free to look around."

Michael tried to look around but was really interested only in the sunburst diamond inside the teardrop. After a moment, the woman finished up whatever delicate work she was doing and smiled brightly at him. "Can I help you with something?"

"Yes," Michael said, feeling almost buzzed with excitement over the prospect of the purchase. "I was interested in the price of this necklace here." He pointed to the one he wanted.

The woman smiled. "The sunshine. I loved designing that one."

"Are you Stella?" he asked as he pointed to a sign that said "Designs by Stella."

She grinned. "That's me. Anyway, the sunshine piece is seventy-five dollars."

Michael didn't hesitate. He pulled out his wallet, snapped down his credit card on the counter, and waited while Stella wrapped the piece in tissue paper and placed it in a little box.

After the purchase was complete, he left the jewelry shop and felt a deep pleasure in knowing he'd bought KC a gift that evoked such strong emotions. Because the strong emotions had to have come from seeing the necklace and feeling the symbolism.

Why else would he feel so . . . he couldn't even describe it, but he almost felt . . .

No. He blinked several times and laughed as he rolled his

shoulders to shake it off, because he almost wanted to say he felt like he was in love with KC.

But that couldn't be.

He barely knew the woman.

And he'd found she had dishonest dealings with her fan base, which was hard to respect, let alone love.

Besides, had he, Michael Arturo, ever been in love aside from that one time in the second grade when his teacher was out for six months due to hip surgery and the school provided a substitute named Miss Angel? Miss Angel had been the real thing—he was sure of it. He'd never spent so long making a Christmas card in his life. His little second grade dreams were shattered when Mrs. Cartwright came back from her surgery fully recovered and meaner than ever.

Michael never saw Miss Angel again.

And that was how love went.

Michael laughed at himself for even remembering Miss Angel, let alone remembering the way his hands shook as they clutched that homemade Christmas card before giving it to her—kind of like his hands shook now while clutching the little gift box with the necklace. There was something to his feelings for KC.

He didn't know what yet, but he felt determined to find out.

His grip tightened on the jewelry box, and he strode to the Fortune Café with long, purposeful strides. He needed to understand more about why KC had the monthly cheat allowance.

He had to understand how he was falling so hard for a woman he barely knew.

Five

For lift and fluff in your pancakes, use seltzer instead of
dairy. This will decrease the lift and fluff in your derrière.
Use science, not substitutions.
—*No Cheat Days*, KC Casey

C waited patiently inside the cozy front area of
Delilah's Desserts while Delilah was busy getting
something out of the back for the customer who'd
come in just before KC. She perused the display cases trying
to find her mood. That was how her mom always described it.
They weren't looking for a flavor; they were searching for a
mood when they made their monthly sojourn to Seashell
Beach's best bakery.

Her mother had been right all those years ago. Moods
mattered, and they dictated a flavor. Some days demanded
tart, vibrant lime. Other days required a dark, silky chocolate.
The mood mattered.

With a day totally hijacked by a handsome man who

made KC's heart feel like it needed a defibrillator, KC felt like a sweet cupcake might be the order of the day.

She hated to break with tradition in any way and buy the cupcake early, but she didn't know how else to fit in the date with Michael and the date with her mom's memory.

Delilah exited the back room with a pink box tied up with a pink and yellow bow and skidded to a halt when she saw KC standing there. The smile on Delilah's face dipped into a frown before she caught herself and forced it back to her lips. She turned her attention to the man waiting ahead of KC and handed him the box.

"Here you go! Turkish Delight Cupcakes."

KC peeked around the man's shoulder. "Turkish Delights?"

Delilah grinned. "Yep, the cinnamon cupcake that's so good, you'd be willing to sell out your siblings for one, unlike those nasty candy things from *The Lion, the Witch, and the Wardrobe*." She looked back at the man. "Not that I'm promoting sibling-sellout or anything. It's just a name. Have you ever had a real Turkish Delight?"

The man shook his head. KC did, too, inserting herself into the conversation.

Delilah shook her head. "Those things are nasty. Seriously. Disgusting. These make up for it."

KC laughed. So did the man. He paid for his box of cupcakes and left. KC stepped forward and smiled at Delilah.

"You're a day early, aren't you?" Delilah asked, looking wary.

"I had to make adjustments. I tell my audience to be flexible and accepting; it's good if I can do the same. Some unforeseeable circumstances have come up for tomorrow."

"Goods ones or bad ones?"

It was KC's turn to frown. "I think good. Are you okay? You look worried."

Delilah rubbed her finger over the counter as if trying to remove some invisible speck. "I am a little worried . . . about you, actually. Some guy came in the shop today, and he asked me some weird questions about you, veganism, and your cupcake habits. And whether or not I carried anything that was vegan in my shop, which you know I don't."

KC's insides tightened until she felt like she couldn't breathe. She understood the implications. Someone was asking about her. And the cupcakes. Someone was looking for a scandal. "Do you know who he was?"

Delilah shook her head, leaned against the counter, and said, "But he said he was spending the day with you tomorrow and that he wanted to surprise you with a treat."

KC's teeth ground together.

Michael.

Michael had been here asking about her, asking about the habit.

"There's more." Delilah's eyes shifted from big and sympathetic to narrow and fiery. "There was a photographer here last night before I closed. He was taking pictures but trying to be discreet about it. When I caught him and asked him what he was doing in my shop, he insisted he was there getting photos for an article in *Vegan Zen* magazine. I scooted him right out and told him that any pictures he used of my shop required my permission since it was private property. I don't know if that's true or not, but figured it was worth a try."

KC closed her eyes and slumped against the counter. "So this is a setup," she whispered.

Delilah must have heard because she said, "I was worried it might be, so I didn't tell him anything. He came in last month just after you were here and asked for a vegan cupcake.

He looked surprised when I told him we didn't make that sort of thing here—sorry, KC. When he came in again, he exuded guilt."

"So he knows." She imagined how it must look to him, how he must perceive the whole situation. "He knows." What did he think of her? He couldn't get too judgmental. After all, he wasn't vegan. He had no moral dog in the race. But if this bothered him enough that he was now digging for information, why did he ask her out for tomorrow? Was he trying to catch her in the act? Did he want pictures? Was this some weird vigilante thing?

She felt no guilt over her actions. Why would she? Honoring her mother one day a month by keeping a tradition was hardly the thing to get bent out of shape over. But as she viewed it through the lens of her followers and her publisher, she could see how everything could go very wrong. Many vegans weren't in it for the health. They did it for the animal rights. They would vilify a person for using a drop of honey in oatmeal. If her followers knew, they would not view it as no big deal.

She remembered a time when someone leaked pictures of an ambassador for a major vegan company. The pictures were of her sitting on her patio gnawing on ribs. The barbecue sauce was smeared up her cheek. The entire internet exploded over the BBQ fiasco. Contracts were canceled. Her sponsors all dumped her. No one even knew her name anymore.

There was also the fitness trainer who took Snapchat videos of herself running a portion of her "daily mile." Someone on the street filmed her doing it in reality, and the world discovered her "daily mile" was closer to a "daily meter." Her run only ever lasted as long as her Snapchat. She didn't even break a sweat as she signed off with a peace symbol and a kiss to the camera.

The fitness trainer was roasted for the disparity between her online personality and her real personality. How could anyone feel motivated by someone who talked the talk but couldn't walk the walk, let alone run the mile? Michael had been the one to blow the woman's cover.

No one could trust the trainer after that. She disappeared into the oblivion KC felt she'd deserved up until now.

What would the industry do to KC? Would she lose her contracts? Would her books be recalled and sold to recycle shops? How could she make them understand that this was something different, separate? How did she make them see that this wasn't a cheat? It was a memorial. But her audience wouldn't care. Animal products were animal products. Even a little still counted.

She straightened. "What did he say?"

"He said he wanted to impress you . . . maybe surprise you. Which, at first, seemed really sweet. But then when he didn't seem to know about your mom dying—and I'm sorry I told him that part—it felt suspicious more than sweet." Delilah looked sheepish. "I was only trying to explain why he really shouldn't get you a cupcake and that came out. I'm sorry."

"It's fine. You're fine. None of this is your fault." KC tried to think. She wanted to figure out how to paint Michael in a heroic light in all this, but all she could think of was that he was trying to set her up.

She didn't know what he intended, but she did know his intentions couldn't be good. Otherwise, he would just come right out and ask her in an open and honest conversation versus all this cloak-and-dagger nonsense. The worst part of such a discovery was that it hurt so much. Why did it hurt so much? Why did she feel like she'd been sucker punched?

"It doesn't matter," she told Delilah at the same time her

heart sang out, *It hurts because you like him, because you know how easy it would be to care deeply for him.*

She ignored her own thoughts. Just because they were true didn't mean she had to listen to them. KC stared into the display case for several broken heartbeats longer before she squared her shoulders and took a step away. "You know, actually, I think I'll just come back tomorrow. We'll stay with routine for now. Thanks for letting me know, Lilah. I appreciate you looking out for me." With that, KC left the shop.

He wanted to surprise her, huh? Well . . . he would get the surprise, because she planned on having that open and honest conversation he was apparently too immature to instigate on his own. Her anger at his sleuthing into her life just so he could get a good story only magnified her hurt. Here was a man who she felt to be her intellectual equal. Here was a man both handsome and intelligent, both interesting and funny.

Yet he was the same man who planned on turning her over to the wolves of a community that could never understand her situation. They weren't there holding her mother's hand after chemo treatments. They weren't there when there was more of her mother's hair on the pillow than on her head in the morning. They weren't there through the lifestyle changes and the crying and the worry.

They weren't there the day her mother declared they needed stress relief and the bakery shop happened to be along the way as they walked to the beach.

They weren't there when her mother's shaking, weak hand held a cupcake aloft and toasted to the good health of them both, irony notwithstanding.

They weren't there when the doctor declared her mother cancer free.

They weren't there to see her mother clutching her and sobbing with gratitude over the news.

They weren't there for the times when KC returned home from school to check on her mom and they always ended up at the same bakery, the same bench on the beach.

They weren't there when that journey to the bakery and the bench was made alone.

They weren't there.

And KC owed them no explanations or apologies. Those memories were hers. That life belonged to her. But they would judge that life that they weren't there for and that didn't belong to them.

They would call her an animal hater for allowing animal products into her life for even a moment. They would call her a liar and a cheater.

Maybe they were right.

Maybe.

It finally made sense that her interview hadn't shown up. Why would Michael do some vanilla interview when he could do a spicy exposé that revealed her for who she really was?

Except the interview revealed far more about her than the exposé would.

She walked to the bench, sat down, and stared at the sea that had been a lone witness to all of it. But there would be another witness come tomorrow.

And he wouldn't like it one bit.

Neither would she.

I

KC had already decided on what she'd wear for her day date with Michael before she found out he was a jerk she had to contend with and not a romantic possibility. The long skirt was both casual and dressy depending on where it was worn.

It was comfortable enough to work for the beach, hiking, or in-town activities. The skirt was her most comfortable clothing item. The fact that it emphasized her frame in all good ways was just a bonus. She considered changing her outfit choice before realizing the day would be long and filled with who knew what. The fact that she looked nice in it didn't matter as much as the fact that it was comfortable. The shirt she'd chosen was clingy and had the appearance of being something dressy and alluring.

She had to stay with the shirt option since it was the only shirt she had that matched the comfortable skirt. And she was sticking with the skirt because the day promised enough discomfort. Her clothing didn't have to contribute to the problem.

Five thirty in the morning found her staring at the outfit spread out over the easy chair in her bedroom. Even though she'd already decided to go with comfort, a new day changed her perspective. Did she wear it and run the risk of him thinking she was trying to impress him when the reality was that she'd as soon knock him unconscious?

Or did she choose jeans and a work T-shirt so he had a clear message from the beginning?

Neither option sounded great. She wanted to stay in her pajamas and not answer the door when he knocked. But that wasn't really an option either.

At least she didn't have to choose immediately. The day started with an early morning run on the beach. That meant her jogging attire would make it clear she wasn't trying too hard to win his approval. She was dressed and ready for the run in less than ten minutes. She had her hair pulled back in a ponytail, her face washed, and her teeth brushed. Michael Arturo would get no more of her time or attention than that.

She jumped when the knock finally came. He was six

minutes late. She grabbed her key, tucked it into the inner pocket of her jogging shorts, and opened the door. She didn't open it very wide, not wide enough to invite him inside or to even really let him see into her home.

Michael did not deserve any more of her privacy than he'd already stolen.

"Hey!" he said as soon as his eyes met hers. He looked legitimately happy to see her, happy to be able to spend time with her.

The woman who'd pretended to jog a mile a day hadn't worked so hard to fool her fans as Michael did to fool KC. His acting job only hurt her more. Because no matter how many times she called him the enemy in her mind, she could not keep her emotions from swelling inside her when she saw him.

She gave a half smile, knowing she'd never been good at faking anything but also knowing she had to try to appear normal. "Hi," she said, and she shut her door with a solid click before he could do anything awkward like ask to use her restroom.

When he leaned in and kissed her cheek, much like he had before at their interview, she stiffened.

"You look great."

She hated how he sounded like he meant it. She didn't know how to respond to the familiarity of the cheek invasion or the compliment, so she said nothing.

He must not have noticed her hesitation because he said, "Got everything you need?"

She nodded.

"Great! Let's go catch us a sunrise!"

She followed him down the stairs and to the road where his car waited under the streetlight that hadn't yet turned off for the day. Something about getting in his car felt like a self-betrayal, so KC stopped at the curb. "It's only two blocks to the sand from here. Might as well start now, right?" She tried to smile, to look bright and at ease.

But what she felt was sad because she'd liked him. Seeing him again reminded her of how much she liked him. She'd admired him for years. She couldn't quite talk herself out of liking him. Not yet.

He smiled back. "You're the boss. I'll follow where you go."

She didn't respond but instead took off toward where the sand met the surf. He laughed as if she was just messing with him by getting a head start and pounded the pavement behind her to catch up.

She didn't make an effort to wait for him, but she didn't really need to. Michael caught up and kept up. He was one of those people who actually ran instead of just pretending to run. Was he surprised to find that she was a practiced runner as well? Had he expected her to be like the jogger blogger who'd probably never run a mile in her life?

They lagged at the dry sand but found their pace again once they hit the place where the sand was packed down by the waves. The sky lightened, setting the clouds on fire to announce the coming sun. The golden clouds reflected off the water, seeming to wash the whole world in a rosy sort of cheerfulness. Even jogging next to someone who wanted to see her fail couldn't take away the quiet peace she felt as she breathed in and out in rhythm to the way her feet and the waves pounded the sand. How was she supposed to stay full of righteous fury when they were doing one of her favorite calm-down activities?

"So . . ." Michael started the conversation. "If I guess what your initials stand for, will you tell me if I'm right?"

More personal information. Did he already know the answer and was baiting her on that as well? What did it matter if he was? She planned on laying it all out on the table before she was through with him for the day. So what if he exposed her full name along with exposing what her community would view as so much more than a flaw?

The cupcake would be reason enough for her demographic to burn her at the stake.

She shrugged, thinking of the public and how they would view her. There were some passionate people in the vegan culture. Some of them were outright cruel—the kind who worked their fingers to the bone to save a cat, but who would have no trouble kicking a human to the curb. But there were others who knew unbound kindness and legitimately lived do-no-harm lives. Those people would understand her choices. They might not agree, but they would understand. Regardless, the opinions of the people on either side didn't matter. She was who she was. And her choices belonged to her, not to the judgmental public.

"Was that a yes or a no?" he asked.

She gave a sideways glance, having forgotten for a moment what he'd originally asked. Her name. He wanted to guess her name. She nodded. "Sure. What have I got to lose?"

"Let's do the first name first," he continued when she didn't argue. "Kate?"

She shook her head.

"Karla?"

"Nope."

He went through dozens of others as they ran side by side, weaving their steps so they stayed out of the foamy waves. Karen, Kylee, Kiki, Kirsten, Kennedy. From the exotic Katya to the more common Kim.

He didn't sound winded as he moved beside her and tossed out guesses. She liked that about him and hated that she liked anything about him.

He began musing out loud. "What if your name is Kaycee all spelled out and perfectly fine, and you're the one who turned it into initials?"

She couldn't help it; she burst out laughing. "My parents would have been the worst people on the planet to give me a name like that when my last name is Casey." She allowed herself to enjoy the laughter for a moment before she sobered and said in a quieter voice, "And my mom was the best person I've ever known. She definitely wouldn't have done that."

She was surprised when he reached out, gave her arm a tug, and pulled her to a stop. "Of course she wouldn't." He seemed to be waiting for her to say something important or to say something important himself, but instead he suggested they walk for a minute to enjoy the sunrise.

"That's right," she said, very aware of his hand on her arm. "We were supposed to be looking at the sky."

"I don't feel like I'm missing anything."

It took KC a moment before it sunk in that he was staring at her, complimenting her. She really wished everything she'd learned the day before wasn't true, because the reality of it was that Michael was missing everything. He was missing what they could have had if he had just printed her interview and then asked her to dinner like she'd fantasized about since she'd met him.

To relieve the tightening in her chest, she said, "Why don't you tell me something about you—something I don't know."

He released her arm. Finally. It felt like he'd left a burn mark where his fingers had been. "I thought I was guessing your name."

"We could be here for months without that going any further than it already has. You should give up while you still have your dignity." She smirked at him because she knew it annoyed him to not know her name and to not be able to guess.

He squinted at her as if trying to see her better. After several long moments where the waves pulled out and crashed in five times, he said, "Keira."

Her breath caught in her throat. Her mouth popped open. "Someone told you." There was no other way he guessed it that fast and with such certainty.

He raised his hands as if to defend himself against her accusation. "I swear. No one told me. It was just a guess." His face broke into a grin. "But it was a right guess? Your name is Keira? Really?"

She frowned and nodded. "You even put the right emphasis in the right places. No one told you? Really?" She felt her doubt in him was fair. He'd dug around in her life enough, it was possible he'd charmed her name out of one of her Seashell Beach friends.

Except . . . how many people knew her real name?

Did anyone?

"Nobody told me," he confirmed. They walked along the water's edge. They probably looked cozy, like one of the couples she always sighed over when she saw them walking along the beach or along the boardwalk on Tangerine Street. The silence didn't seem as awkward as it probably should have considering all the opposing feelings she had of him. But if years of meditation taught her anything, it was to let moments be what they were. If the moment was comfortable, why would she want for anything else?

He broke the silence. "Keira's a pretty name. Why would you want to go by initials? Was it just because KC Casey sounded more memorable as a professional persona?"

Since she realized she'd been staring, she sucked in a deep breath of ocean air and let her gaze slip past him to the ocean at their side. "Profession had nothing to do with it. I was five and starting kindergarten. I told my mom I was afraid because I couldn't say the R part of my name and I didn't want anyone to laugh at me. My mom assured me over and over again that no one would laugh and that most of them probably had letters they couldn't pronounce, but I couldn't be comforted. So she let me pick what I wanted to call myself. The initials seemed simple and easy to remember for me, because picking a new name for yourself means you have to answer it when people use it. I already identified with Casey since it was my last name. The initials were an extension of what I knew."

He stopped walking and turned to face her, not even caring that a wave rolled in too close and covered his sneakers. "That's . . ."

What? What could he possibly say to her five-year-old fears?

"So adorable."

She blinked at the unexpected ending. She wasn't sure what she expected him to say about her mom indulging in an all-out name change, but she hadn't expected his commentary to be nice. She sighed inwardly, reminding herself that his chasing a story didn't make him a monster.

Except it did.

A little.

She started talking again to keep herself from thinking. "My mom didn't think it was adorable. Emotionally taxing, frustrating when it came time to fill out paperwork? Absolutely. But adorable was definitely not a word she used when talking about my name. After a while, she was the only person who ever called me Keira. Because of that, the name grew into something special because it was how she referred to me. That's why I don't tell people. It's something between her and me. It isn't for the rest of the world."

His look became something intense, something undefinable. "I completely understand."

His words had the opposite effect from what she was sure he'd intended because she knew he didn't understand, couldn't understand. Why else was he digging around for her betrayal to the vegan world? She gave a tight smile and started walking again.

He stood a moment, likely sensing her discomfort and likely not understanding that either. KC felt certain that Michael was used to being able to charm a woman with a single glance. He'd certainly charmed her from the beginning. But the charm had worn off for her. That had to be an unexpected occurrence for him. He likely didn't know what to do with the stiffness in her voice and movements. She wished she were less transparent. A little opacity would do her some good. But KC was what she said she was, no matter what he thought of her. She never pretended to be anything other than herself. And if any of her fans really read her book, they'd know that about her.

"So what does the C stand for?" he asked.

"What?" His abrupt change of subject to something so much lighter and more frivolous was a smart move, one she felt gratitude for because she wasn't ready to face the serious stuff. She knew she had to at some point, but not yet. She wanted to be his friend for a little while longer.

"The C. You haven't told me what it stands for, yet."

"You haven't tried to guess," she countered.

They'd run out of sand. Before them stood a fence with a No Trespassing sign that looked like it meant business. On her daily runs, KC usually touched the fence then turned and went back. Even though they were walking now, she still went right to the fence and touched the wood, warmed by the rising sun.

When she turned, he was right there, not even a full step away from her.

He didn't step back or out of her way, and she nearly ran into him. "Are you okay? Keira?" he asked, tacking her name on at the last in a way that felt tangibly affectionate. When was the last time anyone had said her name aloud to her? He seemed immovable in that moment.

And she found she couldn't move either. "I'm fine. Why do you ask?"

"You seem incredibly tense today ... in a way you weren't the other day. I was just wondering if you were okay." His voice lowered to something slight—not exactly a whisper—not as intimate as that, but something like a whisper.

"I'm fine. There's just a lot going on, a lot to think about. Nothing more." She said all this rapidly, as if rushing her words would ease the crackling tension tightening over her skin.

"I'd like to help if I can."

"Help?"

That one word shattered the moment. He wanted to help. But how much could he really want to help when he was the guy who didn't print her interview the way she'd given it without wanting to go all private detective so he could drag her personal life into it? How much could he want to help when a photographer from his magazine was taking sneaky pictures in Delilah's Desserts?

She stepped to the side and began moving forward. "I'll let you know if I need any help, then. Thanks for the offer. Race you back to the boardwalk!" She took off at a run.

She had to run. She didn't know what the day held or didn't hold, but she knew she couldn't stand in that trance any longer without the energy of him overcoming her good senses.

Because she'd wanted to kiss him.

Heaven help her, in spite of everything, she'd nearly done it. The attraction was just so strong. She'd spent too long fantasizing about him as a romantic interest for it to be undone in a single day. And hearing her name again? Was it any wonder she lost her head?

It was a lucky reminder to hear he wanted to help. It brought her back to herself. For all she knew, when he said help, he might have meant he wanted to help her off a cliff. She didn't know what his intentions were. He'd been snooping around her past. Did she have no self-respect at all?

He caught up, but she didn't slow her pace. She had challenged him to a race, after all. So she put on more speed to ensure she won the race. It wasn't that KC was a sore loser; she just really liked to win. Though she might have felt like a sore loser if she lost to Michael. She'd already had too much ego bruising from that man.

The fact that she'd thought about pushing up on her toes to kiss him? The fact that she'd actually lowered her gaze to his mouth?

I'm an idiot, she thought. What woman thinks about kissing a man who could possibly be trying to sabotage her career? So what if he's handsome? So what if he's intelligent? So what if hearing her name on his lips sent a shiver through her? She was not an idiot. She needed to stop acting like one.

She reached the boardwalk with Michael almost immediately behind her. She might have thought he let her win the footrace except he was panting now. He had worked to keep up.

"Dang!" he said between breaths. "I thought that if I won, I could get you to tell me your middle name without having to guess."

MUCH ADO ABOUT CUPCAKES

She shrugged. "Them's the breaks. But since I won . . . what's my reward?"

She might have imagined it, but it seemed . . . it almost seemed like his eyes dropped to her lips. But they snapped back up so fast, she'd likely misread the whole thing. She knew better than to project her feelings on the actions of other people. Just because she felt attraction to the enemy didn't mean he did.

I'm being an idiot, she thought again.

"How about breakfast?" he said, pulling her from her own thoughts.

She stiffened. Was this the moment he'd suggest Delilah's Desserts? She wasn't exactly ready to deal with the situation no matter how many times she'd played through it in her head, but—

"I hear there's a fabulous breakfast café on Tangerine Street," he finished and pointed down the street.

"You must mean Carl's," she said, since it was the only breakfast café she knew of. She felt relieved he hadn't mentioned Delilah's.

"That's the one."

She looked down at her bare legs and jogging shoes. "Should we change first?" As soon as the words left her mouth, it occurred to KC that he might think she was worried about how she looked for him, so she rapidly added, "We don't want to make the regular breakfast crowd sick from our post-run aroma."

He laughed and agreed, and they worked their way to her house with him pointing out a few of the Tangerine Street shops to her as they moved to her street.

He must have done his homework on her hometown, because he'd managed to point out two shops she'd never noticed before.

If she hadn't talked to Delilah the day before, KC would be well on her way to being in love with Michael.

But she had spoken with Delilah. That little black rain cloud over her head diminished even the charm of Tangerine Street. Enough that she felt relieved to be on her own street in front of her own porch stairs.

"It'll be quick. I only need a minute." She didn't know what she expected him to do as she ran up the stairs to her apartment. Did she really think he'd stay at the car? Did she really imagine he hadn't brought a change of clothes and needed a private place to get into those other clothes?

The truth was, she hadn't thought about it at all. At least not until he said, "Mind if I use your bathroom to change out of my running clothes, too?"

She halted on the top stair; his request wasn't exactly unreasonable. He had to get ready somewhere. She hated the idea of it, though. Hadn't he already stolen enough of her privacy? Would he search her cupboards for animal products, her bathroom cabinets for leather?

He wouldn't find any, but she didn't want him looking.

"No problem," she said, giving herself a shake back into reality. He hadn't been a monster when they'd met before for the interview, and she'd admired him and his writing long before that. How hard it was to separate all the emotions she felt! There were so many different ways to look at him, and all those ways swirled over her like a hurricane over water, taking on emotions and then discarding them just as fast. She wasn't sure what thoughts were going through his head as she stood there debating with herself, but plenty were going through hers. Not all of them were unpleasant. But some of them definitely were.

She breathed deeply, trying to meditate away the weirdness of it all as she said, "Sure. No problem."

She didn't turn to look but heard him open his car, rummage for a moment, then close the car door up again before engaging the locks. He then bounded up the stairs two at a time to join her at the top. He had his gym bag in hand and his smile turned all the way up to bright and shiny. His smile faltered a little when she didn't return the gesture. He peered into her face and said, "Are you sure you're okay?"

It took all her strength to plaster on some semblance of a smile before she turned away from him to insert the key into the lock. "I'm fine. This is fine." She pushed the door open and waited for him to also come inside so she could shut it again. Fine?

No, it wasn't. Nothing was fine with him standing in her home. She pointed him toward the bathroom as she hurried to her bedroom and called over her shoulder. "Five minutes?"

Five minutes weren't enough time for him to get dressed and go snooping through her cupboards and cabinets.

At least she hoped it wasn't.

She dressed so fast that as she exited her room, she had to double check to make sure her clothes were actually on straight and hanging properly. She slid her feet into her comfy sandals and then posted herself outside the bathroom door to wait for him.

She jumped when he whipped the door open as if he'd raced as fast as she did. "Oh!" he said, apparently as startled as she felt. "You really meant it when you said five minutes, huh?"

"You said breakfast was on the line. I don't joke about food." She smiled at him and wondered if he'd thought he could get ready faster than she had and go snooping while he waited.

It was as she had those thoughts that she realized he was looking at her.

"What?" she asked.

"What?" he repeated.

"Is there something wrong?"

He sucked in a deep breath and scrubbed his fingers through his dark hair. "You just look very pretty."

Her legs were such traitors! How dare they turn to water and start to buckle just because a handsome man gave her a compliment? "Thanks."

She turned to lead him out of her home, but he stopped her as he pointed to a picture on her wall. "Is that your mom?"

It was like he'd dumped a bucket of ice over her head. "Yes," she said, hating that the ice in her voice reflected her feelings. She walked to the door.

But he didn't move from where he stood. "You look like her."

That compliment affected her far more than him calling her pretty. Looking like her mom mattered to her. Sometimes, she felt like if she got close enough to the mirror and squinted a little, she could see her mother looking back at her. It was dumb, but when she ached with the pain of missing someone, dumb was irrelevant. She felt sad and happy both that a shadow of her mother hid in the lines of her own face. "Yes," she said. "I do."

She opened the door and stepped through, leaving him no choice but to follow her out.

Six

Impress the girl without the use of painful Botox injections.
Antioxidants keep you from aging.
—"Top Ten Reasons to Eat Your Vegetables,"
Michael Arturo

Something was wrong. Michael followed KC out of her house, feeling the tug of her insistence. At moments, he'd see flashes of the warm, funny woman she'd been during the interview and even during their conversation on the phone. At other moments, he almost shivered from the frost in her eyes and voice.

He didn't know what was going on with her, but something was definitely wrong. And somehow, he understood he was the reason for her negative mood shifts.

He wondered if his editor had done something stupid like call her up and confront her with the whole cheat-on-the-vegan lifestyle thing. That was the only thing he could think of that would make her so unhappy with him today.

Not that she was unhappy with him at every moment. There was that second when the public beach turned to private property that he really thought she was going to kiss him. He still felt a sting of disappointment in her turning away instead.

He'd come a long way in the last twenty-four hours. He'd come to understand that KC's mom was the central force in everything KC did in her life. He'd gone home and looked it up when the skinny baker let it slip that KC's mom had died. The owner of the Fortune Café refused to talk to him while he was "intoxicated." No matter how many times Michael promised the restaurant owner that he was completely sober, the old guy insisted Michael was under the influence. Frustrated, Michael had gone home and turned to the internet for information.

KC lost her mom in a car accident. Drunk driver. The drunk survived—they always did. KC's mom hadn't survived. There was an interview online with the drunk driver, a woman named Alison, who'd talked about how KC had visited her in jail after the accident. KC forgave the driver, told her to let the accident do some good in her life and to get the help she needed to walk away from alcohol.

The driver said it was KC's visit that changed her. Michael had pretty much fallen in love with KC as he read that interview. The courage it had to have taken to face the person who stole her mother must have been intense. And not just to face but to forgive?

Michael knew he wasn't that nice of a guy. Sure, he wanted to be, but he was a long ways away from her level of compassion. KC put the human in humanity.

KC. Keira. He wanted to call her by her name again. He could tell it affected her. It softened her toward him. It was after he'd used her name that she'd almost kissed him. He was sure that had been what was about to happen. She'd meant to kiss him.

And he really, really wanted her to.

The entire walk to the restaurant had been the cold KC, not the warm, funny KC. Breakfast had been a little of both: a raised eyebrow covered in frost here and a melty, sunshine smile there. The split personalities were at war with each other in every way, and if he hadn't felt some emotional investment in the whole situation, he would have found the entire thing fascinating. But he was emotionally invested. And it was far more frustrating than it was fascinating.

Had his editor called her? He knew he could ask, but how would he cover up such a question if his editor hadn't called?

They were in a cold spell at the moment, and he wasn't sure how to coax her out of it. She'd liked breakfast well enough. The food was good, and the café had a good vibe. The food came out slowly enough for the meal to feel luxurious and calm.

Now they were on their way to his next planned event— which was a surprise because he'd gotten permission to walk through the old children's museum that had been closed down recently. Another museum was being built away from the trendy Main Street. When he'd seen it on the list of Seashell Beach must-sees, then discovered it was closed down, he'd called in a favor from Paul Studly, who owned the realty firm representing the sale of the building.

Michael hoped to impress Keira with his resourcefulness, but he wanted her to be happy KC when they got there, not this icy, suspicious woman who walked next to him while making him feel she was purposely keeping her distance.

"So hey," he said, trying to fill the silence. "I still haven't guessed your middle name."

"Do you want a hint?" she asked.

A hint? That sounded promising. "I'd love one."

She leaned her head in and lowered her voice to a conspiratorial whisper, "It begins with a C."

He burst out laughing. Even as ice, the woman had a humor he knew he would never grow tired of. "Best hint ever," he said, hating that she leaned away again. But at least now she was smiling.

"Carla?" He jumped right into the guessing.

She raised her eyebrows and gave her head a little shake. She glanced past him, and the smile slid from her face into something unreadable. He followed her line of sight and found they were walking past Delilah's Desserts.

Maybe she was unhappy with him because he was taking her away from her routine of the day. The ritual of the last Friday of every month belonged to her and her alone. And as far as Michael could tell, no one else had ever been able to get her to agree to being unavailable for it. But his coming in like he had and asking her to be with him during the total working hours of the bakery meant the only way she could partake in her ritual would be to drag him along.

He didn't think she would let him take part with her, and maybe that was why her personality was so inconsistent. He was a source of confusion and pain for her because he was keeping her from something that mattered to her.

That had to be it.

This new explanation made more sense than his editor being stupid enough to call.

With that puzzle figured out to the best of Michael's abilities, he felt free to work his hardest to distract her. "Corinne?" he said as he walked faster in an effort to pass the offending bakery sooner. "Cathy? Clementine?"

"Do I really look like an orange?"

Finally, her eyes were back on him. Michael considered going to the obvious quip about her being a lil' Cutie but decided that reached a new level of ridiculous, even for him. "Camille then? No, no wait. I've got it. Cornelia!"

She laughed.

He loved that sound. And they were past the bakery. He threw out guess after guess: Chloe, Cara, Connie, Constance, Carli, Cameron. He even threw a few non-names but still C words in there: crazy, crinkled, crisp, congratulations, and confetti. "I think I've guessed it," he finally said, "and you're just not telling me."

"Oh really," she said. She'd moved closer to him so she could hear his guesses. Her hand brushed his. He thought that was a good sign until she folded her arms across her chest to keep it from happening again. "And just which of those names do you really think could be mine?"

"Crystal was a good guess. It's pretty and has some classic charm to it. I think you could be a Crystal."

She tsked. "While I like the explanation, that's definitely not my name. Your problem is that you're thinking of the hard letter C. Think softer."

Finally. A real clue. And given of her own free will. She'd never told any of her interviewers what her initials stood for before, but her letting him guess had to mean something, didn't it? He listened to the sounds of their footfalls against the boardwalk as he contemplated softer sounds of C and how they would correlate to names.

"Cindy?"

She shook her head. She obviously liked the game of guessing. Maybe that was why she was going along with him. Maybe it wasn't because she liked him or felt he was worthy of such information. Maybe it was just a game to her. Maybe. But he didn't think so.

He believed that she had to like him as much as he liked her, or she wouldn't have agreed to meet him for activities that would occupy her all day on a day when she had always required some personal alone time. She had to have liked him if she was willing to give him this insight into her actual name.

He kept guessing: Cynthia, Celia, Cecelia, Charlie, Charlene, Cierra—even though Keira and Cierra would sound really dumb together. He didn't mention that part in case her middle name was something equally strange. Parents did all kinds of weird things when they named their children. Sometimes because they thought they were funny, and sometimes because they weren't thinking about how it all went together.

They arrived at their destination, and he still hadn't guessed. She patted his arm and called his efforts valiant. She looked up at the building they stood in front of. "Why are we here? This place is closed down"

"I read about it on the Seashell Beach website and found out that a local artist, Roxy Somebody-or-other, did about a dozen murals inside. I wanted to see them before the building is renovated. It was a pretty big deal, and I thought it might be worth looking at. Kind of like going to our own private art exhibit."

"I never even thought to come in here when it was open. I love unique art. How did I not know anything about all this?"

"I know you do." He'd read that online, too. He had finished eating that chocolate cupcake he'd bought and devoured every interview, article, blog post, and anything else regarding KC Casey at the same time. He felt like he knew everything about her. Knowing what he knew, he felt anxious to please her, to make up for what he'd been about to do with her interview.

Because, when he was honest with himself, he probably would have done the exposé interview with KC Casey the way his editor wanted if he hadn't already done all the research on her and decided he was smitten. He wanted to believe he wouldn't have done the exposé, wanted to believe he was a nice enough guy to just let it go and let her live her life whatever way she felt okay with.

The truth was, it bothered him that she got after him for being disingenuous regarding not being a vegan when she was making her living off of pretending to be a vegan when she wasn't.

Yes. It had bothered him a lot.

But now? Now that he knew it was something more, he wanted to help her keep her secret. He still didn't necessarily agree with it, but he would not be the guy to out her. KC had been through some things. Like him, she was an orphan. Like him, losing her parents had led her to her current lifestyle. And he decided somewhere between his time with the skinny baker and his time as a stalker on the internet that he wanted to date KC and get to know her better.

To see how delighted she was with the museum art exhibit felt like a total win to him. He pulled out an old-fashioned brass key that the realtor had loaned him and opened the door. They stepped into the deserted building.

"This is incredible work!" KC said in an excited whisper. "Look at the detail!" They stood in a room painted to look like a large ballroom in a castle. A set of thrones for the king and queen stood at the front, and a wardrobe full of royal play clothes sat at the back of the room. The murals on the wall made the tiny room feel palatial and opulent. Michael almost believed they were in a castle somewhere and not in a museum just off the boardwalk of Tangerine Street.

Each mural seemed more detailed than the one before it, as if the artist were in competition with herself to improve with each room. KC declared her devotion and love to every mural until they were exiting the museum. "I loved that. Thank you."

He'd loved it, too. They'd played with the wooden fruit at the grocery store and plugged in and turned on the plasma globe, though he was pretty sure they weren't supposed to be doing that. He looked at his watch. They'd been in there for over an hour. He never would have imagined touring a closed-down children's museum could be so entertaining. He gave her a grin. "You're welcome. Caroline!"

She laughed. "I already told you. Think softer."

"There aren't any other softer C names."

"Sure there are. There's Cheryl. You hadn't guessed that one."

Water from the splash pad misted over them as they walked past. "Is it Cheryl?"

"No. It's just in the right direction."

"Are you giving me hints because you want me to know or because you're tired of me guessing?"

"Probably both." She pulled off her sandals and walked barefoot over the warm cement. Michael couldn't say why, but that was the single most provocative thing he'd ever seen a woman do. It made him forget they were playing a guessing game. It didn't help that the light from the midday sun teased around the individual strands of hair that had fallen loose from her ponytail so that it looked like they were dripping sunlight.

He wanted to touch her hair, to run his finger across her

cheek, to see her tilt her face up at him like she had this morn-ing, to have her raise up on her tiptoes with her mouth smiling and accepting of the kiss he badly wanted to give her.

"What?" he asked. He'd been so distracted imagining her, he'd missed her question.

"My favorite murals were the scenes from The Jungle Book. The detail and feeling of the forest were seriously amazing. What was yours?"

"I'd have to say I loved the one in the space station best. It kind of felt like I was looking out a portal to the universe."

She sighed. "I think this Roxy is my new favorite artist. I'll have to look her up and see what else she's done."

Michael sighed, too, though likely not for the same reason.

His sigh brought her attention back to him. She surveyed him for a long moment, her face falling from the lighthearted musings of artists to something he couldn't read. "So what else do we have planned for today?" she asked after a moment.

He'd had a whole day planned: some time at the farmer's market, lunch, and tickets to a local play in the early evening. But he felt the seriousness of her expression required a conversation. She was missing her monthly ritual, and it was his fault. He was sure that was the reason for her unhappiness. If they got it out of the way, she would be free to enjoy herself, to enjoy spending time with him.

"I do have plans, but I think I'm going to alter them a little. Let's go," he turned his body so it was facing the direction of Delilah's Desserts, "this way."

Her expression darkened a little, then smoothed out into something calm and unreadable. "That's a very good idea," she said. Though she didn't sound like she felt it was a very good idea at all.

Seven

It's okay to be confused in a world where
vegetable soup is made with chicken broth.
—*No Cheat Days*, KC Casey

*H*e was taking her to Delilah's. KC was sure of it. In some ways, she was glad, grateful even, to have the moment of open honesty finally come. In other ways, she felt an incredible loss. The day had been great so far. He was funny in all the right places, poignant in all the right places. Here was a man she wanted to spend time with, and she was probably going to have to tell him off.

Why did he have to be a part of her industry? Why did he have to go snooping around in her private life like some idiot gumshoe detective instead of just calling her and asking her outright? Why couldn't he be Michael the wonderful love interest instead of Michael the chump journalist?

Stop it, KC, she admonished herself. Because maybe he

wasn't the chump journalist. Maybe he had a good explanation for prying into her personal life. She would hear him out, let him talk, try to understand his motivations and intentions.

Please don't be the chump journalist, she thought over and over in her mind.

The fact that he was walking her straight to Delilah's meant he wanted to talk about it. She'd already decided she was going to confront him at some point in the day. She just hadn't wanted the point of the day to come so soon. Because what if he was the chump? What if he meant to do to her what he'd done to the jogger blogger?

She'd be heartbroken. And her career would be smudged. She would lose followers from her fandom—the diehards who judged the world based on menu choices. Of course, she would recover from that. It wasn't the end of the world. But just because something wasn't the end of the world didn't mean it was something anyone wanted.

Michael stopped walking at Delilah's door. He took a deep breath. She waited. But he seemed to be waiting, too.

He took another deep breath. And when it seemed he'd figured out she was allowing this to be his party, he launched into his reasons for bringing her to the bakery. "I know about the last Friday of every month." He said the words in a rush as if they would burn his tongue if they stayed in his mouth any longer. He fished in his pocket and finally pulled out a small mesh sachet closed with a drawstring.

She lifted her eyebrows at the object and waited for him to continue.

He seemed confused by her determination to let him speak. "Ssssooo . . ." He sounded like he'd sprung a leak. "I was wondering if you wanted to talk about it."

"I'm not really sure what it is you want to talk about." KC

had imagined being the one to bring him here. She'd imagined demanding to know why he'd pumped Delilah for information. She'd imagined demanding to know what he meant by sending in photographers. She'd imagined demanding to know what he planned on doing with his information.

Instead, she stood staring at him with her eyebrows raised, and her words all gone. She didn't want to talk about it. Some of that came from the fact that she didn't know what "it" was.

She'd enjoyed her time with him, was insanely attracted to him, no matter how stupid that was, and she didn't want to demand anything.

At the moment, she wanted him to give her a reasonable explanation for his actions.

"I know about your cupcake ritual," he finally continued. "And I know the bakery doesn't make the exceptions necessary for a vegan diet. So I guess what I brought you here for, what I wanted you to know is that it's okay. I can live with it."

She processed the words, translating them in her head, and frowned. Okay? He can live with it?

The conversation was not at all what she'd imagined. It was actually a little worse because it sounded like he had passed judgment on her. He'd declared her ritual something that had to be lived with.

He continued. "I actually made my peace with it at the jewelry store. I saw this . . . the jeweler called it a sunshine. It reminded me of you: sad and full of light at the same time. I understand now." He pushed the sachet into her hand. "Sure, I was mad when I found out about the cupcake. That's why I didn't publish the interview. I wasn't sure how to put you in a good light when you said one thing and did another. We've already discussed how little I can tolerate hypocrisy—"

He didn't.

But he did. He'd actually called her a hypocrite.

"Stop," she said. "Back up to what about my life is hypocrisy in your opinion."

"Well, you know. You make your living off of telling people how to be. It's not exactly honest for you to tell them all one thing and then to be doing something else entirely." He must have seen the heat flooding to her face because he rushed on to say, "But that's what I'm getting at. I'm okay with it. I understand why you do what you do, and I'm not going to hold it against you. And I'm not going to rat you out. I plan on putting out your article in the next publication as it was when I first wrote it. Your secret is safe with me."

He smiled, wide and expecting.

But what exactly was he expecting?

Applause? A gold star on his forehead? Her gratitude for his willingness to hide what he considered her dirty secret?

"You're kidding, right?" She finally found her words. All of them were angry. She couldn't talk to him like this. She knew she needed to calm down first.

His smile dropped. He shook his head, and his mouth made an O shape like he planned on speaking, but she jerked the door to the bakery open and left him standing out on the sidewalk in front. He stayed there a moment, likely processing her tone before he opened the door and followed her in.

When Delilah saw Michael, her mouth fell open, her eyes widened, and she turned her astonishment to KC for an explanation. KC didn't explain anything. Instead, she scanned the display case quickly and then ordered two cupcakes, the raspberry chocolate ones with the filling that always made her need to close her eyes so she could savor the pleasure of it.

Delilah pulled the cupcakes out slowly. She kept one eye on KC and the other on Michael. KC understood the woman's confusion. She felt confusion as well. "We won't need a bag," she said when Delilah's hand reached for the stack of bags near the display cases. Delilah nodded and handed the cupcakes over to KC, who thrust one into Michael's hand. Delilah turned to her register to ring in the purchase.

"How are you doing today?" KC asked her, knowing small talk would be more polite than the silence.

Delilah sketched a glance at Michael before responding. "I had a rough start this morning. But, you know . . . everything's good." She shot another glance to Michael before asking, "How about you?"

"I'm fine. Just figuring things out."

"Oh." Delilah's noncommittal noise would have made KC laugh any other day. But today it felt like a punctuation mark on emotions that weren't sure what they wanted to be.

When Delilah announced the total due, she didn't make eye contact with either KC or Michael. She likely didn't know who was paying the bill. KC dropped the sachet into her purse, not really registering it for what it was, and handed over her credit card before Michael could even reach for his wallet.

He still reached and looked a little stupid doing so since KC's card had already been swiped.

"You should have let me pay for that," he mumbled.

KC didn't respond. She raised her cupcake in the air, thanked Delilah, and left the bakery.

"This one's for the camera," she said to Michael as she raised her cupcake to her lips and took a bite.

"Camera? What are you—there is no camera!" he insisted, but he looked around in a way that made it seem he wasn't really sure if there was or wasn't. As if needing to prove his point, he took a big bite out of his cupcake, too.

KC had expected the first bite to fill her nerve endings with calm and peace like it usually did. But for reasons she couldn't explain, she felt even more confused. Angrier. She looked at Michael. This was his fault. Her cupcake meditation had always worked until he came into her life.

She sucked in a hard breath because the idea of him being the reason she was losing this part of her life that she loved made her sad.

So incredibly sad.

She turned away from Michael and started walking. She didn't look back to see if Michael kept up as she fled to the bench—her refuge.

When she arrived at her destination, she sensed he was behind her, though she didn't turn to look. "Sit," she said.

Michael sat. He looked as mixed up as her insides felt.

She did not sit.

He opened his mouth to talk but didn't say anything.

She took that as her cue to speak. "I need to ask a few things." The confusion felt overwhelming. "I want some clarity here. Okay?"

He nodded.

"You were in Delilah's yesterday trying to investigate the crime of my infidelity with veganism. True or false?"

He shifted on the bench. "True." The word came out slowly, as if he planned on changing it halfway through but then decided to just finish it the way he'd started.

"Delilah told me." She explained this because he seemed mystified that she knew. "She told me because she said you exuded guilt like it was last year's cologne. You knew you were being a tool and did it anyway."

"Also true." Michael hung his head.

"And your magazine photographer was also at Delilah's last night taking pictures for the article you intended to write regarding my guilt. True or false?"

His head shot up. "False!" He started to get to his feet to

defend himself, but she glared him back into his place. "KC . . . you have to believe me. No one from the magazine was taking pict—" He seemed to rethink his statement and quickly amended it. "At least, not that I know about. No one told me anything about a photographer. I would have canceled it if I had known."

She believed him. He'd looked too surprised by the information to be lying. "But you're not surprised that someone at the magazine knew enough to send a photographer, and you aren't sure if someone took pictures of us leaving Delilah's just now, which meant you had intentions, Michael."

"Of course I did. You said yourself in your email to me that you believed the industry was filled with liars who did what they wanted but got paid for saying what the companies wanted. You said you didn't like the hypocrisy either. So why wouldn't I have intentions to reveal what I knew?" He stood up, probably as angry as she felt if his reddened face was any indicator. "But I changed my mind. I already told you I changed my mind. Delilah told me about your mom. She gave me the rest of the story, and I realized this is your deal. Your secret. I already told you I'd keep it. That I forgave you. So you've lied to everyone. I'm trying to explain that I don't care that you lied. I get it. I forgive it."

He said he got it, but he clearly didn't get it. His magnanimous gift of keeping her secret and offering forgiveness were the reasons she felt so angry. Because what those things meant was that he was calling her a liar. The word made her blood boil. But even as the anger almost consumed her, she felt like her anger was misplaced somehow. She shook her head to try to clear her mind. She needed to focus. "That's just it. I don't require the forgiveness of anyone else. My time with my mom is my time. My meditation. Could I choose to do it differently?

Could I go to a different bakery? Could I light a candle instead? Sure. But I didn't make that choice because it was mine to make, not anyone else's."

He breathed in several deep breaths, likely trying to find his composure. They worked in an industry of aligned chakras and soft answers of wisdom. She doubted he'd ever shouted at anyone. She certainly hadn't. But she wanted to at that moment. She wanted to shout and stomp and shake her fists at someone.

"Look," he said. "I like you, Keira. I like you a lot. I'm willing to overlook this . . ." He waved his hand at his half-eaten cupcake and then at the bench, "because I want to get to know you better. I thought there was some serious potential here to tap into."

He'd called her Keira again. He knew her name, but he still didn't understand the problem between them. The problem was that she liked him, too. She'd also seen the potential. But he didn't stand by this thing he couldn't understand about her. He wanted to hide it, not support her in it. She needed his support, even if her time with her mom every month was a little strange or even a sign of mental cracks—she certainly felt like she was falling into a mental crack at that moment. But what she needed from a relationship was someone who would stand with her, not someone who would send photographers after her, and certainly not someone who would hide her in a closet and call her a liar.

There. That was why she was upset. He had tried to hush up who she was. He hadn't wanted to support it. He'd turned something important to her into something base and immoral.

She slumped to the bench. She figured she might as well

since he refused to sit. There was no reason for the bench to be neglected.

He watched her carefully, finally looking like he might be calming down a little. When she didn't say anything, he began again. "I said I like you. I care about you. And I think you feel the same. But if you tell me you aren't interested, I'll go away."

Eight

Eat healthy food.
Or as your grandparents called it: Food.
—"Top Ten Healthy Foods to Eat," Michael Arturo

He'd done it. Michael laid it all out on the table. He'd never actually had a conversation like this with a woman so soon into their relationship. And most relationships were surface intrigues at best even after several months. Why did he care so much? Why was he trying so hard? The answer was because none of those relationships felt like this. He knew if he walked away from what he'd felt here with her, he'd regret it for his whole life. But he also felt an irrational sense of irritation with her and the whole situation. The whole thing was ludicrous. Couldn't she see that? He bit back the irritation he felt, not wanting to say anything more, not sure he could trust the way he felt at the moment.

She took a deep shuddering breath. "You say you care about me. And honestly, I do feel the same about you. I see the

329

potential. I can't help but feel attracted. But you didn't even read my book, did you?" she asked softly.

He opened his mouth to argue, but the reality was that he hadn't. He'd been given a review copy, and he'd flipped through it a few times and highlighted a few talking points for the interview, but he hadn't read it cover to cover. He'd meant to up until he saw her with the cupcake, but then he felt too annoyed with her for her disingenuous public persona. He slowly shook his head, wondering why that mattered.

"Did you even open it?"

He snapped his head up, his shame firing into indignation. "Of course I did!"

She studied him a moment. "But you didn't really read it, or you wouldn't feel like I have anything to hide here. I don't keep this a secret because I feel like it's something to hide or to be ashamed of. I do it because it hurts. And my hurt is no one else's business. Not anybody's."

He knew he had been lumped into the sum of those who did not belong in her business. He hated being in that category of her life. "Look, I don't know what you think you know about me, Keira. But I wasn't going to run to the public with this information." He couldn't stop himself from using her name, from reminding her that he knew this detail in her life, that the whole her mattered to him.

"Then why a day outing that soaks up every minute that the bakery is open? Did you want to get pictures of the event? Did you want to see if I kept my routine even with another person around? What did you want from this?"

Michael couldn't answer. He didn't know. Some part of him had been looking for the story. Other parts of him wanted the truth—not for anyone else, but for him. Other parts of him wanted the whole thing to be wrong and for it to be okay for him to like her the way he wanted to like her. He wanted to be morally free to date her in earnest, to be allowed into the small group of people allowed to call her Keira. "Writing the story was a possibility. I'm not going to lie about that. Up until I met the skinny baker, I planned on the story. After that . . . I guess I wanted to know who you were."

She barked out a small laugh and rolled her eyes. "I'm an open book. You could've read all about the woman who is not ashamed of who she is. Of a woman who isn't a liar or a hypocrite." She stood and pulled a book, one of hers, from her bag. She set the book on the bench. "Goodbye, Michael. Good luck with whatever version of this twisted story you decide to print. Just know I've already directed my agent to deflect and handle all responses. I won't be reading the article because, in the end, it doesn't really matter."

He wanted to stop her from walking away but felt rooted to the spot by his own stupidity and confusion. He was mad at her for being mad at him. It was a childish response, he knew. But childish or not, he couldn't seem to shake his irritation with her. He should've talked to her about it outright before today, before his editor got involved and sent photographers. Andy had to have sent the photographers. It was just like him. Michael should have brought the whole crazy subject up and got it out of the way back when he saw her with the first cupcake. But how was he supposed to have had that conversation and keep their relationship pro-fessional? No. He couldn't have talked to her about it then. Maybe he should have, but he didn't.

And now? Now the whole thing felt blown out of proportion. It was a cupcake, for crying out loud!

Except it wasn't a cupcake. It was an ideal. It was a moral code. It was a guy who was falling for a girl who now hated him because he became irrational and angry with no good reason.

The longer he stood there, the better he felt, the calmer he became.

As the anger drained, the guilt rose.

He stood there a long time staring at nothing before he actually looked at the book on the bench and noticed a slip of paper sticking out the top.

He opened the book and read the chapter heading: "The Cheat Chapter." He straightened and kept reading.

This book is called No Cheat Days. *No cheating means no lying to yourself about what you are and are not going to do. Does this mean you give up every indulgence that feels like a party in your mouth and a sigh on your lips? No. It means you need to know in advance what you need. Give yourself wild card days, days where you need a little sweet to soften the bitter that is sometimes reality. Knowing in advance means planning in advance. What allowances will you make? What treats are just simply necessary for you to live a happy, balanced life? What celebrations are coming up? What family gatherings or parties will you be attending?*

I give myself one treat day every month. Notice I called it a treat day, not a cheat day. It is a day where I allow myself to be a human who needs a little boost. My treat isn't huge by anyone's standards. But it is exactly what I need. Find out what you need and make room for that in your life.

"I'm a jerk," Michael said aloud. The answering cry from a flock of seagulls was a wave of laughing agreement. He sat on the bench and watched the sun set. All the volatile emotions he'd felt with KC waned with the light.

By the time it was dark, he wondered what all the fuss had been about. Why had he felt upset? Why had he acted so unreasonably?

He didn't know.

What he did know was that he felt ashamed of himself for being so disagreeable and judgmental.

What he did know was that he'd given a necklace to KC. And now he had an apology to give along with it.

He just needed to figure out how to make that happen, since he felt certain she wouldn't want to ever talk to him again.

Nine

So you messed up. Don't beat yourself up.
Do overs are acceptable.
—*No Cheat Days*, KC Casey

*K*C felt awful. Worse than ever as she walked toward her home eating her cupcake as tears rolled down her cheeks. If anyone saw her, they would be horrified. She was horrified. Her reactions to Michael were so over the top it felt like someone had taken a magnifying glass to them. It wasn't like her feelings weren't valid or that her anger wasn't justified, but she handled it all so poorly that she could only feel embarrassed and ashamed.

Even more shaming was the thought that kept echoing in her mind as she went through the rest of her day: *I should have kissed him when I had the chance.*

It was a stupid thought. She should *not* have kissed him. She knew that. But she regretted not doing it, just once, just to see. She imagined such a kiss being epic and amazing. And she loathed herself for even thinking about kissing the same guy who'd dared to call her a hypocrite and liar to her face. She found the sachet and clawed it open when she got home and felt she understood what Michael meant when he said it reminded him of her. The sunshine, as he'd called it, felt like her. She put it on her dresser and blinked back tears.

She put on her activewear and parked herself on the couch, knowing that was not the purpose the clothing manufacturers had imagined when designing the stretchy, formfitting clothing. They *should* have imagined such uses, because activewear was the most comfortable loungewear she'd ever owned.

With her remote control in hand, she streamed romance movies until her eyes felt like they might leak out of her head. At least someone was getting a happy ending.

She went to bed feeling as tangled as she'd felt walking away from Michael. She woke up feeling the same way.

A week later, the feelings had abated some, but not entirely. When she went to collect another lunch takeout order from the Fortune Café, Cái pursed his lips and gave her the stink eye. "I thought I told you to stay away from food magic." He shook his head and disappeared into his back kitchen. He'd taken her lunch with him, otherwise she might have just left a twenty on the counter and taken her food to the gym, where she had classes to teach. She didn't have time to indulge Cái today. And she honestly didn't feel up to humoring him and his eccentricities.

When he came back, he gratefully still had her lunch order in one hand. In his other, he had a cup of tea. She reached for her lunch, but he pulled the sack back. "No," he said. "Not until you drink the tea."

"It's hot outside. I don't want tea."

"Drink. Or you get lunch from someone else."

Scowling, she took the teacup from his hand and drank. Did any other restaurant owner hold their customers' food hostage like this?

Once the cup was drained, KC handed it back to Cái. When he smiled knowingly at her, she smiled back and ... oddly enough *meant* the smile she gave him. She actually *did* feel better. "Thanks, Cái. I don't know what was in that and don't know that I want to know, but thanks."

"You should call him."

She narrowed her eyes. "Yeah, that's not going to happen."

"You're being stubborn."

"Stubborn? He called me a liar."

Cái shrugged and rang up her lunch order. She handed over her credit card and hoped he'd leave the subject alone.

He didn't.

"When you meet someone who you can spend hours talking with and not get bored or distracted, you've found something special." He handed back her card and smiled wide as he lifted one shoulder. She knew this gesture to be Cái's innocent look. "It's worth a try."

"Special people don't fling accusations," she countered, stuffing her card back into its slot in her wallet with a little more force than necessary. Maybe that tea hadn't done as much good as she'd first thought.

"But were those accusations done in spite or in a sincere desire to understand?"

"It doesn't really matter, Cái." She adjusted the strap on her shoulder bag and tightened her grip on her takeout order. "Because I am over it. I'm not thinking about it any longer."

"Right. That's why you shared the whole sad tale with an old man?"

She rolled her eyes. "You are not an old man. You're my personal chef and favorite confidant."

"Then as a confidant . . . you should read the article he put out in that magazine you were so excited to be interviewed in."

KC's heart skipped a beat. She squared her shoulders and shook her head while taking a step away from the front counter. "What he wrote or didn't write doesn't concern me. See you later. Thanks for lunch."

She made her way out of the restaurant and stood on the sidewalk for several long moments sucking in deep gulps of air. His article was published. Out for the world to see. KC's agent hadn't called her yet. Did she even know the article had released? Was she already fielding the hate mail filling her email box from those vegans who would call KC a traitor to the cause?

KC closed her eyes and tried to find some sense of calm in the whole thing. She tried to picture something peaceful, something beautiful.

Oddly, the thing that came to her mind was the mural she'd seen in the children's museum, the one of the jungle scene. The problem with that scene was the person she was with when she'd been introduced to it. Scowling, she went back to the gym to teach the rest of her classes.

Her agent called seven times before KC finished her work for the day. But because KC was at work, she couldn't answer. Anytime someone addressed her personally, she prepared for some sort of snide remark, attack, or, worse, sympathy over the whole article.

But no one at the gym said anything. She knew the silence didn't exist because there was nothing to talk about. The fact that her agent had called seven times meant there was plenty to talk about in whatever Michael had decided to publish. It probably just hadn't reached her friends and coworkers yet.

KC didn't have the strength to listen to messages at the gym, so she hurried home, where she could wallow in peace.

She entered her home, dropped her bags with a thunk at the front door and went to the kitchen to down a glass of water. She did not want to face reality without at least hydrating first. She finally turned her phone on speaker.

The first message was cryptic. "KC, call me back. The interview went live. It's not to be believed. Call me!"

The second message was an apology. "That last one probably scared you off. I meant it wasn't to be believed in a good way. Call me."

The third was a demand. "If you aren't going to call me, then go read it for yourself. You will definitely be happy with how this all went down."

The next several messages were variations of the same thing.

The article wasn't bad. It was enough that her agent felt she'd be happy. KC did the thing she swore she would never do. She opened her laptop and clicked on the link that took her to the place she least wanted to go.

The article was called "Top Ten Ways to Earn My Respect."

The first item on the list was *Be Who You Say You Are.*

KC's heart sank. How was this something she'd be happy about?

Out of sheer morbid curiosity, KC kept reading, dreading each word. The paragraph under that first item was basically all the things Michael had told her. It went into an explanation of how important integrity was to him. How he valued people who valued their word. And then he shared a little story of a time his mom kept her word to him at a time when she could have made excuses and done what would have been easier and less stressful for her. But instead, she kept her word and explained to him that a person's word was one of the most important and powerful possessions.

KC felt sufficiently wretched by the time she'd finished reading the first item on his list and wondered why her agent had assumed she'd want to read this.

The second item was *Love People More than Anything.*

The paragraph under it mentioned a friend of his, someone who he thought he'd known all about and had been excited to meet. He talked about how he'd witnessed her doing something that he felt violated her code of ethics when in reality, the behavior exemplified her code of ethics because it proved she put people, especially those people she loved, first.

Her. Michael was talking about her.

KC's pulse quickened as she realized what he'd done.

The last item on the list confirmed it. Number ten was *Be KC Casey.* The paragraph underneath her name was the information he'd gleaned from the interview. It was sweet and funny and put her in a good light.

His article had become his apology. She sped through the list, recognizing the places where he'd found the generosity to admire her instead of censure her.

She thought about what Cái said when he'd admonished her to call Michael. He said she'd found something special. Was he right?

Maybe.

She read the list again.

Probably.

She read it a third time.

Definitely.

Michael had extended an olive branch.

It was now up to her to take his offering and give some-thing back in return.

After considering her options—calling him or emailing him—she decided to do the thing that was a little of both. She texted him and asked him to meet her in the morning at the bench.

And then she started to plan.

The next morning, KC woke early, earlier than she had when she'd met Michael for their sunrise run. She dressed quickly, taking care to put on the necklace, and ran to Delilah's, where she banged on the door several times before Delilah heard her from the back room and came to the front to let her in.

"Should I be worried?" Delilah asked.

"Worried?"

Delilah brushed an arm over her face. "The last time you came in with another person, and now? Now this is the wrong day."

KC contemplated the question before shaking her head. "I don't think you should be worried. Things are definitely changing. But I don't think change is bad, do you?"

Delilah shook her head.

"What about you? Are you doing better today than you were the last time I saw you?"

Delilah grinned. "Today feels like it's going to be a great day."

KC agreed.

She bought two cupcakes, paid for them, and rushed to meet Michael.

She hurried through the alley that connected Tangerine Street to that side of the beach and scrambled up over the rise of sand that blocked her view of the bench.

Michael wasn't there.

"Oh," she said softly. She looked around, hoping maybe he was just stretching his legs or something. But no. He truly and really hadn't shown up. She checked her watch. Two minutes late.

A little late. He was just a little late. That didn't mean he wouldn't come. Did it?

"You brought breakfast."

The voice from behind her startled her, and she whirled to see Michael approaching from over the small dune. "You came!" she very nearly shouted in her relief to see him.

He seemed wary as he approached her and halted a couple paces away. "Did you read the article?"

She nodded.

He took a step closer. "So you forgive me?"

She nodded again. "Do you forgive me?"

He took another step closer. "You didn't do anything wrong."

"I yelled at you," she said quietly.

"Well, I might've deserved it. I *did* threaten your career and entire existence."

"Yeah, you kind of did do that." She smiled and nodded her head toward the bench. "We both messed up. I propose a do over. Have a seat."

Michael did sit, much to her relief.

She sat as well, keeping the bag from the bakery between them. "Today," she said, unfolding the top of the bag and opening it up, "I'd like to start a new tradition. This is the last cupcake I will be eating from Delilah's Desserts, and I'd like you to share it with me."

Michael was already shaking his head. "KC, you don't have to change this. I thought I made that clear in the article. I like you as you. I want to get to know you as you. No conditions. No expectations. It's like that necklace." He nodded toward where the pendant dangled at the end of its silver chain. "You are you. I expect nothing more."

"I know. But this . . ." How did she explain? She wasn't sure she really understood the intricacies herself. "My mom was my best friend. A lot of this tradition came because I was lonely without her. And I've been thinking . . . she wouldn't want that for me. She'd want me moving forward and meeting new people and forging new friendships, not having dates with the past. So I propose"—she pulled out a cupcake and handed it to Michael, then pulled one out for herself—"a toast." She held her cupcake aloft. "To new friendships."

"To new friendships." They each took a bite. Michael tried to maintain eye contact with her, but his eyes fluttered closed at the flavor in his mouth, and a small moan escaped him. "These really are the best things I've ever eaten in my life."

As KC chewed and allowed herself a moment to close her own eyes, she couldn't help but agree.

They ate in companionable silence. The clouds brightened from a smoky pink to a fiery rose as the sun announced its intentions.

When the cupcakes were gone, KC felt that euphoric lightness she'd come to expect when she finished a confection from Delilah's. Only this morning, it felt different, more hopeful, more solid, more ready for changes and chances.

She peeked at Michael and found he was staring at her. "Thanks for the necklace. I really do love it." She scooted closer to him and turned her body in his direction. She leaned in, giving him permission to close the distance.

Michael did close the distance until she could feel his breath warm on her lips. He moved a hand up and traced his finger along her jaw, sending shivers through her in anticipation of what would come next.

Instead of kissing her the way she thought he would, Michael smiled and whispered, "I know your full name."

She smiled, too. "You think so, huh?"

"What do I get if I get it right?"

"To watch the sunrise with me."

"We're already doing that." His eyes followed along as his fingers trailed over her face, her neck, threaded into her hair. Every nerve in her body reacted to his touch. She felt emotions rise up in her like the swell of a wave that never seemed to crash down. There was a future with this man waiting for her. Every cell in her body thrummed with the acknowledgment that here was a man worth having.

"A kiss, then?"

His smile widened. "That's a promise, *Keira Charlotte Casey*."

She blinked and pulled back slightly in surprise. "You really did get it."

His fingers, which had been threaded in her hair, traced down the curve at the back of her neck and lightly pulled her toward him.

As his lips settled on hers, the sunlight hit the sand and the tops of the waves as the sun rose into the sky.

But KC forgot to look at the sunrise as her own heat and light rose up within her, and the kiss deepened into a different promise—one of changes and chances.

"What is it?" Michael asked as she smiled against his lips.

"It's just that . . . Delilah's right," she murmured. "Today is going to be a great day." To prove it, she kissed him again.

Dear Reader,

We hoped you enjoyed *Delilah's Desserts*! This has been a fun project, and reviews help us spread the word. Please consider reviewing *Delilah's Desserts* on Amazon, Goodreads, Barnes & Noble, GooglePlay, Kobo, or iBooks. Or if you'd like to contact one of us personally, our websites are listed in our author bios.

Sincerely,
Melanie, Heather & Julie

THE **Tangerine Street** ROMANCE SERIES:

Melanie Jacobson

Melanie Jacobson is an avid reader, amateur cook, and champion shopper. She consumes astonishing amounts of chocolate, chick flicks, and romance novels. After meeting her husband online, she is now living happily married in Southern California with her growing family and a series of doomed houseplants. Melanie is a former English teacher and a sometime blogger who loves to laugh and make others laugh. In her downtime (ha!), she writes romantic comedies and pines after beautiful shoes.

Visit her website: melaniejacobson.net

Twitter: @Writestuff_Mel

Instagram: @writestuff_mel

Heather B. Moore

Heather B. Moore is a USA Today bestselling author of
more than a dozen historical novels and thrillers, written
under the pen name H.B. Moore. She writes women's fiction,
romance and inspirational nonfiction under Heather B.
Moore. This can all be confusing, so her kids just call her
Mom. Heather attended Cairo American College in Egypt, the
Anglican School of Jerusalem in Israel, and earned a Bachelor
of Science degree from Brigham Young University in Utah.

Please join Heather's email list at:
hbmoore.com/contact
Blog: MyWritersLair.blogspot.com
Website: hbmoore.com
Twitter: @heatherbmoore
Instagram: @authorhbmoore

Julie Wright

Julie Wright started her first book when she was fifteen. She's written over a dozen books since then, is a Whitney Award winner, and feels she's finally getting the hang of this writing gig. She enjoys speaking to writing groups, youth groups, and schools. She loves reading, eating, writing, hiking, playing on the beach with her kids, and snuggling with her husband to watch movies. Julie's favorite thing to do is watch her husband make dinner. She hates mayonnaise but has a healthy respect for ice cream.

Visit her website: juliewright.com

Twitter: @scatteredjules

Instagram: @scatteredjules

CPSIA information can be obtained
at www.ICGtesting.com
Printed in the USA
LVHW081959220719
624870LV00018B/1768/P